LORD EDGINGTON

BOOK 7

THE CRIMES OF CLEARWELL CASTLE

A 1920s MYSTERY

BENEDICT BROWN

COPYRIGHT

For my father, Kevin,
I hope you would have liked this book an awful lot.

NOTE TO READERS

Like all the "Lord Edgington Investigates…" novels so far, this book is a spoiler-free mystery. It does not give away the solutions to any of the mysteries from the earlier books and makes limited reference to previous cases. All you need to know to be able to enjoy it is that a famous lord and his novice grandson are rather good at investigating crimes together.

This book is set in the real village of Clearwell in Gloucestershire. I really enjoyed researching the area, and I've tried to make my version of the town reflect the real place. However, this is a work of fiction, and I've had to take some liberties with the geography and certain details from time to time.

I hope you really love this story full of mystery, intrigue and humour, (not to mention cakes. There are always a surprising number of cakes!)

Clearwell Castle in the Forest of Dean

PROLOGUE

Young Cole Watkins was a cheerful drunk.

Everyone in Clearwell knew him and, come the weekend, if he wasn't in the street, drinking a tankard of cider and singing an old folk song, you could be sure to find him at the bar of The Wyndham Arms… drinking a tankard of cider and singing an old folk song. He had a sweet, high voice which carried across the village in fair weather and foul.

**"Come, landlord, fill a flowing bowl, until it does run over.
To-night we all will merry be, to-morrow we'll get sober."**

More often than not, no one asked him to perform, but the villagers rarely complained. He was part of the colour and character of the place, as much as the sound of woodpeckers in the forest or cattle lowing in the fields. He seemed to know more ancient verses than the rest of England combined and could be relied upon to impart his wisdom whenever the moment called for it. Though certain members of the parish disapproved of a few of his bawdier verses, it was widely agreed that Cole was a harmless sort.

**"The maiden who enjoys a kiss and comes back for another,
She's a boon to all mankind and soon to be a mother."**

If you had no interest in his songs, he would charm you with a story. Young Cole liked to think of himself as the walking history book of Clearwell village and the Forest of Dean at large. He knew all about the local manor and the people who'd lived there, right back to the first owners in the fifteenth century. Rich families had come and gone to Clearwell over the years. The manor had been destroyed and rebuilt as a castle, but folk like Cole lived on to maintain such stories for posterity.

"As it happens," he would happily explain, if you were so generous as to buy him a pint of his favourite scrumpy, "my great-grandmother was the daughter of the second son o' Michael Wyndham, the Earl of Dunraven. Not that the family ever acknowledged her. You see, my great-great-grandfather had a bit of a way with the ladies, and the Wyndhams kept it quiet." And then he'd go back to his song.

"But he who drinks just what he likes and getteth half seas over,
Will live until he die, perhaps, and then lie down in clover."

He didn't always get the lines in the right order and occasionally repeated himself, but you could be sure that he'd get the song sung by the end of the night. And what nights they were when the pub was full of locals and the whole place would sing along with him. At times like that, the landlady, Florence Keyse, would keep Cole's drink flowing, and the songs would come one after another.

He'd sing ballads of medieval knights, tragic maids and, most of all, men in their cups. And if you paid careful attention to the lyrics that came out of him, you could fall into the stories, just like magic.

"He that courts a pretty girl and courts her for her pleasure,
Is a fool to marry her without a store of treasure."

In fact, it was on such a night – the night before the 1926 Clearwell fete – when Cole put on his finest performance. There were Morris dancers all the way from Oddington. He was accompanied by his friend Jed Gibson on the accordion, and folk said he had never sung so brightly. Kate Yarworth, the butcher, didn't look like she wanted to drown him (for once). Mrs Fox, the baker, was clapping along, and even a couple of Wyndhams from the castle had made an appearance.

"Now that was a real party," lovely Florence proclaimed from behind the bar when they were the last two remaining.

"It were more than a party," Cole replied a little grandly. "It were a celebration!"

She laughed at him one last time, and the pair of them said goodnight. When Cole staggered outside, he was still singing his favourite song.

"Come, landlord, fill a flowing bowl,
Until it does run over.
For tonight we'll merry merry be,
For tonight we'll merry merry be,
For tonight we'll merry merry be,
Tomorrow we'll be sober."

Swaying all the way, he crossed the cobbled square, bowed his head respectfully to the medieval cross, then walked to his usual spot upon the small well outside Lieutenant-Colonel Stroud's cottage.

And do you know what he did then? Well, he sang, of course.

You see, Cole didn't actually need an audience. There was nothing that gave him greater pleasure than his own dulcet voice. Like a robin in a tree, he sang for the joy of exercising his vocal cords and to feel the air rush out of him.

"He that drinketh lots of beer and goes to bed quite mellow, Lives just as he ought to live and dies a jolly fellow."

By the time he finished his final verse, the inhabitants of Clearwell were tucked up in their beds for the night, and there was no one to see the look of delight on his face. No one except the shadowy figure who grabbed poor Cole Watkins and pushed him to his death down that well.

CHAPTER ONE

My exams were over. School was over, not just for the summer, but for ever.

I was free. Free to experience the world without the shackles of The Oakton Classical and Commercial Academy for Distinguished Young Gentlemen weighing me down. Now that I'd finished my education, I thought I might finally learn something useful. Perhaps optimistically, I hoped to discover what I wanted to do with my life.

"Of course, there are plenty of things I'll miss about Oakton," I told my friends on our last day there. "After all, we started school when we were five. If I added up the hours, I've probably spent more time here than in my own house."

"Go on then," Billy demanded. "What will you miss?" He didn't sound particularly happy with my appraisal.

"Well..." I began, struggling to think. "I'll miss the four of you, of course. And there are a couple of teachers who were perfectly decent, too. Herbie and..." Perhaps I should have said there was one teacher who was perfectly decent. "...and I suppose Mr Bath wasn't too bad when he wasn't making us run around a boggy field... or calling me tubby."

"And that's all?" William definitely wasn't happy with me and, as for Bill... well, he looked as though he'd passed out on his bed.

"I'm sorry, but I'm not going to say I'll miss this cold, uncomfortable room, if that's what you mean." I glanced about the dormitory that had been stripped of all personal possessions. It looked fit for demolition. "Or the food in the cafeteria. I'm not going to miss detentions or being made to feel like a fool in geography class because I wasn't sure how a map worked."

"Make him stop!" Bill moaned, but Marmaduke – our bulldog and bodyguard for that last year – thought this was hilarious.

"I'm with Chrissy. The sentence we've served is finally over, and it's time to forget about Oakton. We've called this dusty old institution home for far too long, and I, for one, cannot wait to find out what the rest of the world has to offer."

"But we won't see each other anymore." William's voice had almost disappeared within him, and I could only just make out these words.

"We'll stay in touch," I tried to reassure him and walked around my bunk to put one hand on his shoulder before he could burst into tears.

"Absolutely, we will!" Marmaduke managed to sound enthusiastic. "I'll tell you what. We'll make a pledge. Chrissy and I promise that, no matter what we end up doing, we'll come to visit the three of you in Oxford at least once a term. How does that sound?"

I thought it sounded rather lovely, and the emotion of that moment welled up in the pit of my stomach. My heart stung a little and my throat had become very dry for some reason.

"It's perfect." I walked to the aisle between our stripped bunks and put my hand out in front of me. "Come on, you lot. Make the pledge."

Billy immediately jumped forward and placed his hand on mine, but William and Bill were more reluctant. Perhaps they thought it was all a ruse – a way to stop them complaining before we left and never looked back.

"I really mean it," Marmaduke reiterated. "We'll come every term like clockwork. It's your job to get to know the city, find the best places to eat and discover where the pretty girls spend their time. But then Chrissy and I will be along to visit before you can say…" He thought for a moment but, rousing himself, Bill beat him to it.

"Einstein's theory of critical opalescence!" In case it isn't obvious, he was planning to study physics at university.

"Urmmm, yes… that."

William was the final holdout, but we'd done enough to sway him. And so, with all five hands piled on top of one another, we made our promise.

"Three times a year… minimum," I stated, and the words came back to me in a slightly pagan chant.

"Three times a year, minimum!"

I don't know who started laughing then but, within a few seconds, we were all at it. Smiles reflected from boy to boy, and I realised that there was more to miss about Oakton than I'd previously considered. The beds may have been as hard as boulders, but the camaraderie I'd experienced there certainly made up for any such minor discomfort.

I can't have been the only one who noticed this as, out in the yard, half the boys were in tears. I never thought I'd live to see the day that Oakton's savage bullies, Edward and Percy Marshall, would be sobbing their eyes out in front of everyone.

"I just don't know who I am without this place," Percy complained, and his brother did his best to make him feel better.

"Don't worry. We'll find someone to rag at university just like we did here. Think of all those new lads who we can impress with our twisted nipples and barley sugars. We'll be the talk of Cambridge."

The fact that these scarlet fools would be attending one of the most prestigious universities in Britain made me wonder whether such a college would have accepted me after all. I still hadn't ruled out the idea of a degree in… something, but there would be plenty of time for that later. For the moment, I wanted to live my life and discover where it would lead me.

My four friends and I took one last look at the long rectangular dormitory and waved melodramatically. All that was left after that was to say goodbye, which was more difficult than I might have expected. I admit, I may have had something of a glaze over my eyeballs, but it was a windy day; I probably just had a spot of grit in them.

"I'll see you when we're next together," I told them rather enigmatically.

Marmaduke saluted me, – the ridiculousness of which helped tamp down any excessive emotions – and I left the tears and commiserations behind to make my way off the school grounds for the final time.

"Congratulations!" approximately twenty-seven people screamed at me as one.

"My goodness," I said. "I really didn't expect any of you to… to…"

Righto, I'm going to tell the truth. I wept like a baby when I saw my whole family there (along with every last member of staff from Grandfather's estate, his dog and my two bright young friends from London whom I hadn't seen in months.) They even had a banner! It said, "Well done, Chrissy!" and I'd never felt quite so proud of myself.

Mother stepped forward to wrap me up in her arms and Grandfather, perhaps inevitably, cleared his throat to make a speech.

"We couldn't let this day pass without properly marking the occasion." He turned to his audience, many of whom had climbed onto one of his luxurious cars to get a better view of the proceedings. "Today, my dear grandson, Christopher, stops being a schoolboy and becomes a man. Today is the day that he is freed from the yoke of his parents' decision making and can choose his own path in the world."

I'm not sure that my parents were too keen on this statement, but he quickly hurried us along. "Christopher has worked ever so hard this year to pass his exams and I am immensely proud of him."

"Hear, hear!" my soppy brother cheered before giving me an affectionate punch on the arm.

"You've done so well, Chrissy," my mother said, and I hugged her all the tighter.

"My grandson truly is the most–" Grandfather didn't manage to finish his speech as his staff rushed forward to surround me.

They were chattering with great fervour, the noise of which soon drowned out the old lord's words entirely. I was afraid they would pick me up off the ground and throw me into the air in jubilation. I've never been very good with heights, so it was lucky that they resisted any such impulse and made do with hearty pats on the back and some generous words.

Cook was there to pinch my cheeks. Our footman Halfpenny gave one of his typically formal bows, as though I'd just asked him to put an extra log on the fire or inform the kitchen that I needed a new pot of tea. But it was the younger figures whose presence there really moved me. Our chauffeur Todd, Alice the maid and even the delegation of my friends from the Gargoyle Club all looked so happy for me. It was quite unexpected.

"Ladies and Gentlemen," Grandfather raised his voice to regain everyone's attention. He'd been forgotten for literally seconds. It must have been terrible for him. "Cook has prepared a champagne reception back at Cranley Hall, and you all have the afternoon off to enjoy yourselves and celebrate my youngest grandson's success."

My mother went over to whisper something in his ear, and I heard the words "Big Francis" and "stunning impression of Aunt Belinda" before Grandfather addressed us once more.

"Or rather… We will celebrate my second youngest grandson's success."

"I beg your pardon, M'Lord," Halfpenny began, but his master predicted what the man's complaint would be and was having none of it.

"No, Halfpenny, you may not be excluded. You will have the

afternoon off like everyone else. We can serve our own drinks for once."

With these orders issued, everyone piled back into the cars. Mother was brave enough to drive in the cockpit of Grandfather's Hispano Suiza Speedster, and so I went with my brother in his new Salmson AL3. I didn't know anything about such cars except that they were French and could barely fit two people inside. I hadn't felt so squashed since I was twelve years old and "Stinky" Simon Speight had to bunk in with me after he wet his bed.

Even more uncomfortable than the poky car was the look on my brother's face as we climbed aboard. Albert had spent the last five years since he'd left home either fussing over a girl he adored or complaining because said girl hadn't returned his feelings. But this was different. He looked oddly… Well, I don't quite know the word for it.

He took his place in the driver's seat without cranking the engine and sat there sighing as the other cars drove away.

"What the blazes has got your goat?" I eventually asked.

In response, he sighed once more and mumbled a phrase I hadn't expected to hear. "Somebody loves me." He shook his head as he spoke, clearly finding it just as difficult to fathom as I did.

"Gosh. Who is she? Has she met you in person?"

My response clearly deflated his balloon a smidgen. He realised that we were now the last car remaining and exited the car to start the engine.

"Yes, thank you very much, little brother. She and I have met in person." He turned the handle with as much gusto as he could summon, but it still took him a few rotations before the machine sputtered into life. "Her name is Cassie, and she's the prettiest, most sophisticated, cultured, debonair, intoxicating…"

He'd gone back to his sighing again, as I waited for this very long list of qualities to reach a conclusion.

"Oh, my goodness. You're happy, aren't you? (It's just not natural!)" I didn't actually voice this last comment, but you can be sure I was thinking it.

"Yes, I think I am." It was a relief that he hadn't started dancing or broken out in song.

"Well, she sounds just charming." I was trying to be diplomatic. Though, if it were Cassandra Fairfax who'd bagged him, my mother had informed me she came from a family of rotters. "I can't wait to meet her."

"Me neither." My brother was already off with his thoughts, somewhere far far away – no doubt running hand in hand through a meadow with his beloved.

This time, when he sat back in the driving seat, he managed to drive away, and it was my turn to feel emotional. We travelled across that leafy domain, and I wondered if I would ever set foot in Oakton again. I kept my eyes on the imposing red-brick tower until it had become a speck at the end of the long driveway and, when Albert pulled onto the country lane outside, I felt some small piece of me snap off and stay behind.

Was that it? Was I now an adult?

I wouldn't be eighteen for over a month – and my twenty-first birthday seemed a lifetime away – but for all intents and purposes, I felt I had come of age.

CHAPTER TWO

As my grandfather, Lord Edgington, had anticipated, there was quite the party to enjoy that afternoon on the terrace of Cranley Hall. All of my cousins were there – though I hadn't seen them since Grandfather's disastrous spring ball. There were famous (and not so famous) detectives from Scotland Yard, friends of the family from across Britain, and even a celebrated cricketer made a special appearance. I was jolly lucky to be me that day, and I had a sense of what it must feel like to be a prince or a popular actor.

Cook had made a selection of delicious hors d'oeuvres to my precise tastes – which meant they were approximately eighty per cent pork pie and twenty per cent cheese. Todd who, despite being our chauffer, spent more time tending bar than behind the wheel, had prepared some fresh lemonade for me, and the maids had decorated the place with garlands and an "appropriate quantity" of flowers. It was almost exactly how I would have organised the party if I'd been in charge.

For all the frivolity of that afternoon, a strange mood hung over me. Even as everyone sang 'For He's a Jolly Good Fellow' there was something I was eager to discover. Grandfather was in fine form, chatting away to his guests like the entertainer he was but, try as I might, I couldn't get his attention. Admittedly, as soon as dessert was served, I got distracted filling my stomach with sweet pastry. Then afterwards, there were photographs to be taken and speeches to be made. In fact, it wasn't until the evening was upon us, and the last guest had left, that I finally found a moment to talk to him.

I'd accompanied my family back to their cars and found the old chap sitting on the terrace with his golden retriever, smoking a cigar. Or rather, my grandfather was smoking a cigar, not his dog, Delilah. At first, he didn't look at me but peered across his impressive estate. There were swallows and swifts carrying out a series of daring dogfights over the lakes. Their wings occasionally touched the surface of the water as though one of their engines had blown.

"I haven't smoked a cigar in fifteen years," he told me, and I realised that I hadn't actually spoken. I was simply standing there, marvelling at the magnificent fellow. "I don't have the taste for them anymore, but I thought I'd do something special to commemorate this momentous day." He took one last drag on the noxious tube and released a spiral of smoke into the air before stubbing it out.

"Momentous is a bit strong, don't you think?" I'd been feeling shy over such overblown language all afternoon. "I'm so thankful for everything you've done, but surely most children who start school eventually finish it."

He leaned back in his chair to get a different view of me. "That may well be, Christopher, but not one of them can claim to be my assistant. Not one of them has helped me in quite the way you have. Not your cousins, or your brother or any of the other boys from Oakton."

He'd made me blush and my voice came out a little squeaky. "I admit, I am very good at chasing around after you and asking silly questions."

He laughed at this and Delilah, who was sitting at his side having her ears ruffled, turned to look at me.

"I don't agree. You're good at all sorts of things." Grandfather leaned forward and placed his fingertips together in front of him as the pace of his speech increased. "You've become more observant and inquisitive. You endear yourself to our suspects in a manner of which I can only dream. And, what's more, you are beginning to formulate exceptional ideas on our cases that I doubt I would have had the capacity to envision when I was your age."

He fired his words at me like a spray of bullets. "You seem to be under the impression that you're not very clever based on the fact that you have the power to empathise with those around you, but–" He stopped himself then and looked a trifle puzzled. "But that's not why you wanted to talk to me, is it?"

What colour is redder than red? Whatever it is, that's the shade my cheeks turned. "No, I'm afraid not. I wanted to ask you…"

"Out with it, boy." He had become incredibly serious, and his pure white moustache had squared itself off on his lip.

"Well, I was wondering what comes next?"

What exactly do you mean? he said with his eyebrows alone.

"You must know that, if it hadn't been for you, I would have gone straight to university as my parents expected. So… what should I do next?" I thought this was a fair enough question and hoped he

20

had a good answer, as I still hadn't a clue what I was supposed to do with my life.

"Next, you take a break from questioning what comes next." There was an inscrutable smile on his face once more. "Next, we're going on holiday."

I had secretly hoped this might be the case, and I made an audible gasp. "Where are you taking us?" I'd thought of little else through my gruelling exams than our travel destination for the summer. "Spain, Belgium, India?"

"Better than that." His moustache moved in unison with his eyebrows. It was quite a talent, and I felt he could have made good money in a circus with such an act. "We're going to Gloucestershire."

"Oh," I tried to inject some enthusiasm into this sound and failed.

"We'll visit The Forest of Dean."

I tried again, but could only muster another, "Oh."

He clearly wasn't happy with my response. "Really, boy, you could at least pretend to be interested."

I thought that was exactly what I'd been doing. "I'm sorry, Grandfather. It's just that... well, I was rather hoping we'd be going somewhere more exotic than the West Country."

"The Forest of Dean is exotic. It has the largest concentration of Britain's only poisonous snake. They say there are more adders in Gloucestershire than the rest of the country combined." He sounded terribly excited about this, but it only reinforced my opinion.

"Grandfather... I don't like snakes." My words came out in a small, sad voice.

"That's not the point, Christopher." He stood up to convince me but, on reading the expression on my face, appeared to relent. "Perhaps I haven't explained myself well enough. We may not be going to the continent or Hindustan, but I can assure you that we will have the most wonderful time together."

It was hard not to believe him when he looked at me with those intensely grey eyes. He must have thought I needed more persuading, though, as he soon continued. "We're going to stay with a cousin of your grandmother's whom I haven't seen in almost two decades. Algar is a fine old chap and I'm sure you'll get on very well indeed."

"That sounds wonderful." He'd lost me yet again and even my best acting couldn't convince him.

"But there's more." His voice was more animated than usual, and he waved one hand through the air like a master of ceremonies at the circus – reinforcing my idea that he was born for such a profession. "Your distant cousin Algar, the Earl of Dunraven…" He paused for an imaginary drumroll. "…lives in a castle."

"A castle?"

"Yes, a castle in the Forest of Dean." He was determined to make the most of this point.

"Does it have a moat?"

He held in his answer for a few seconds and Delilah barked at him to hurry up. "Well, no. It's not that sort of castle. I doubt it ever saw battle in fact, but it has towers and battlements and that sort of thing. And, from there, we'll drive on to visit the Mendip Hills and the sandy shores of Cornwall. Believe me, Christopher, when we sit on the pristine sands at Kynance Cove, with its turquoise waters shimmering in the sunlight, you won't wish to be anywhere else on Earth."

He'd finally convinced me, and I felt a touch ungrateful for doubting him. "Can I plan the journey?" I asked, as I'd picked up a love of maps from my dear mentor during a previous holiday.

Standing up, he put his arm over my shoulder and led me towards the house. "Of course, my boy. But it would be even more enjoyable if we could plan the trip together."

Delilah let out a soft moan. She could be as soppy as my brother sometimes and required a word from her master to cheer her up. "There's nothing to worry about, girl," he said, looking over his shoulder. "You'll be there with us all the way."

The three of us ran across the terrace to enter his vast library, with its endless bookshelves and a desk in the middle with a map of Great Britain already laid out upon it. I wanted to take a pencil and chart a course across England. I was eager to learn about each square of the map we would visit. Unlike my old-fashioned teachers, Grandfather had instilled in me a sense of wonder at the rich history that had shaped the world around us. It could still be seen in the roads and houses, churches and monuments that peppered our verdant landscape.

Staying in a castle sounded like a real treat, but it was the path that led from there that most excited me. The Marquess of Edgington (as I rarely referred to him) and I huddled together at his desk, and he pointed out the wonders of South West England that I couldn't have found on my own. He spoke of incredible sights such as The Valley of Rocks on the Exmoor coast, the natural arch in the sea at Durdle Door and the stretch of cliffs around Lyme Regis where the pioneering fossilist Mary Anning had discovered the remains of ichthyosaurs and plesiosaurs over one hundred years earlier.

I, meanwhile, realised that South West England was very much the destination for me. I should have remembered that, according to legend, King Arthur himself was born on the Cornish coast. Number one on my list was his birthplace at Tintagel. After that, there were any number of wild islands off the coast that we could visit. I knew absolutely nothing about sea birds and looked forward to misidentifying any number of them.

"Well, we could do all that," Grandfather said, after we'd been making this plan for the best part of two hours. "Or we could drive on to Wales instead. They have excellent cheese in Wales." His eyes became a little misty. "Just think about what Cook could do with a few pounds of creamy yet chalky white Caerphilly."

I have no doubt that there were more wonders to discover in that fine Celtic nation than merely its cheese – its cakes, for example – but Grandfather had done a poor job of convincing me to change our plan.

"I appreciate the thought, but let's leave Wales until a later date, shall we? There's still so much of England to discover."

He straightened up from the table and, unlike me, did not appear to have an achy back. "Very true. And if we work through each country by geographical distance, I should make it to Greece by the time I'm one hundred." I couldn't fathom why he'd mentioned that far-off land until he added a brief but significant point. "I've always wanted to go to Greece."

It was terribly difficult to keep pace with his lightning-powered intellect, which could jump from topic to topic before I knew what he was talking about. Rather than reply, I stood waiting for my brain to catch up with the conversation.

"Look at the time." He took my arm to lead me from the room.

"We've an early start tomorrow, and you must get some sleep."

He deposited me in the corridor, and I stood there trying to determine whether, come the morning, we would be leaving for the Forest of Dean or Mount Olympus.

CHAPTER THREE

If I'm being totally honest, what I really wanted was a whole day of doing nothing. I'd spent most of the last month panicking over my exams and had only just got the confirmation that I wasn't a total dunce and would not have to retake my final year. While setting off on another of my grandfather's grand tours was undeniably exciting, the thought of a day spent lazing at home was simply heavenly.

In my dream that night, I didn't have to get up early to throw my possessions into a trunk. Instead, I ate a long, leisurely breakfast with seventeen different kinds of cake and several freshly squeezed juices to go with them. I went for a walk in the gardens, had a nap on the great lawn and very much enjoyed my lunch and dinner. It was a perfectly boring dream by most people's standards, but just what I needed. Quite inexplicably, when I woke the next morning to the sound of Delilah nosing about in my room, I felt refreshed and ready for our journey.

I packed my travelling case with ease, and the only real trouble I had was deciding which books to take with me. My five favourite Dickens were an easy pick, and I included my copy of Geoffrey of Monmouth's 'Historia Regum Britanniae' to brush up on my knowledge of King Arthur. But then I came unstuck. I couldn't decide whether to opt for Jane Austen's 'Persuasion' or Thomas Hardy's 'The Mayor of Casterbridge', Agatha Christie's 'The Secret of Chimneys' or G.K. Chesterton's 'The Innocence of Father Brown'. Six books certainly wouldn't be enough – we could be going away for months for all I knew. The only solution was to take every last one of them and hope, even then, that I wouldn't get through them too quickly.

To my surprise, by the time I'd pushed my luggage downstairs, my bossy travelling companion still hadn't made an appearance. I was frankly over the moon. I sat down in the breakfast room, rang the bell for Halfpenny to attend me and was cutting up my first piece of bacon when Grandfather stuck his head around the door.

"There's no time for that, Christopher. If we don't leave now, we'll never make it to Gloucestershire before dark. We've several stops to make along the way."

He marched from the room without giving me a chance to reply, and so I did the only rational thing available to me; I loaded my plate with food and took it with me. One of the staff had already put my case in the car, and I was free to carry my delicious breakfast. I had bacon, eggs, three pork sausages, some roast tomatoes, black pudding, white pudding, fried potatoes and several mushrooms. I would have taken more if I could have carried it, but beggars can't be choosers.

To my surprise, when I reached the front of the house, I discovered that Grandfather would not be driving. He was sitting in the back of the largest of his Silver Ghosts, with his chauffeur being put to good use (for once) in the front.

What has got into you, Christopher? He didn't actually say these words, but I could tell from his face it was what he was thinking.

"If you insist on departing before a boy has had a sensible breakfast, don't be upset when said boy takes said breakfast along with him in unsaid car." I handed him my plate and climbed aboard. There was plenty of room for him, me, his dog and my breakfast, so I really don't know why he looked so bemused. Delilah was particularly happy for me to gobble down my moveable feast, and I gave her a sausage to reward her for her loyalty.

"Off we go, Todd," Lord Edgington said with a shake of his head, once the spectacle of seeing me in the back of his car, working away with my knife and fork, had subsided.

I must confess, it was a little more difficult to perform this task once the car had left Cranley Hall and Todd accelerated along the country lanes. Luckily for me, our footman had provided a stack of neatly triangled toast. This meant I could pile the food on top and avoid the need for cutlery. Thankfully, I also had a napkin and made light work of any spills.

Grandfather was still shaking his head when we passed Guildford. "You do realise that you are…" He had to pause to count. "…fourth in line to the Marquisate of Edgington?"

Like an arrow from an ancient hunter's bow, my response came quickly and deadly-ly. "And you do realise that I could wither and die without sufficient sustenance in the morning? Besides, I don't know why you're fretting; Delilah ate every scrap that fell on the floor."

He was still shaking his head. "Just promise me that, should your mother, cousin and brother die before you, you will never entertain visiting peers in such a manner. Tables were invented for a reason, Christopher."

With his part said, and my plate licked (by Delilah, not me – I didn't want to give the old fellow a heart attack!) the journey continued in a more sedate fashion. It felt a real treat to glide along the smooth roadways in the back of that enormous, motorised carriage. Nothing in the world makes you feel quite so regal as travelling in a Rolls Royce.

I've said it before – and I'll surely say it many more times – but England on a sunny day is my idea of paradise. The sky was a blue that the old masters would have struggled to capture, and the few rogue clouds above us were mere paint dabs stuck to that vibrant canvas. But what would our sceptred isle be without the green of the trees, fields and hedgerows? That bright verdure hemmed us in on the road and, when we arrived at our first stop, it felt as though we'd been trapped entirely.

"It's remarkable," I said, jumping from the car and peering up at the high cliffs on either side of us. I doubt I'd ever seen such luminously bright foliage as that which clung to the high, craggy rocks. The road we were on snaked along the canyon and–

"It's a gorge," Grandfather said, to correct my thoughts. "This is Cheddar Gorge. Isn't it majestic?"

It truly was, and I would have waxed lyrical on the topic if a thought hadn't entered my mind. "Is this where cheddar cheese comes from?"

I was afraid that I'd said something ever so stupid, but his expression relaxed, and he confirmed my assumption. "That's right. In fact, they use the ancient caves to age it. But fear not. I have no plans to venture underground today." Leaning on the bonnet of the car, he pointed to the sky with just his eyes.

"No!" I felt this word perfectly encapsulated my feelings on the matter, and so I repeated it several times. "No, no, no!"

"I'm not expecting you to scale the rock-face, Christopher. There's a staircase in the town that leads to the top of the cliffs and, from there, it's a pleasant stroll to the gorge."

I instantly climbed back into the car in the hope this would make it more difficult for him to enact his plan. Sadly, it had the opposite effect. He copied me and we were soon rolling towards the town of Cheddar.

27

"Drive on, Todd."

I attempted to put my objections in order in my head before speaking. "You do realise that I like neither heights, nor stairs? Why do you persist in choosing such vertigo-inducing places for us to visit? The Monument to the Great Fire of London, the sky itself in a hydrogen balloon, and now Cheddar Gorge. At least when we went ballooning, there was a parachute to protect me. If I fall from a cliff, I will not survive."

I saw a smirk form on his face then and, for once, I was able to read his mind.

"How rude of you to think such a thing, Grandfather. No matter how large a breakfast I consumed, I still won't bounce!"

Even our normally subtle chauffeur laughed at this, and we were soon all at it.

"Perhaps with a few more sausages I might manage it, though." Sometimes, the best jokes are made at one's own expense.

Grandfather was equally happy to contribute. "I've often told you, Christopher; you must eat more black pudding."

After this welcome distraction from my impending doom, Todd parked the Rolls on the other side of the gorge and settled down to read his book.

"You won't join us?"

"No, thank you, Master Christopher. I'll keep an eye on the car."

"Oh, me too," I added, but Grandfather was already pulling me from the vehicle.

"If you don't climb to the top, you will regret it for two reasons."

"Oh yes, and what might they be?" I huffed, whilst Delilah went to dash up the stairs.

Lord Edgington was the most incredibly upright man at the best of times. At that particular moment it was as though a puppeteer had attached a cord to the top of his head and was pulling on it. "First, you will miss out on one of the most spectacular sights in the whole of Great Britain."

He did not continue, so I had to ask the question he required. "And second?"

"And second, if you don't come with me, I won't buy you any cheese when I return. Off we go."

I looked around the rather touristic spot in which we'd parked. All along the street, there were signs for cave-matured cheddar, not to mention cream teas and fresh sandwiches. Much like my grandfather, I realised that the promise of cheese was enough to conquer any fear, and I hurried after him.

Two hundred and seventy-two steps, that's how many there were to the top – I know because I counted. It was known as Jacob's Ladder and, when I got to the summit, I really did feel as though I'd walked far enough to reach that celestial realm. Instead, there was a shed offering refreshments, a wooden observation platform known as The Mystic Tower and some old people eating scotch eggs and looking unimpressed by their surroundings. Who's to say that heaven isn't much the same?

Our journey was not yet complete, as there was still some way to go to have the best view of the chasm. Delilah raced ahead of us, but I was impressed by just how agile my grandfather was, too. The man really was a whippet – while I was more of a dachshund, or perhaps a sleepy bulldog.

We wound through forest and ferns and finally made it to the horseshoe bend we had driven along. I must admit, it was spectacular to see from above. There was a perfect snaking S in the rock that I hadn't appreciated from below. It was as though God had reached down to Earth to rent the land asunder and, for a brief moment, I was transported out of my body and up into the sky to contemplate the planet at just such a scale. I could see every hill and mountain, every river and tree, and the beautiful complexity of our world suddenly made sense.

Grandfather sallied over to a rocky promontory. He stood at the limit of the cliff and peered across the landscape with the tails of his coat buffeted by the warm breeze. It reminded me of that painting of a wandering man on a mountain above a sea of fog. Though I couldn't remember the name just then, the old chap in front of me was, in every respect, a romantic figure.

Delilah was braver than me and went to stand beside her master to complete the picture. I stayed at a safe distance, but I was glad I had accompanied them. Sometimes facing one's fears is just what is required… especially when you get to eat cheese afterwards.

CHAPTER FOUR

"A friend of mine, a chap by the name of Tommy Thynne, owns half of the gorge and much of the county," Grandfather told me when we drove into the city of Bath.

I'm terribly sorry. I mustn't get ahead of myself. Here I am, rushing along with the story, with nary a mention of the cheese. Well, fear not on that score. We stopped at William Small's Genuine Cheddar Cheese Depot, which claimed to be the oldest cheese shop in the world and, not only did I get to taste various different varieties of their produce, Grandfather bought me my own truckle of cheddar to take home!

Suffice it to say, the cheese did not make it back to Surrey.

"Tommy Thynne?" I replied. "He sounds like a market trader."

Grandfather laughed at this, as Todd looked for somewhere to station the car.

"He is not a market trader, Christopher. Thomas Henry Thynne is the fifth Marquess of Bath."

I looked out of the windows at the elegant city we had just entered. "Does he own this place, too?"

Grandfather considered the possibility. "Not all of it, but he certainly has a lot of property here. If I'd planned ahead better, we could have visited his house at Longleat. It makes Cranley look rather drab."

We were passing along a busy road, not far from the Roman baths that gave that fine city its name, when the engine produced a clunking noise, and we only just made it to the desired resting place.

"Looks like we might have a problem with the Rolls, M'Lord," Todd turned to his master to explain. "I'm sure it's nothing serious."

Grandfather's acting was almost as bad as his chauffeur's and, with one finger to his cheek, he pretended to think. "Perhaps you can find a mechanic to have a look at the car. Though you had better call Halfpenny and tell him to bring the Lagonda in case we're stuck here for any length of time."

"Very good, M'Lord."

I allowed their little drama to play out before challenging them. "There's nothing wrong with the car, you hams. That was the exact same noise it made whenever I stalled it on my lesson last month. You did it on purpose, didn't you, Todd?"

The cheerful chap looked pensive, and so Grandfather replied for him. "You know, it is possible to have too suspicious a mind, Christopher."

He got out of the car and sauntered along the pavement before a row of neat stone houses. Delilah followed him and it was clear that I was expected to do the same. One day, the tables would turn, and I would be the one rushing off ahead, though I suspected that day would take some time to arrive.

"Don't worry about it, Todd," I reassured him. "I'm sure you're only doing the old boy's bidding. If Halfpenny turns up with Cook in tow in the next hour, I'll know he put you up to it."

My grandfather had a habit of bringing a gang of his servants along on our escapades, though I still couldn't say for certain why.

"I don't know what you mean, Master Christopher." Todd turned a little red about the cheeks. It was rare to see him so shy and, having ensured that his employer was out of earshot, he added, "Though you may be right on some of the details."

I gave him a smile and went after the irascible lord.

"Lord Edgington…" Two middle-aged ladies with cotton parasols nodded to the dapper gent as we passed, but I had more important issues to address.

"You know, it's no skin off my nose if your staff join us. You don't have to keep fashioning such elaborate excuses."

"That's a relief. I was struggling to think up a reason for why I invited the gardener." He turned to tip his hat to another pair of blushing belles.

I had been to Bath only once before in my life, and it seemed unlikely there was anywhere else quite like it on Earth. Perhaps Venice or Rome had achieved a similar standard of elegance. Though, as my father would have pointed out, neither were British and so they really didn't count.

It wasn't just the wide streets, stately buildings and exquisite fashions on display that made it so special. Walking through that charming city, I felt as though we'd stepped back in time to the days of Jane Austen. Even the trams which jangled along on the road beside us and the young lad on the corner selling the Bath Chronicle looked somehow more sophisticated than they would have in other parts of the country. It was simply that kind of place.

"Lord Edgington!" a really very young woman yelled as she stepped out of a haberdasher's on the other side of the road. She bustled over to us at double speed – luckily, there was no traffic just then. Taking my grandfather's hand in her own, she became quite emotional. "I simply have to tell you how impressed I've been by your detective work this past year. I've been following your cases in the newspaper, and you truly are a marvel, M'Lord."

"You are too kind, my dear." The old devil clearly loved the attention but was good enough to divert some in my direction. "Though if you know about me, I trust you have also heard mention of my grandson?"

She turned to me then and her eyes grew five times bigger. "Christopherrrrr!" She practically swooned as she said my name.

"It was very nice to meet you, mademoiselle. But we must be going." Grandfather tipped his hat once more, and we moved off along the street as the poor lady gazed after me.

I was sad that we couldn't stay to get to know her but realised something interesting. "This place really is nothing like London, is it?"

"Nothing whatsoever."

I had to take one last look at the beauty who had nearly fainted in my presence. "Incredible."

Lord Edgington would not go two minutes without stopping to acknowledge a well-wisher. He was in seventh heaven. "Bath is a nice place to visit, but I certainly couldn't live here. One can be overly adored, don't you think?"

I didn't know what to think. I couldn't remember a time when I'd been particularly adored in the first place, so it seemed unlikely that I had passed my quota of adoration. We cut through the centre of town, past the baths themselves and into a Romanesque building along from the abbey.

"I'm sorry, Delilah," Grandfather told his faithful hound. "The Pump Room is one of the most refined spots in the whole of England. Dogs are not permitted to enter."

The normally peaceful creature looked quite furious. She stared at her master and would not blink again until he spoke some soothing words. "Very well. I will send someone out with a bowl for you. They say that the spring water here has medicinal properties. You may yet outlive us all."

Perhaps he'd got into the habit by this point, or he was merely being polite, but he tipped his hat to the delightful beast and the two of us stepped inside. A white-gloved doorman bowed to my grandfather and admitted us to the Grand Pump Room itself.

My jaw instantly dropped in wonder. What a space it was, complete with large electrolier chandeliers, ornate mouldings with stone columns running around the outside of the room and, in the centre, all the very finest citizens of one of the finest cities known to man. I doubt that the lost kingdom of Atlantis could hold a torch to Bath... well, it definitely couldn't after it had been flooded!

There must have been one hundred people there. Arranged on rows of chairs, the women wore long dresses and feathered hats, while the men stuck to the outside of the room in small groups – no doubt discussing vital matters such as the aftermath of the general strike, the mood in British coalmines and the literary merits of D. H. Lawrence's banned novel 'The Rainbow'. Only joking! They were probably just talking about cricket or complaining about the money their wives spent on hats.

We took our place on two seats somewhere between those gendered groupings. It turned out that there were no waiters in the Pump Room and customers were required to walk over to the small enclosure where a multi-spouted fountain administered water that had been diverted from the nearby spring. This was not a problem for my grandfather, though. The manager, or what have you, immediately rushed over with two glasses for us.

"If you could take a bowl of water to my dog, I'd be ever so grateful," Lord Edgington told him. "You can't miss her. She's a cheerful golden animal with big eyes. There's a good man."

I had expected some resistance, but the obliging chap raced off to do as he'd been told. As I sipped what turned out to be my rather sour beverage, Grandfather was free to examine all those people who were examining him. I noticed that conversation had died away somewhat since we'd entered and, despite their best pretences, it was obvious that our fellow water-drinkers were staring at the distinguished character.

34

I heard some whispered comments of, "...back from the dead..." and, "claims to be a great detective..." from the gentlemen, while the ladies seemed content to smile and, if brave enough, wave across the room to my companion.

I suddenly had the most terrifying thought. "Grandfather, you didn't come here to find a new wife, did you?"

I thought he would either dismiss the idea out of hand or tell me that such delicate matters were not to be discussed in public. Instead, he let out a "Hmmmm..." as though he was considering the possibility. "What an interesting question. I can't say it's my first concern. All I can tell you is that I loved your grandmother very much."

I thought this a rather clever fudge. He hadn't answered my question, and there were certainly a lot of women batting paper fans in his direction. Though, being a deeply naïve seventeen-year-old, I couldn't say for certain why.

Apparently taking pity on me, he changed the topic. "You know, Christopher, I thought you might like to know one particular detail of the castle we'll be visiting this weekend." He giggled to himself silently and did not wait for my answer. "Though only built in the eighteenth century, Clearwell Castle has quite some stories to tell. People even claim to have seen the ghost of a wronged woman wandering its halls."

"A ghost?" I imbued these two words with a suitable amount of amazement. "A real ghost?"

His smile disappeared. "No, obviously not. I very much doubt such a thing exists. Now, that's enough chatter. There will be plenty of time for discussion on the final leg of the journey. Let us simply enjoy the harmony of this beautiful space."

I had a bone to pick with him. "I thought we came here to eat."

"Eat?" He made it sound as though I'd suggested that we take our clothes off and run laps of the room in nothing but our undergarments. "You don't come to the Pump Room to eat, my boy."

His words took their time to settle in my brain as I looked around the handsome venue. I remembered it from a scene in Jane Austen's 'Northanger Abbey', and I believe that Charles Dickens performed there on a number of occasions. Austen writes that "Every creature in Bath... was to be seen in the room at different periods of the fashionable hours". Her observation held true, and yet I couldn't work out for the life of me what any of them were doing there.

A dark thought crossed my mind, and I questioned whether the stale-tasting waters were keeping them all young. Like some vampiric horde feeding on blood, perhaps they needed Bath's spring to survive.

I didn't put this idea to Grandfather, of course. "If we aren't going to eat, what *are* we doing here?"

He took the last sip from his crystal tumbler and, before he could respond, another thought occurred to me.

"Are we on a case?" I gasped then as the possibility seemed a realistic one. "Do you suspect that one of these people is about to be murdered?"

"Don't be ridiculous, Christopher," he said, whilst still smiling at a group of onlookers. "I have no suspicions of any crime. We came here to be seen. And with that task now achieved, we are free to go."

CHAPTER FIVE

Considering the fact that most people in my family tended to dismiss my ideas out of hand, there were all sorts of habits in sophisticated society that simply made no sense. What was the point of a place if there was nothing to eat there? I'd much rather go unnoticed in a pie shop than be seen in Buckingham Palace if it meant I could have a good meal.

Luckily, my grandfather seemed to agree. With our public appearance concluded, we sought out a delightful French bistro near the Royal Crescent. Grandfather insisted that we visit that singularly gorgeous street before we sat down for lunch. Though I might normally have admired its unique proportions, uniformity of design and exquisite Georgian architectural flourishes, it was very hard to concentrate when, since breakfast, I'd only eaten half a pound of cheese.

We had Concombres à la Crème, Jambon de Prague sous la Cendre, Coeur de Laitue aux Oeufs and Poussin en Casserole. Which, no, I can't translate, but I can tell you that each of them was delectable. And perhaps even more importantly, dessert consisted of Fraises glacées à la Vanille which, the international language of deliciousness informs me, were glazed strawberries with vanilla. And now I'm going to stop talking about lunch because I'm beginning to sound like Mrs Beeton.

I was eager to start my holiday in earnest. We'd spent enough time visiting beautiful places and eating exquisite food. I wanted to get to the potentially haunted castle. I wanted to climb its spiralling staircases and mount the barricades. I even wanted to go hunting in the forest for the snakes Grandfather had mentioned (and then run in the other direction as soon as I spotted one.)

By the time we got back to the Rolls, half of Cranley Hall's staff had appeared. We were now a convoy of three cars, with our gardener, Driscoll, transporting his wife in the Aston Martin. Our footman, meanwhile, was driving the blue Lagonda with our maid/weightlifter, Dorie, and our cook, Henrietta, in the back.

"Thank you so much for including us, M'Lord," the cheery Irishman beamed as we climbed aboard the Rolls.

"Think nothing of it, young man," everyone's favourite Marquess replied. "Remember, this is no holiday. You have a job to do, just like your colleagues."

I, for one, was still unclear what our gardener's job entailed. This must have been the fourth time in a year that we'd taken so many staff travelling with us, and I was yet to see Driscoll do anything but drive and occasionally tell Grandfather the name of a plant. I had a sneaking suspicion that my soft-hearted forebear was primarily interested in expanding his staff's cultural horizons without admitting to any such thing.

"To the tunnel," Grandfather called to his gang of chirpy followers, and we all cheered in reply. "We have a train to catch."

It reminded me of the only excursion I went on when I was at school. My monstrous history teacher, Dr Oberon Steadfast, chose to take us to a hop farm, of all places, so that we could learn about making beer. As we were not quite ten years old at the time, he was the only one who showed any interest in the destination, but I certainly enjoyed the trip in the omnibus with my friends.

When looking at the map, I had assumed that Grandfather would have wanted us to make one last stop in the city of Bristol, which was well known for... well... the slave trade, I suppose. It was not to be though, and we drove on towards Pilning railway station. Perhaps it was the joyous companionship I'd felt which meant that I hadn't questioned why we would require a train or what a tunnel had to do with anything but, once we arrived at the station, it was very exciting indeed.

Grandfather stood on the platform admiring the speed at which the navvies worked to load our cars onto the wagons in order for us to pass under the Severn Estuary. That's right, I said *under!*

"It is simply incredible to think of all that humankind has achieved." He was shaking his head again; he'd found a lot to disbelieve that day. "While the last century brought us new advancements – from the railway to the telephone and modern cameras – I believe the twentieth century will be focused on developing those forms of technology." I thought he had finished his speech, but then he barked again, "Convenience! That's what the future will hold, all sorts of convenient developments that will enable us to live faster, freer and more efficiently."

I had some doubts on the matter. "How long does the train take to arrive on the other side of the water?"

"A mere twenty minutes."

"That is impressive," I had to concede. "But we got here forty-five minutes before departure, and we'll presumably need a similar amount of time at the other end. So how long would it have taken to drive around the river to the north?"

He was rocking in amazement at the spectacle. "Approximately an hour and a half. But it's not simply the time; think about the petrol we'll save."

I might have pointed out that the tickets we'd bought cost a lot more than the fuel we would have consumed, but he had the joy of a small boy stamped all over his face, and I didn't like to disillusion him.

With the cars secured, we climbed into a passenger carriage and the shunting engine arrived to manoeuvre us onto the line. The tunnel under the water wasn't quite as thrilling as I'd hoped. In fact, it was pitch black, but even this didn't dent my grandfather's excitement and he peered out of the window as though he were gazing at the Eiffel Tower or the Great Pyramid of Giza.

Once we'd emerged into the light and the cars had been unloaded, we could enjoy the rest of the journey. It looked even greener across the water. We were still in England, but Wales wasn't far away, and I think I had a sense of what that mystical land would have offered if we'd continued westwards. Instead, we drove north towards the Forest of Dean and, by six o'clock, had reached the village of Clearwell. I doubt it was what any of us had envisioned.

"Oh, my good Lord," I heard Henrietta gasp from the car in front of our own as it ground to a sudden halt.

It took me a moment to realise what she'd spotted, but as I took in the rows of pretty, white-fronted cottages in the main street of the tiny village, a hideous sight came into view. We had reached a small square with an ancient stone cross elevated above the level of the road in the centre of a three-way junction. The ground all around us was covered in gallons of thick red liquid that I could only assume was blood.

If the grotesquery had ended there, I might not have been so repulsed, but there was worse to come. A small parade was dancing along the street. There were ten or so men in black gowns, and the one at the front was dressed as a diabolical creature. I could see nothing of his face, as it was covered with a horned mask that seemed to have been constructed like some Frankenstein's monster from various different creatures. The horns were short and spiralling, the skull oddly flat. I noticed cuts of what I had to conclude was bacon, attached here and there. It was a truly macabre sight, but the movements of the dancers were quite jolly, and they'd drawn a crowd.

A line of onlookers stood before a pub called The Wyndham Arms. I noticed a man of advancing years in a neat blue military blazer with shiny brass buttons. A peasanty sort of fellow with a piece of grass in his mouth stood next to him, and there was a pretty young wench nearby. I say "wench" merely for the fact that she was holding two overflowing tankards of beer in either hand. I could only assume she worked in the pub.

The dancers were dressed, cap-a-pie, in black and made a terrible noise as they paraded. A couple of them had bells, one a drum, and the others simply shouted out ghoulish wails. There did not appear to be any rhythm to the sound they were making, and I wondered if it was some ancient tradition designed to ward off evil. If this was the case, I couldn't make out why one man at the back had a bucket of blood that he occasionally tipped over the road, the pavement and, at one moment, himself.

Our three cars had come to a standstill in the middle of the chaos, but no one paid us any attention. In fact, the miniature crowd had fixed their eyes on the strange ritual and would not let go. Although silent, they looked quite furious.

"It must be a local tradition," Grandfather attempted to explain, but even he sounded bemused.

The cacophony ended and the two men at the front of the chain came together to create a new sort of monster. The man in the mask climbed onto the shoulders of his partner and the long black cloak he was wearing covered the two of them. Together, they formed one immense, devilish beast.

"These are the crimes of Clearwell Castle. These are the crimes of the Wyndham family!" the fearsome voice began. "People of Clearwell, you have blood on your hands. For two centuries, your thoughtless overlords have gone unpunished for a terrible injustice. A good woman from the town of Scowles Folly was murdered."

"Who killed the bears?" the peasanty-looking chap yelled over this announcement. "Who killed the bears?"

I really didn't have the first idea what we were witnessing, and my mind ran with questions. Where did bears come into this? Who was the good woman that the monster had mentioned? Would I ever be able to go on holiday with my grandfather without someone being murdered?

"The crimes of this town are manifold and will not be forgotten," the demon continued in his slightly squeaky voice. "Heed my warning! A great wrong has been committed and it will be righted before the weekend is done."

CHAPTER SIX

So that was a lovely welcome to the neighbourhood. We'd been in Gloucestershire for approximately thirty minutes and we'd already – quite literally – seen blood spilt. After some more haranguing between the two groups, the devilish interlopers climbed onto a horse-drawn cart and rolled out of the village. The locals screamed after them the whole way, with the same refrain consistent throughout.

"Who killed the bears?"

The main monstrous character stood on the back of the cart and shouted back with relish, "Who killed Lady Morgana?"

Grandfather watched all this with interest, then shrugged and called to Halfpenny, who was driving the car in front of our own. "Turn right towards the castle. We're almost there."

The footman did as he was told and, like a circus convoy, we moved off once more. Within a minute, we'd reached the impressive medieval gatehouse. I hadn't known what to expect, but it was the kind of fantasy castle a child would have drawn in school. The gatehouse itself was surprisingly grand, and the high wall it divided stretched right around the property. It was all thick stone, coats of arms and crenellated battlements. We drove through the pointed arch, and I leaned out of the car to look up at the impressive fortification. I admit that I half hoped to see a portcullis, but in every other respect it was perfect, and we hadn't even reached the main house yet.

I caught a glimpse of it through the abundant trees, but the road led us around a little wood before coming out again in front of Clearwell Castle. And what a beauty it was. Just the place to… well… pretend you were a knight, I suppose – or perhaps a king if you were feeling ambitious. It was a symmetrical stone keep with a high tower on either side and mullioned windows on four levels. The left-hand wall was covered from ground to roof in thick green ivy, while the opposite one had been consumed by the neighbouring forest. A circular lawn was laid out in front of the seemingly ancient building, and the picturesque scene was completed with a row of blooming rose bushes on either side.

"What did I tell you?" Grandfather asked, though in truth, the answer was *not very much at all.*

"It's beautiful. When was it built?" I climbed out of the Rolls to marvel a little longer.

Grandfather came to join me, and we stood there gawping. "Two hundred years ago, I believe. It's neo-gothic in style, rather than genuinely medieval, though no less lovely for it."

"Edgington!" a voice bellowed from just inside the castle. "I'm so glad you're here."

Our second procession of the evening came to greet us, and I'm glad to say that this one was far less disturbing. Four members of the Wyndham family appeared and raced down the steps one by one. They certainly suited their abode. The man who had spoken had a long, curly beard and a round tummy like some ancient ruler. His wife was tall and haughty, and their pretty daughter was wearing what I can only describe as the robes of a princess. Her dress was made of velvet. It had long sleeves that came to a point, and the skirt trailed behind her as though it was her wedding day. The beauteous damsel's brother was the last to arrive. He was about my age and looked a bally good egg.

"It's wonderful to see you, Algar," Grandfather told his friend, as he seized one of the man's sizeable mitts in his own and shook it affectionately. "It's been too long."

"It has indeed," the mother said, and she took the opportunity to offer my grandfather her cheeks for a friendly kiss.

"Christopher, allow me to introduce you to Algar and Cressida Wyndham."

They even had medieval names! It was as though the whole lot of them were playing a game of historical make-believe. At least the boy's clothes were a little more neoteric. He wore white trousers, a matching short-sleeved shirt and a cream Aran sweater, which was draped over his shoulders despite the scalding temperature.

"The grandson, eh?" the Earl of Dunraven enquired. "Your grandfather speaks highly of you, Christopher."

"These are our children, Gertrude and Dante," Cressida added, and I was happy to know that their names were just as antiquated.

"Hullo!" Dante said in an excited voice before beating me about the back most enthusiastically. "I believe we're distant cousins or some such. I'll be your guide for the weekend. No doubt a fellow like you and a chap like me can get up to all sorts of mischief."

"No doubt," I replied, and I knew that I'd finally met someone in the family who was just like me.

Gertrude said nothing but, like the romantic figure her attire recalled, she sighed and peered across the neatly manicured garden.

Looking a touch uncomfortable at his children's behaviour, Algar put his arm around my grandfather's shoulder to lead us towards the house. As he was rather short of stature, this was not an easy task.

"I hope you didn't have any trouble coming through the village. It's *that time of year,* you know?" He spoke as if the meaning of his words was obvious, but I hadn't a clue to what he could be referring. Where I was from, there was certainly no *"time of the year"* when people dressed up as devils and splashed blood about the place.

"I'm eighteen," Dante said, copying his father's gesture to steer me inside. "What about you?"

And so began a short exchange of facts that would act as shorthand for our personalities.

"Still seventeen for another month or so," I replied.

"I like exploring the forest, stuffing my face with chocolate and reading fantastical novels. How about you?" He had a suave, liquid voice and a cheery disposition.

"Birdwatching, cake and nineteenth century literature. But that's close enough in my book." I produced a hearty laugh, and he did the same.

"You're my sort of fellow, Christopher. It looks as though we'll be best of friends before the day is through."

Gertrude trailed behind mournfully, while her mother instructed our staff (and dog) as to where they could find their lodgings. We mounted the short stone staircase with its moss-covered balustrade and stepped into the house. The entrance hall was just as I had imagined it, with dark metal sconces all over the walls and an iron candle ring that was suspended from the ceiling on a thick chain. There was little decoration except for the natural beauty of the stone walls, and I felt as though I'd travelled hundreds of years back in time. All that was missing were a few suits of armour and a healthy arsenal of weapons, though I'd soon spot such things once I explored the castle better.

"I hope you don't mind eating an early dinner?" Cressida enquired before leading us to the neighbouring dining room.

"I've yet to come across a type of dinner that I mind," I replied with enthusiasm, as heady scents wafted over from the kitchen. "Just as long as it's delicious."

"Hear, hear!" Dante concurred and stood aside for me to walk ahead of him.

My trip through time was short lived; the new space we entered brought us straight back to the twentieth century. The room was long and rectangular and had all the comforts of a modern home. There was a shiny mahogany dining table, with the matching chairs around it upholstered in red velvet. The walls were smooth and white, with nothing but hunting scenes attached to them. There must have been ten paintings of nearly identical composition. They featured horses, dogs and men in red coats over and over in slightly different configurations.

The table was laid, and a number of servants were already on hand to take our surplus garments. Grandfather would obviously not allow anyone to remove his usual grey morning coat. I sometimes wondered if he was a snail, and his neatly tailored clothes were his shell. He clearly felt naked without them.

We were given time to wash our hands – what with the long journey and all – and by the time we returned, drinks had been poured.

"To old friends," Algar said once we were seated.

"And new," Dante added.

I would have offered a *hear, hear* in reply, but I was busy hiding the fact that red wine is approximately as tasty to me as a bucket of mud that's been left out in the rain.

Our first course was served by two footmen and a butler in royal blue waistcoats. I couldn't begrudge them foregoing full liveries in the summer, though the thick castle walls did keep the place cool.

"I would have asked even if you hadn't raised the matter," my grandfather began once everyone was seated. "But I must know. What in Heaven's name is going on in the village? We almost drove into the devil, and there are gallons of blood on the streets."

"Oh, not the blood again," Cressida replied and quickly made the sign of the cross. "I had hoped they wouldn't do that this year."

"I'm afraid it's a very long story." Algar held out his hand to comfort his wife across the corner of the table, but she didn't take it.

"Two hundred years, to be precise." Gertrude spoke for the first time, her gaze still fixed despondently on her plate.

Her father continued as though he hadn't heard. "The neighbouring village has never forgiven us Wyndhams for something that happened in the eighteenth century. No one knows the exact sequence of events now but, in short, my great-great etc. grandfather was due to wed the daughter of a rich family from Scowles Folly."

Dante cut in then with the juiciest detail. "A short time before the wedding, poor Lady Morgana was murdered in her bed."

"I thought she was pushed from a tower?" his sister replied.

This got my grandfather thinking, and I could see how excited the old boy was. I'm sure he was contemplating the skills it would require to solve a mystery from the distant past.

"So why do they blame you?" I felt I should ask, as two centuries is a long time to hold such a grudge.

Algar looked at his wife then, but her eyes were closed, as if she couldn't bear the sad story.

"My ancestor went on to marry an exceedingly rich woman who provided him with the money he needed to finish building this castle," he began. "Over the decades, there have been various clashes and confrontations between the two villages, but it mainly comes back to that first scandal. Since then, the folk from Scowles Folly make a big scene on the night that Lady Morgana Mordaunt died. Things quietened down for a while, but their mayor, Jimmy Mordaunt, has taken things a step further. It's now a whole weekend of fun and games, and you have arrived just in time for the drama."

What about the bears? I thought and, approximately one eighth of a second later, my grandfather asked, "What about the bears?"

Dante laughed at the question. "It appears you already know something of our local customs."

"There's really no connection between the two events, but it proves yet again what long memories folk around here have." Algar sighed, and it reminded me of his daughter's melancholic display. "Some years ago, a troupe of French entertainers were travelling through the forest with a pair of dancing bears. There were rumours that the animals had attacked a mother and her child, so a group of miners from the area went off in search of the foreigners and killed the poor creatures."

"They killed the Frenchmen?" Yes, it was me asking this question.

"No, they killed the bears!" Algar allowed himself a brief chuckle. "Of course, the animals were entirely innocent, and the miners were brought before a magistrate and made to pay a substantial fine. As they were mainly from Scowles Folly and Cinderford, it's become an insult that the people of Clearwell like to deploy."

"How fascinating." Grandfather rippled his eyebrows, clearly intrigued.

"The second centenary of Lady Morgana's death will be tomorrow night," Dante added with a hint of glee in his voice.

"Have you tried to make peace with them?" I am ever the optimist.

Cressida's weary eyes clicked open at this moment and there was a strange intensity to the woman's gaze as she looked at me. "After the years of harassment we've suffered, do you think they deserve forgiveness?"

Her husband leaned over to pat her arm. "As it happens, I have tried. As did my father before me. The Mordaunt family are not the people they once were. They have fallen on hard times and, short of giving up Clearwell Castle, there is nothing I can do to make them see sense. If you're unlucky enough to visit Scowles Folly, you'll find that retelling the tale of Morgana Mordaunt is their favourite pastime. Sadly, with each recital, the part my family played becomes more sinister."

"Every year, their thirst for revenge grows, and their tomfoolery becomes more despicable." Dante had lost his cheerful air. "I blame that mayor of theirs. He's the one who keeps the hatred alive."

I found myself thinking of the monster and all the blood we'd seen in the streets that afternoon and I started shivering – though, as I mentioned, it was comparatively cold within the castle walls.

Algar noticed the discomforted look on his wife's face and realised that the time had come to change the topic. "Let us talk of happier things. How are your children, Edgington? Belinda is the oldest, isn't that right? And your boy would be... Maitland? I remember him as a bonny lad."

CHAPTER SEVEN

Here's a tip if you ever have to entertain guests in your home: in order to have a pleasant evening, it's an awfully good idea not to start with tales of murder, ancient feuds and revenge. Politics and religion seem positively mild in comparison. Of course, you could make things easy on yourself by talking about the weather, but if you insist on broaching more grisly, gristly topics, at least wait until the main course is over.

The impression that the Wyndhams were a perfect, easygoing family was quickly dispelled, and I began to see what lay behind their quaint, faintly medieval façade. I suppose I must have known right from that first meal that each of them had a secret, but some were hiding it better than others.

After a relatively pleasant welcome, our four hosts seemed to have transformed into caricatures of themselves. By the time dessert was served, Gertrude had become even more sullen and withdrawn. Her mother's intensity had risen to the surface, and any topic of conversation my grandfather broached was met with closed eyes or gasps of disgust. Her conversation mainly consisted of such proclamations as, "The wickedness of man!" and "Every creature who walks the earth is born into sin," which is hardly the cheeriest message to enjoy around the dinner table.

In response to this, Algar and Dante did what they could to maintain a convivial mood. The Earl of Dunraven rushed to change the subject whenever his wife said something gloomy and looked quite on edge when his daughter failed to answer a question or looked dejectedly out of the window. His son, meanwhile, did his level best to cheer us all up with pithy comments and so much youthful slang that even I had trouble understanding him.

"You know, I'd be off my bean if I couldn't keep my pecker up, but I suppose I'm just that sort of bird," he said at one moment, and in response I nodded, allowed a brief laugh and then gave a serious look in case what he'd said wasn't meant to be taken lightly.

"Well, quite!" Worried that this was not a sincere enough response, I quickly added, "I said the same thing this very morning."

I could tell that my grandfather was just as puzzled by the scene as I was. He listened intently as we skirted, though rarely delved into such topics as the history of the castle, the growth of Clearwell Village, the recent loss of a beloved member of the community and Gloucestershire County Cricket Club's uneven form. It was a most unusual evening.

It was clear that something significant had occurred to distress these (in all senses of the word) distant relations. I couldn't begin to imagine what it was – the death of a pet, perhaps? – but each of them had reacted to the problem in a different way.

"I've never noticed that painting on the wall," Dante said once we were well fed and perhaps a little more relaxed.

"What are you talking about, boy?" his father responded, and our eyes all turned towards one of the many examples of hunting art on display. "It's been there since before you were born. Sometimes I despair of you, I–"

He didn't finish that sentence as, when he turned back to see his son's reaction, the boy was nowhere to be found. There was a wall and a fireplace, but no Dante.

"Silly ass," his sister whispered, as I tried to comprehend how my new friend had disappeared.

"He does it all the time," his mother explained, and even my grandfather looked a little impressed. "There's a tunnel hidden in the side of the fireplace. If you push against the wall, it gives way."

"The house is full of such tricks," Algar added. "My ancestors were clearly petrified that someone from Scowles Folly would come for them as they built any number of escape routes."

"How remarkable." Grandfather was up on his feet, examining the apparently solid brick wall that was built at a diagonal to the chimney breast.

"Why don't you go after him, Christopher?" the earl suggested. "You'll probably find him waiting for you at the end of the tunnel. There's nothing my son enjoys more than showing off our labyrinth."

I was hesitant to agree, but Grandfather had already worked out how the passage opened and beckoned me over.

"What remarkable workmanship." He was shaking his head again. I was surprised he didn't have a bad neck.

Without a word, I pulled the swinging stone door open and ducked through it. It was dark, cold and musty in the tunnel, but I wouldn't be deterred by such minor inconveniences and pressed on towards a faint light. It turned out that this first tunnel led to a second perpendicular one, and I zigzagged about like that before emerging from a hole some yards from the property boundary. I could barely see the castle for the trees.

"Good-oh, you made it," Dante said, once I'd disentangled myself from the long chains of ivy. The entrance to the tunnel was well hidden, and I don't think I'd have been able to find my way back inside if he'd turned me around three times.

"There's nothing like that at Cranley Hall," I admitted, still marvelling at the fact I had completed my journey without entering any other room.

"Yes, it's terribly handy when I don't want the old folk knowing what I'm up to." He was sitting on a tree trunk, smoking a thin cigarette.

Though we were born but months apart, he seemed a great deal more sophisticated than I. Not that I had any interest in smoking. I didn't understand the attraction for a second and, had I wanted to have a good cough, I would have stuck my head in a smouldering bonfire.

"Secret passageways!" I said to reiterate my surprise. "Will wonders never cease?"

He stubbed out his cigarette with his foot, then picked up the butt to put it in his pocket. "Come along, you. Let's go to the pub. Tonight should be a good one."

He didn't wait for my answer but disappeared off through the trees. The sun was already setting on the horizon, and I wasn't sure how my grandfather would feel about me wandering off the grounds, but it was the first night of my summer holiday – the first night of my independent life, in fact – and I was determined to do all the things that my fears would never normally allow. Walking into a public house was quite honestly more terrifying than the time I'd parachuted from a hydrogen balloon, but I would not be intimidated by a room full of noisy, drunken strangers. Well, maybe I would... just a tad.

I ran after Dante as fast as my legs would motor. The forest around the castle was dense, and I had no wish to get lost in such a place, so it was a great relief that I caught up with my guide.

"What did you make of my family?" he asked as I drew alongside him. It occurred to me that, for all our similarities, he was a great deal more outspoken than me.

"They seem lovely." I used my most diplomatic voice.

"Get off, would you! We're a bunch of loons, and you know it."

I laughed nervously. "That's possible too, I suppose. But my grandfather says that, without eccentrics, the world would be a terribly dull place."

He lost a little of his usual joie de vivre. "I think there's a difference between eccentricity and outright madness."

I wanted to ask him more. I wanted to know why his mother sounded so scandalised and scared all the time, and why his sister was unable to look anyone in the eye. Instead, I laughed and kept my counsel.

Leaving the forest, we joined a footpath around the edge of the Clearwell estate, which would lead us to the village. I could hear nightingales in the bushes along the path, and I'm certain I heard a barn, tawny or possibly little owl overhead. The temperature had barely dropped a degree since lunchtime, and I was soon sweating, even in my light summer clothes.

"A pint of lager will cool you down," Dante told me.

"A whole pint?" I replied quite involuntarily. "Don't they sell beer in children's sizes?"

"Chrissy, you are too funny. I like you already." He hit me about the back again, and we marched off towards the local tavern like two old friends. I was both excited and unnerved for our adventure. I only wished that they sold drinks outside pubs in order to give a fellow the Dutch courage to step inside.

CHAPTER EIGHT

By the time we reached the village, someone had cleaned up after the strange procession we had witnessed. The stones around the cross were now clean and, though there was no sign of the rival villagers, the locals were ready for them. There were roadblocks at either end of the street and metal buckets with small fires inside. In a sense, this really was a method of keeping bad forces at bay; I could see black figures in the distance, loitering beyond the flames.

In a happy contrast to the dark scenes outside, we could hear the joyful sound of The Wyndham Arms even before we saw it. It was not merely the hubbub of a large group of rowdy people. A song floated over to us.

> **"Who killed the bears?**
> **Who killed the bears?**
> **Those pesky teddy-killers turn up everywhere.**
> **And every time I see one, I shout 'Who killed the bears?'"**

Though the subject matter already felt a little tired, the tune was undeniably catchy. It helped me overcome my apprehension as we entered the building, and I was so glad that I did. The little pub with its low ceiling and old, oaken beams was the picture of cosiness. It was no stately home, but the people of Clearwell gave us quite the welcome.

There were folk squashed in everywhere. Some were lucky enough to have seats, others were crushed into the corners, and one man was forced to perch on a table. I noticed that Delilah had a chair of her own, though it took me a few moments to realise that there was anything strange about finding her there.

An accordionist kept the song going between verses and then there were calls of, "Lord Edgington! Lord Edgington!" and my imperious grandfather jumped up from his seat behind a pillar to (presumably) improvise a stanza of his own.

> **"Who killed the bears?**
> **Who killed the bears?**
> **The case is most perplexing, and I find it quite unfair,**
> **Those poor beasts were both slaughtered, and yet no**
> **one seemed to care!"**

There was cheering and laughter as he took a foppish bow. To my horror, this was followed by a call from the corner where a rather handsome chap was playing the fiddle.

"Master Christopher!" Todd yelled, and his colleagues from Cranley Hall soon echoed him.

Even my own grandfather encouraged the idea that I should be a participant in the jolly endeavour. "Ladies and gentlemen, my grandson, Christopher Prentiss."

I can't honestly say that I was breathing very easily at that moment. If entering such an establishment weren't gut-stingingly frightening enough, now I was expected to sing! I opened my mouth to do just that, but nothing would come. A few bars of music repeated and, when I had my chance again, I closed my eyes and did the best I could.

> **"Who killed the bears?**
> **Who killed the bears?**
> **The folk from Scowles Folly are quite beyond compare,**
> **Ummm... Something something something... Who**
> **killed the bears?"**

Admittedly, I struggled with this last line, but no one seemed to mind. In fact, it inspired the biggest laugh of the evening, and several people sang it back to me.

> **"Something something something... Who killed the**
> **bears?"**

Dante pulled on my arm to take me over to the bar, and I noticed several other familiar faces. Algar was sitting at Grandfather's table with a large metal tankard in front of him – well, how else would a medieval lord drink? Our cook, Henrietta, was dancing with one of the many local farmers and had her skirts in her hand, while Alice and Driscoll were cuddled up to one another in the corner.

I spotted a free stool in front of the bar and was just about to claim it when the pretty wench I'd seen when we arrived in Clearwell put her hand out to stop me.

"Not there, lad," she said firmly but politely.

"Yes, not there, Chrissy," Dante echoed. "That's Cole Watkins' stool."

The accordionist standing next to me suddenly stopped playing, and the pub fell oddly quiet. "We always leave a space at the bar for Young Cole." I realised then that the jovial musician was the peasanty chap who had been outside the pub that afternoon. He still had a piece of grass in his mouth and pulled one hand free from the accordion to offer it to me. "The name's Jed Gibson, and I like to think that, in some ways, I'm here to upkeep the traditions that Young Cole set for us."

I had no idea what he was talking about, but nodded and said, "Oh, yes. That's very good of you."

"So this would be the Cole Watkins who died recently?" my grandfather swooped in to enquire like… a bat. A big, grey bat.

"Tha's right, mister. Our Cole were a merry old soul indeed." Jed found his own joke very funny. "He would sit on this here stool and sing his little heart out – and drink his cider of course – from noon till night, Thursd'y to Sund'y."

"What did he do the rest of the time?" Grandfather's eyes narrowed.

"Bit o' this. Bit o' tha'. I s'pose it depends who were asking." It was this sort of opaque answer that made investigating cases in the countryside far more difficult than in the city.

Grandfather had picked up a scent and pushed the man further. "How did he die?"

Jed shook his head. "Fell down a well he did, poor chap. But as I say, I've tried to maintain his traditions. I've been coming here in his stead this last month to lead the place in a song whenever I find the time. And, just as Cole liked to tell stories of the village, I've been trying to remember as many as I could. Like the time the old school mistress, Mrs Breakwell, went out to fetch eggs from her henhouse and, to her surprise–"

"I see," Grandfather interrupted before I could find out what happened in the henhouse. Something had clearly piqued his interest and, perhaps to confirm his suspicions, the gorgeous young landlady spoke up. She had large brown eyes and a button nose. She was almost lovely enough for me to consider taking up drinking on a regular basis.

"As you're interested," she said, leaning over the bar as though to share a secret, but then speaking as loudly as before, "you might like to know my theory. You see, I reckon someone must've pushed him."

"Be off with you, lass!" Jed laughed at the idea and delivered a short wheezing melody on the accordion. "Who done it? The Lieutenant-Colonel when Cole wouldn't stop singing?"

"I'm serious!" She certainly sounded it. "Cole used to sit on that well for a good few hours most days, and no matter how drunk he were, he never fell in. I served every drink he had on the night he died, and I were the last to see him. I'm telling you; he weren't so sozzled that he could've fallen down Lieutenant-Colonel Stroud's well."

On mention of the military man, Grandfather's eyes scanned the room and quickly came to rest on the blue-blazered soldier who was sitting in the corner, quite apart from the other drinkers. He had a rather sour face and was clearly now a suspect in Grandfather's largely speculative murder enquiry.

"And that's not all," the landlady continued. "Late one night a couple o' weeks ago, when I were locking up the pub, I saw smoke coming out of the chimney at Rosebank Cottage." Both Grandfather and I waited for an explanation. "That's where Cole lived, you see? There's been no one else in there since he died."

I thought we might finally have discovered something worth discovering but, instead of pursuing such a line of enquiry, Lord Edgington turned back to the accordionist. "You say he knew stories about the village. What sort of stories?"

Jed looked cheered to be addressed once more. "Well, Cole liked to believe he were descended from the Wyndhams, but I always thought that were a tall tale. Like I were saying before, though, his favourite yarn were about old Mrs Breakwell when she went out to get eggs one morning and found a Roman coin in her garden. Must have been buried there for centuries, but them chickens make a mess of the earth and had turned it up."

To tell the truth, it was not the thrilling conclusion to the story for which I'd been hoping.

"I see." Grandfather seemed to lose not just his enthusiasm but his interest altogether. He pulled back his shoulders and, with a brief,

"Thank you both for the information," returned to his table.

Dante found nothing strange in the encounter and bought us both a drink. I really didn't understand why everyone insisted on consuming such gigantic servings of alcohol, unless it was for the joy of holding very large vessels that made their hands look small.

"Get that down you, my good lad," Jed Gibson said with gleeful *ha-ha* as an absolute bucket of cider landed in front of me. I would have trouble lifting the thing, let alone drinking it.

At that moment, another song struck up, and the focus of the public house returned to the free and easy revelry that the people of Clearwell clearly enjoyed. It was a perfectly joyous night. I watched as my beloved friends who had accompanied us on the journey let their hair down. But it was the locals in whom I was most interested. It was evident that Lieutenant-Colonel Stroud had something on his mind. Once he'd drained his small glass, he kept glancing at the bar before pulling out a piece of paper on which he scribbled down a quick note. With this done, he wandered over to us.

"My dear Florence," he said in a rather pompous voice. "I will have one more drink before I leave for the night. My brother was expecting me hours ago."

The previously jolly landlady poured out a measure of sherry and put it down on the bar for the old soldier to pay his account. He raised the glass to her, but she was soon busy with another customer and paid him little attention.

"She is quite lovely, isn't she?" My cousin gave the chap a cheerful nudge in the ribs.

"I hadn't noticed," the Lieutenant-Colonel replied, and I believe it was the only time I saw him smile that weekend.

I was impressed by just how much the people of the village loved Dante. Despite being from "the big house" as the locals called the castle, he had a real rapport with them and everyone from the butcher to the baker (there was no candlestick maker, as far as I could tell) treated him as one of their own children. His father held great respect there, and it was terribly nice to see all levels of society mixing together as one. The only disappointment was that the matriarch and daughter of the family hadn't come with us to enjoy the happy scene.

Perhaps feeling the need to compete with my grandfather,

Algar even got up to accompany Jed in an old ballad of a murdered highwayman in the forest. It was quite chilling, and the place fell silent as he sang in his truly deep baritone voice. After that, he spent most of the evening at the bar chatting to the charming proprietor and trying to make her laugh – he had better luck than poor Lieutenant-Colonel Stroud, and it was clear to me that Florence Keyse was quite the heartbreaker of the village.

To distract us both from having to look longingly at that singularly lovely young lady, Dante introduced me to practically everyone else in town. There was really only one man who seemed out of place there. He was a young chap in a flat cap and coarse woollen waistcoat, who sat quite alone at a table. He drank his pint in silence and made no attempt to talk to the others, but his presence was clearly tolerated.

"Who is that man?" I asked my newly discovered cousin once the unnamed figure had finished his drink and left with the Lieutenant-Colonel.

Dante's eyes sparkled. "That's Jimmy Mordaunt's nephew, Sam. We call him The Infiltrator."

"Mordaunt?" I said, thinking back to the conversation at dinner. "You mean to say he's from Scowles Folly?"

"That's right. He appears most nights, has one drink and then leaves. At first, people took exception to him coming here, considering everything that his family has got up to over the years. But he seems harmless enough."

I went to the window to see the apparently shy figure say a few words to the military man, who shook his hand in farewell. He picked his way down the road among the fiery barrels, and I might have forgotten all about him if, a few minutes later, the pub hadn't been rocked by an explosion.

"The Mordaunts!" old Jed Gibson shouted. "We're under attack."

He had a short baton about his person for just such an occasion and immediately turned his table over in order to barricade the window. This would not be of much help, however, as the assault had been launched from some way away.

"Outside, lads," one of the young farmers I'd met shouted, and his friends snatched cricket bats, scythes and clubs that were hanging from the walls.

Quite caught up in the drama of it all, I was too excited to remember to be nervous and rushed outside with them. At first, I thought the street itself was on fire. Whatever the people from Scowles Folly had used as an incendiary device, it had overturned two of the barrels, and a channel of fire scarred the main street through town. It was far enough from the houses not to be a threat and would soon die out on the tarmac, but it made for a terrifying sight as, in the distance, the figures in black raced away.

"You Scowles Folly swine!" Dante shouted to appreciative cheers from his people. "If that's all you've got, do your worst."

CHAPTER NINE

By this point in my life, I'd got used to all sorts of things. I no longer had a distaste for peas, for example – an aversion which had caused my mother any amount of consternation when I was a young child. I'd learnt how to overcome my crippling mediocrity to pass my school exams as well, and I was surprisingly composed around corpses thanks to my grandfather's efforts over the previous year.

As a matter of fact, the sight of an explosion, mere feet away from where I'd been enjoying a raucous evening in a public house, did little to frighten me. Overall, I'd say the experience was positively sedate compared to some of the things I'd lived through. And so, instead of walking back to Clearwell Castle fearing for my life, when we'd had our fill and it was time to go home, I nattered to Dante about all that we'd witnessed.

"That's nothing," he said rather heroically. "I've seen far worse. The Mordaunts really are a gang of fools."

"Easy, Dante," his father complained in a soft voice. "There's no sense in making things worse between our families. The Mordaunts were once wealthy folk, just like us. We should think ourselves lucky not to have trodden the same path as them."

The boy waved away the earl's concerns. "All I was going to say was that nothing they did tonight could scare me because I've seen more frightening sights in the castle." He looked about us then; I've no idea why. "I'm talking about Lady Morgana. Her ghost walks the halls late at night."

Before I had time to react, I spotted a black shape on the path ahead. We were on the long straight road that led from the town to the castle gates, and I was certain I saw someone skirt the wall. Todd was a few feet ahead of us and must have spotted the same thing.

"Hey," he called. "I saw you, fella." The carless chauffeur dashed off along the road with his usual rapidity but, by the time he reached the property, the chap must have vanished into the forest.

"You see, Father. It will be a Mordaunt or one of their kin causing trouble. What sense is there in treating such savages with any kindness?"

Algar didn't answer except to sigh a little, and no one said another word until we were back inside. I must say that, unlike the terrifying moments I'd experienced on earlier cases, there was a theatricality to that night in Clearwell. It was as though the explosion had been planned for the spectacle it provided, rather than any damage it might cause.

To be perfectly honest, the courage I'd shown scared me far more than the scenes outside the pub had. You see, if I became brave all of a sudden, that would mean I was more likely to do something foolish and end up with a knife in my back, a bullet in my brain or eating a delicious cake laced with poison – admittedly, where cake was involved, I would always rush in where angels fear there might be arsenic.

My cowardice had served me well for just short of eighteen years. Where would I have been without it? Dead in a ditch, that's where! Bravery is a very frightening thing indeed. Who knows what my chances of survival will be the next time some madman starts assassinating people if I don't take the appropriate cowardly precautions?

The awfully discreet castle staff showed us to our rooms in the eastern tower. I'm very happy to say that there was a spiral staircase to reach them and the candles on the walls leant a terribly atmospheric… umm… atmosphere to the place. The back of my neck tingled as I thought about coming face to face with Lady Morgana, that poor wronged woman who had died at the hands of… someone. I couldn't be certain who the ancient killer had been, and as Grandfather was now busy investigating the case of a drunk chap from the village, it seemed he would have too much on his plate to answer the question.

Our rooms were next to one another on the highest floor – whereas our staff had all been assigned beds in the gatehouse. My own stone box reminded me of the cells that monks occupy in a monastery. I found that I was both excited about this medieval experience, and a little worried that the mattress would be too lumpy. Grandfather, of course, was afforded far greater luxury. He had a four-poster bed, exquisite tapestries on his walls, a roaring fire already ablaze and no interest in swapping rooms with me.

To be fair to the accommodation – and perhaps the half pint of cider I'd managed to imbibe before feeling queasy – I slept like an old dog that night. I dreamt of heroes and villains, maidens and muggers and, when I woke, the sun was low on the horizon. I was eager to see more of the forest, so I dressed quickly and, allowing for the warm weather, selected a pair of pale blue dungarees with a seersucker shirt. Realising I looked like an overgrown baby, I immediately changed into a pair of linen trousers instead.

It turned out that I was not the first member of the household to rise. Down in the breakfast room, Gertrude was already reading the newspaper. I was surprised to see that she looked rather happy. It was quite a contrast to the night before, and I wondered if she was one of those strange characters who are really only themselves in the morning.

"How nice to see you again, cousin," she said with a smile.

I must admit that I'd been so distracted by her frown the previous day that I'd barely noticed how terribly handsome she was. She had brown hair that had a reddish gleam when it caught the light. It was arranged in neatly defined waves that seemed to cling to her scalp, before cascading down her shoulders. I really couldn't fathom how she controlled her hair just so. Do women have some sort of glue they apply for such purposes? All I can say for certain is that it was terribly attractive and, with her light green eyes, perfectly straight nose and warm smile, so was she.

"It's lovely to be here," I replied quite genuinely. "And it's lovely to see you looking so…" I didn't know how to finish this sentence without implying she'd been grumpy the night before. "…ummm… healthy."

Her lips turned up a fraction, and I could tell she had to suppress a laugh. "Well, thank you, Christopher. I am feeling quite well this morning. I trust you are too?"

"Yes, I'm very healthy, thank you. Very healthy." I thought that, if I kept repeating this word, I could make it sound more natural. This was not the case. "It's funny that we've never met one another at family parties and such."

She looked down at her paper. "Hardly. Mother rarely goes anywhere except the church down the lane. Our ancestors bestowed St Peter's on the village, so perhaps she wishes to get her money's worth. I've pointed out that my great-great-grandmother also paid for the construction of the primary school, and yet she has shown little interest in attending classes there."

There was nothing I would have liked more at that moment than to enquire whether she could explain the cause of her mother's frigid nature. After I'd spent the previous night in her father's jolly company, it was even more difficult to comprehend Cressida's attitude. Of course, I was far too polite to say anything and had to cross my fingers that some inspirational topic of conversation might materialise in my brain.

"Hops!" I said when it very much didn't.

"I beg your pardon?" It was hard to say whether Gertrude was offended or merely bemused by my outburst.

"I said, 'hops'. You know, the plants they use to make beer?" I didn't wait to confirm her knowledge but pressed on with the topic. "It turns out that they're a type of flower and are used to add a touch of bitterness to the drink. It's amazing the things one can learn on a school trip."

She smiled again, and I felt a heady mix of relief and pride. "I wouldn't know. I've never been to school. My mother insisted that she educate my brother and me here. Though if it was only beer-making you studied, it sounds as though I haven't missed out on much."

"Oh." I rewarded her quip with one of my most nervous laughs. "Indeed."

I have no idea why I was behaving like such a buffoon. I'd met plenty of pretty girls in my life – and spoken to at least five of them! I really thought I'd become more debonair in my conversation. Perhaps it was the fact I'd never had breakfast alone with a woman other than my mother before, though I felt there was more to it than that.

I noticed that Gertrude's sense of dress had travelled even further back through time than her previous ensemble. She now wore a Grecian gown with no sleeves and a jewelled clasp at the neck. This elegant robe was made of cream silk and, though loose and free flowing, enhanced her perfectly willowy figure. I wondered if she was the kind of person for whom men would do anything. My terribly severe paternal grandmother had warned me of such women, but I'd rarely experienced that magnetic pull before.

Admittedly Gertrude was approximately my third cousin, but even the fact that we shared a bloodline wouldn't have deterred me from running to the gardens to collect a bouquet of flowers for her or writing a sonnet in her honour. It was most unnerving, and I was very glad when a servant arrived to offer me some breakfast. It was a relief to be able to concentrate on the one true love who had remained constant throughout my life: food.

By the time my selection of breads, rolls and jams arrived, the rest of the family had woken. Algar accompanied his wife into the room, his arm threaded through hers and a faint smile on his lips. Cressida, meanwhile, looked just as horrified as she had the night before. I half expected her to deliver a sermon on the wickedness of using too much butter on one's bread after the look she gave my breakfast.

Instead, she kept her thoughts to herself and took a place at the far end of the table. I had the sense that she would like to have criticised her daughter, too, as her eyes flicked across at Gertrude every few seconds. I could only assume that it was propriety that kept her from launching into a tirade and, by the time Dante arrived, all four members of the Wyndham clan had returned to their usual roles.

Gertrude had become colder, calmer and quieter. A distant, martyr-like look had taken possession of her features, and I wished that I'd made better use of our time alone together instead of babbling on about the production of a drink that I didn't even enjoy.

I could see that it was the job of the two men in the family to animate the others. Algar did his best to cheer his daughter with jokes and anecdotes, though even he didn't risk enraging his wife. Dante was so uneasy that, at one moment, he juggled three apples whilst singing 'Burlington Bertie'. In response, Gertrude stared at her paper all the more intently, and her mother said a prayer that was little more than a hoarse, crackling whisper before starting on her breakfast of dry toast.

I'm sure it was a great relief for everyone when Grandfather popped along to make things less awkward.

"Good morning, everybody." His jubilant tone seemed to warm the room by a few degrees. It was a rare moment to catch him in his waistcoat and shirt sleeves. I could only assume that his coat was being cleaned. "What a fine day it–"

His arrival was sadly overshadowed by the appearance of a grey-faced butler, who rushed into the room just behind him.

"I'm sorry to disturb you, M'Lord, but Jed Gibson is waiting to speak to you."

"Well, show him in, man," King Algar summoned, and his nervous minion scurried off to fulfil his task.

"I'm terribly sorry to bother you, Lord Dunraven," the local character began in a hesitant voice, as he stepped into the handsomely appointed breakfast room. "I thought I'd better bring the bad news in person." With this said, he stopped speaking.

"Perhaps your visitor would like some privacy to deliver his message," my grandfather suggested and sat down so that he could graciously stand back up again *tout de suite*.

"No, no, M'Lord." Jed peered around every face at the table before his gaze came to rest on mine. I had to infer that he was searching for the least intimidating member of our party to address. "You see… a body has been found."

"In the village?" the earl asked and, across the table, his wife released a cry.

"A dead body?" she asked, though I rather thought this went without saying.

"That's right, M'Lady." Even now, Jed struggled to continue. "It's Florence Keyse… the landlady o' The Wyndham Arms. It appears she's been murdered."

CHAPTER TEN

I had expected my grandfather to take the lead at this moment, but he did not move a muscle. He stayed exactly where he was and watched our hosts to see the gamut of emotions that the news triggered.

Horror, fear, anger and disgust were plain on their four faces. I didn't know what to make of this display, but evidently the great detective in our midst had gathered the information he required and began to issue orders to the returning butler.

"If the police haven't been called, then get to it. You should mention that I will soon be at the scene of the crime. With that done, you must tell my chauffeur that his services are required. I'm sure that he will know to bring my dog." He walked over to the window that faced the town, then changed his mind and came back towards the servant. "And one more thing. I will need my coat."

"Your coat, M'Lord?" the upright butler enquired with all the pomp expected of his position. "But it must be eighty degrees outside."

"That's right, my good man. I requested my coat, not a report on the weather. Now off you go."

The blue-waistcoated retainer raced from the room and Algar finally spoke. "Is there anything that we…" His words ran dry at this moment. I could see the impact the news had made upon the poor fellow. "Is there anything I should do?"

"No. Not for the moment." It was odd to hear my grandfather reply so bluntly to his old friend, but there was only one person in that room who had his wits about him. It wasn't me, and it certainly wasn't Algar Wyndham. "Look after your family and station a man at the gatehouse to make sure the castle is secure."

"Do you think this is the Mordaunts' doing?" Dante spoke in a low, shaken voice. Grandfather have heard him from across the room, and as his head flicked over in that direction.

"I knew this day would come," Cressida screeched, and something within her seemed to reach out to attack her troubled husband like the claws of a wolf. "'They that plough iniquity, and sow wickedness, reap the same.'" I was fairly certain this was something that our school chaplain had quoted to us on occasion. He always chose the most damnatory verses from the Bible, and I'm sure he would have got along just swimmingly with the Countess of Dunraven.

My cousin Gertrude was the only member of the family who had remained silent until now. Her mother's intervention must have sparked some change within her as, in the space of a moment, she began to cry. It was quiet yet violent; she laid her head on the table and the movement of her bare shoulders demonstrated the pain she was suffering.

"You have no need to worry," Grandfather assured them, as the butler returned with his grey morning coat. "You are all perfectly safe here. No one can harm you."

He nodded to me then, and I'd quite forgotten that I was to be anything but a spectator. I didn't feel quite right about leaving Clearwell, and it wasn't merely because I would like to have eaten more breakfast. I saw the shock still present on Dante's face and felt that I might have been more useful staying to comfort the family.

"Off we go, Christopher," Grandfather said and, as he hadn't questioned whether I would be joining him, I found it easier to accept the idea.

Todd had prepared the Rolls on the oval drive in front of the house. Delilah was sitting in the backseat already, and a few of our staff had evidently heard the news from their Clearwell counterparts. They were standing beside the gatehouse with sombre faces as we passed. Todd slowed the car just long enough for Grandfather to issue orders to his guard dog – the human one, not the friendly canine.

"Dorie, I'm trusting you to keep an eye on everyone here. There may be people nearby who wish to hurt the Wyndhams."

The giantess looked concerned for a moment but then smiled – presumably at the thought that she might get the chance to punch somebody. "Yes, Mr Lord Edgington, sir. Of course, Your Highness." And then she waved us off with one meaty mitt.

Driving just a few hundred yards in a Rolls Royce seemed opulent, even for a lord, but I suppose that time was of the essence. When Todd pulled the car to a stop outside the pub, there was a policeman already standing on duty.

"Morning, Superintendent Edgington," he said with a tip of his helmet and a nod of the head.

"Constable," Grandfather responded. "Would you mind telling me what you know so far about the incident?"

The bell-shaped chap in the blue uniform moved his chin lower to his chest as though he were trying to hide the fact he had a neck. "I haven't been in there, Guv'nor. I'm not paid enough for that." Though clearly scandalised by the idea of doing his job, he maintained a civil tone.

Grandfather sounded shocked by this attitude. "But there's been a murder. A woman is dead and even a momentary delay could lead to the killer going unpunished."

"Well, that's as maybe, but there's a dead body in there." He paused to allow the full significance of this information to be absorbed. "I've been on this planet for forty-nine years without seeing a dead body. I'd prefer to keep it that way."

Such logic was impossible to counter, even for my wise grandfather, and so he gave up trying. Instead, he let out a huff and, taking a handkerchief from his pocket, opened the door to the pub.

He paused on the threshold. "I don't suppose you have any objection to my taking a look?"

"Be my guest, Guv'nor." The constable made sure to look away from the building at that moment, so as not to spy even a glimpse of the dead woman through the open door.

Without any lamps lit, it was far darker inside the pub than it had been the night before. The ceiling was low and the windows small. The place smelt of the fire in the grate and the locals' tobacco, which seemed to permeate every surface. There were still dirty glasses and tankards on the tables, and the floor hadn't been swept.

Grandfather moved around the bar with quiet reverence. Though I enjoyed criticising the odd foible in the old chap's behaviour, he was undeniably respectful when dealing with the deceased. It did not take us long to find that day's corpse.

Poor Florence Keyse. She was by far the loveliest landlady upon whom I'd ever set eyes, and now she was lying dead in the very spot where she'd worked so cheerfully the night before. I still found it difficult to see a good, kind person such as her robbed of that vital ingredient which makes each of us so special. Her light had been extinguished, and Grandfather and I stood without saying anything. We were unable to start the investigation until we'd acknowledged the tragedy of a young woman's life being so curtailed.

When a suitable time had passed, he kneeled to look at the corpse. "I believe this was a pre-meditated attack." He nodded to himself and inspected the stretch of rope that had been pulled tight around the woman's neck.

I really didn't see how he could have divined such a thing, not only in this incredibly short time, but without carrying out a detailed examination of the scene.

"Interesting," I said, as I was hardly going to admit what an ignoramus I was. "You mean because of the choice of weapon?"

"That's right."

Fantastic, I'd made him believe I knew what I was talking about. Now I just hoped he would explain what it was that we both understood.

"This place is like an arsenal," I prattled when he didn't utter another word. "There must be a hundred weapons the killer could have used, from cricket bats to bottles of cider. And the length of the rope is just right for garrotting someone. Whoever killed her came here with a purpose."

He stopped the inspection and looked up at me. I couldn't quite read the expression on his face, but it was not one with which I was familiar. "Christopher…"

I thought I'd done something terrible then, and the most intense feeling of guilt stung my insides.

"Christopher, those are the exact thoughts I had when I saw her."

Even after he said this, it didn't feel quite right, and I raced to apologise. "I don't know what's come over me, Grandfather. I really don't. Perhaps I should lie down."

He shot to his feet and seized my hand to give it a hearty shake. "Not at all, my boy. You've just done something most impressive. You've extracted a key piece of information from the scene of the crime. While any number of motives are still possible, the evidence before us is exactly as you read it."

I didn't know how to reply, and so I hummed for a while and hoped the funny spell would pass.

"In fact…" There was a great smile on his face and, if this wasn't a bad enough sign, he went digging in his pocket for something. "…I think you should put these gloves on and search for clues yourself."

I'm fairly certain I'd had a voice once. I distinctly remember using it from time to time, but it had deserted me, and I very much doubted it would return. Of course, this meant I couldn't argue with the forceful fellow, and he somehow managed to thread my fingers into the white cotton gloves.

"There we go." He nudged me down to the floor with a knee in the back of my leg for assistance. "Now. What can you find?"

I would love to have immediately surged into action, but there was a slight problem; I'd caught sight of the poor, lifeless creature before me. I was filled with such sorrow that I couldn't bring myself to disturb her any further. For a moment, all I could do was kneel there and think of the life she would have had if some monster hadn't murdered her.

I saw her wedding to a cheery young farmer and a family photograph of the pair of them in their twilight years, surrounded by loved ones. There were children and grandchildren, and every last one of them was smiling at dear, sweet Florence, the landlady of The Wyndham Arms. But what stood out to me most was the brown of her eyes. The photograph in my imagination blended with the sad scene before me, and I saw that those pretty orbs were flooded with channels of red where the blood vessels had burst.

I was certain that my grandfather was going to hurry me along, but his hectoring never came. He stood behind me and allowed me to take my time. And when I felt I'd paid sufficient tribute to the slain woman, I did my best to make sense of the scene.

"Perhaps she was attacked from behind?" I half suggested, half enquired.

Grandfather did not respond for a moment. "Hmmm... Why do you say that?"

"Well..." It was harder to put things into words sometimes than simply guess them correctly. "Less force would be required. The killer wouldn't have had to wrap the cord around her neck several times." A thought occurred to me, and I stood back up to peer over the bar. "And there was a struggle."

"Good again, Christopher." His eyes scanned the upturned stools and fallen chairs that had barely registered in my mind as we'd entered. "I believe that Florence was in here tidying the bar when someone entered. It's impossible to say whether he threatened her, or she realised she was in danger as soon as she saw the nasty fellow, but it looks as though she charted a course around the tables before running behind the bar where he caught her."

"Perhaps if she'd run in the other direction, she would have made it to the door."

Grandfather exhaled despondently and looked around the narrow space where the body lay. "There." He pointed his finger at a double-barrelled gun that was attached to the wall at the end of the bar.

"It wouldn't be loaded, would it?"

His eyebrows shot up his forehead as though to say, *there's only one way to find out.* I felt a little guilty about stepping over Florence, but it had to be done. With the white cotton gloves still protecting the evidence, I seized the weapon.

It probably comes as a surprise to no one to say that I'm not much of a hunter and, on the one occasion my uncle Maitland had forced me to hold a gun, I was terrified I would shoot myself in the head. This time, I had more composure about myself. I carefully removed it from its bracket and passed it to my grandfather. I was sure he knew his way around a shotgun and would be less likely to murder us both with it.

He pushed a hidden lever on the top of the... the... ummm, what's the bit on the top called? Well, regardless, he pushed the lever and broke the barrels to look inside the chambers.

"It's loaded," he confirmed. "Though that's probably not so rare in the country. Guns are tools out here. There's no need for one in Leicester Square, but farmers use them all the time."

This didn't make a great deal of sense to me. "So a pub in a small village kept a loaded shotgun in case of... what? Rogue deer running down the high street? An infestation of rabid rabbits?"

He laughed to himself and walked around the bar. It felt odd to remain there, and I wondered if he expected me to serve him a drink.

"You may have a point, but there's something we're both forgetting."

I had rarely heard my grandfather admit to doing anything so human before and was curious to discover what this was. "Oh, yes?"

"Yes. We've forgotten what happened here last night."

"The explosion," I replied, recalling the scene of chaos we'd witnessed.

"That's right. The locals all seized arms. The gun may well have been loaded then."

This seemed something of a moot point, as it was not the murder weapon and merely explained Florence's attempted escape from her assailant. It occurred to me, though, that this analysis was not for Florence's sake or even the investigation's. Grandfather was putting me to work to see where my capabilities (or otherwise) lay.

I returned to the body as Grandfather secured the shotgun back on the wall. I noticed that he first removed the two shells and put them in his pocket, presumably in case anyone else in the village should have murderous thoughts.

"I'm afraid there's one vital clue that you've missed, Chrissy." He walked along the bar to point out a small metal object that had come to a rest beside one of the huge barrels of beer. I took the brass button between gloved fingers and held it up for him to see.

"The Lieutenant-Colonel!" I exclaimed, dreaming that we had solved the case in record time, and that I would now be free to spend the rest of my weekend exploring the forest with my cousin. "It must have fallen off when he murdered her. He's our man."

"Not on that evidence, he's not. The button you are holding is from the uniform of a soldier in the Royal Army Medical Corps. Lieutenant-Colonel Stroud was in the Royal Artillery."

I was taken aback. "You can tell that just by looking?"

"Yes, of course I can. The Royal Artillery badge features a crown and canon, with the Latin motto Ubique Quo Fas Et Gloria Ducunt underneath. As you will notice, the button in your hand has the serpent-entwined Rod of Asclepius within a wreath of laurel."

I wondered for a moment whether the Latin he had recited would prove of major significance to the case – though thought it more likely he merely enjoyed showing off his knack for reciting chunks of an old, dead language.

"So if it isn't the Lieutenant-Colonel's, to whom does it belong?" I was incredibly pleased with myself as I thought this quite the most essential question we could ask. My big head was soon deflated.

"No, no, my boy. The question we must answer is how it came to be here in the first place."

I tried to do just this, but soon gave up on the task. Instead, I gave

Florence one last look. I don't know whether it was my own instinct to be a shining knight to every damsel in distress we encountered, but something about her death cut deep within me. I couldn't just leave her there until a doctor came, so I knelt down and closed her eyes. It was a futile gesture but helped me feel I'd at least tried to help her.

"It's such a tragedy," I said, as I rose from this sad act. "What I want to know is why anyone would want to kill her in the first place."

Back to his normal self, he was unimpressed by my comment. "Obviously, boy. That's the whole reason we're here!"

CHAPTER ELEVEN

We left the gloomy pub, and it felt in that moment as though it were not just Florence Keyse who had died, but the village itself. There was no sign of life on the high street and, as we strolled back along the scorched high street towards the Rolls, the only person I saw was the Lieutenant-Colonel. He was lingering in his front garden, clearly interested to discover what we had found.

"That poor girl really is dead then, is she?" Though somewhat younger than my partner in crime detection, he had a rather ancient air about him. His face was grey and pinched, his wiry hair yellow, as though stained by the sun, and his sentences came out in short stabs.

"That's right." Grandfather clearly wasn't going to divulge any unnecessary information. "Do you know who found her?"

"It was the brewer's boy. He comes most mornings to deliver fresh barrels of beer. I was reading the paper in my breakfast room." He pointed over his shoulder to one of the windows at the front of his small, thatched house. A sign beside the door read 'Dunraven Cottage'. "I heard him run out screaming, and we rang the police from here."

"It seems that Clearwell is a dangerous place to live." Grandfather glanced about the garden and his eyes came to rest upon the circular well that was further along the pavement from us. I had to assume it was very old as the wall appeared to have been built around it.

"The world is dangerous wherever bad people roam." The old soldier sighed, and he seemed to be just as depressed about Clearwell's lost landlady as we were.

"Do you know why anyone would have wanted to kill her?" Grandfather asked, and our witness-cum-suspect turned his head at an angle, perhaps thinking that the great Lord Edgington should have already formed his own conclusions.

"I would say that was obvious, under the circumstances." He adjusted the rather wilted flower in the buttonhole of his blazer, as though this were more important than answering silly questions.

"You're referring to the Mordaunts of Scowles Folly, I presume?"

When the man looked back at us, he was most aggrieved. "I very much am. Those savages have been terrorising this village for decades. I remember the current brood's grandparents being quite abhorrent when I was a child. But they've taken it too far this time, don't you think?"

"It could simply be a case of–"

His muscles tensed and he turned towards the pub. "I suppose you'd like me to believe that it's just a coincidence. You're suggesting it's merely chance that, on the two-hundredth anniversary of Lady Morgana's death, our own local beauty should be murdered in the middle of the night."

Grandfather would not be baited and kept his voice calm. "I was going to say that it could have been a case of a jealous lover or a disagreement in the village."

"No, it couldn't." I'll give him this; he was quite adamant on the matter. "You can mark my words; I know all that goes on in Clearwell. Although every young man wanted to be with her, Florence wasn't interested in any of them." His voice faded out then, and I think that just the mention of her name brought back the reality of her death. "It was those Mordaunts. And, if you ask me, they were behind Cole Watkins' murder as well."

This was an interesting point I hadn't had time to consider. Two members of a tiny village had died in suspicious circumstances within a month of one another. Surely my grandfather would be eager to find a connection between the deaths.

"How long have you been living in Clearwell, Lieutenant-Colonel?" Or perhaps not.

As though his credentials had been questioned, he shot bolt upright and barked out some facts. "I was born and raised here, as it happens. There's evidence of my family in these parts going back eons." His cheeks were as red as the roses climbing in his garden, and the veins in his neck bulged like swollen rivers. "My great-grandfather helped raise the original church back before St Peter's was–"

"I see," Grandfather interrupted before the man could burst. "So you know the place rather well." He turned away from the conversation and peered back towards the high street. There was a petroleum garage a few houses down, a bakery on one corner, and a butcher's opposite. "No doubt you've grown up with stories of the feud with Scowles Folly?"

"That's right." Stroud made no effort to hide this fact. "And what of it?"

Grandfather brightened for a moment and replied with an angelic grin. "Oh, no reason. I merely question whether the ingrained hatred that exists towards the rival town might fuddle people's thinking."

Like a boar protecting his territory, the old soldier stamped his foot. "I am in no way mistaken. I know for a fact that the Mordaunts were here last night, and the end result is plain for all to see. You heard the explosion, didn't you? You saw the damage they did?"

Grandfather walked a few feet away, as if no longer interested. "I saw some theatrical effects and a brief combustion in the street. But, no, I did not notice any real danger."

The old soldier opened his mouth to speak, but Lord Edgington had more to say. "It's much like any country rivalry – all talk and no action. The people of St Mary-under-Twine, which borders my estate, haven't spoken to an inhabitant of Mill's Steeple for over a century. Even our postman leaves his letters in a box on the outskirts. But despite a lot of talk and the occasional kerfuffle between youngsters, there's no real danger in the rivalry. It's a pastime, much like croquet or painting."

He smiled to himself then, and I had no doubt he was considering his continuing passion for amateur art. He'd been trying his hand at impressionism recently and... well, impressive is not the word I'd use.

"They hate us, and we hate them." Stroud looked in danger of bursting an artery, if he hadn't already. "It's more than just a rivalry. There's been no shortage of violence over the years, but this is murder."

"Murders plural, weren't you saying?"

I often felt the need to study my grandfather rather than our suspects during interviews. His reactions were far harder to decipher but tended to be worth the effort.

Stroud gave another irate stamp and pulled on his sleeves. "That's right. Two murders – first Cole Watkins and now that tragic creature who did nothing but good for other people."

Just when we seemed to be getting somewhere, Grandfather would pull the conversation off in another direction. "Florence was a kind person, was she?"

"The very best sort of Gloucestershire lass. She took over the pub when her parents were killed in a tragic threshing accident. She was barely twenty-one at the time, but she put aside her inexperience to keep the heart of the village alive."

"And what about Cole Watkins? Was he your sort of person?"

The Lieutenant-Colonel appeared to have two moods: angry and enraged. He could veer between the two at a moment's notice. "He was a harmless sort of young person. Harmless, shiftless and more or less useless, but not the type to cause too much trouble."

"That's not what we heard last night from some of the townsfolk."

The soldier's eyebrows attempted to jump from his body just then. "Oh, yes? And what did they tell you?"

I tried to remember this myself, and Grandfather put one hand to his head as though struggling to recall. "I believe it was the accordionist, Jed Gibson. Now, what did he tell me had passed between you and Young Cole?"

The conversation we'd had in The Wyndham Arms suddenly came back to me. "He said that Lieutenant-Colonel Stroud didn't like Cole because he was always sitting in front of his house singing. I don't suppose you pushed him down the well, did you? The well just in front of your property."

"Are you intentionally trying to antagonise me?" the cantankerous fellow asked. "I told you, it's the Mordaunts with whom you need to talk. Clearwell is not a large village. If I went about murdering everyone, the population would shrink far too quickly for my liking."

"Of course it would." I believe there was a touch of sarcasm in Grandfather's voice. "But just so that I'm sure of the facts, would you mind telling me where you went after you left The Wyndham Arms last night?"

He glanced along the road and shook his head. "I went to see my brother in The Pludds. I was there all night and didn't come back until an hour ago. That was shortly before I saw the brewer's boy in such a state."

"I'm sorry, 'The Pludds'?" I couldn't let this pass without comment.

"That's right, boy. It's a village out near Ruardean. Is there something funny about it?"

"Oh, no, of course not. That's a perfectly reasonable name for a village."

I had to ask myself what was wrong with my country? Why had our ancestors chosen such outlandish monikers?

"I can give you my brother's telephone number if you wish. He'll confirm that I was with him all night." The retired soldier did not seem nervous about his alibi, and a note of amusement entered his voice. "We stayed up until late swapping war stories. To be perfectly honest, he only made it to the rank of major and has never lived it down."

"Very good, Lieutenant-Colonel. You should pass that information to the officer in charge of the case… whenever he appears." Grandfather was all grace and manners once more. "Meanwhile, I think it's high time we travelled to the cesspit of immorality about which we've heard so much."

"You're going to Scowles Folly?" The soldier sounded shocked and perhaps a little impressed. He was not the first person in Clearwell to suggest that any such visit would lead to untold risk.

"That's right." Grandfather glanced about once more. "Now, where's my dog? Christopher, did we forget to bring Delilah?"

"Oh, dear. I think we must have left her at the castle."

Without another look at our *wit-spect* (or perhaps *sus-ness* would be better?) Grandfather trundled back to the Rolls. "Back to Clearwell Castle, Todd. Delilah will not be happy with me."

Before our chauffeur could reply, the placid beast stood up on the back seat of the vehicle where she'd been sleeping. She told her master exactly what she thought of his absent-mindedness.

"What do you expect from me? I have rather a lot of things on my mind." Grandfather was quite indignant, and I could only imagine what the crowd of people who had gathered opposite the pub were thinking as he conducted a brief conversation with a canine.

Luckily for all involved, there was a distraction at this moment. The doctor had arrived, and the locals were suitably impressed by the dashing run the young chap made from his car. I don't know why he bothered; a few seconds quicker wouldn't do Florence any good.

This raised an interesting question. "I didn't consider the time of death when I examined the body," I said as I climbed in beside the somewhat placated Delilah.

"It was your first attempt at truly examining a crime scene, my boy. You can't be expected to think of everything."

I liked his turn of phrase and rather wondered if such a sentiment would one day be etched on my tombstone.

Here Lies Christopher Aloysius Prentiss

Born 18th August 1908
Died 24th June 1926

He couldn't be expected to think of everything…
Though perhaps it would have been a good idea
to look both ways before crossing that busy road.

I noticed that a few familiar faces were mingling with the crowd by now. Jed, the previously jolly accordionist, had returned from the castle. A number of young farmers from the night before had arrived, and Dante had walked over to see what was happening. Feeling rather like King George, I gave them all a solemn wave as we roared past them in our car.

CHAPTER TWELVE

"Scowles Folly, Todd," Grandfather announced. Our capable driver had an instinctive knowledge of the direction in which to point the car, and we shot off along a stretch of densely forested road. It was my first venture deep into the woodland that so characterised that part of the country and, despite the sad circumstances of the day, it felt rather wonderful to fly through that beautiful tunnel of trees, which the sunlight penetrated like a rain of diamonds from heaven.

Clearwell's rival village was only a few miles away, but it in no way matched the picture I'd crafted in my brain. Every hamlet we'd passed through the day before had been quaint and well preserved. Scowles Folly was... well, it was not.

As the forest spat us out beneath a clear blue sky, I spotted the first signs of the distressed state of the place. Pieces of agricultural machinery were piled up at the side of the road. Countless motors, trailers and disembodied cogs lay in small heaps at the entrance to the village and I wondered how anyone could allow such messiness to remain there.

The sign welcoming us had been splashed with more blood, which I thought an odd thing to do in one's own village. The small settlement had no tarmac on the road, and it felt for a moment as though we had stepped back into some long past epoch – the stone age perhaps, or medieval times if I was being generous.

Todd pulled the car to a stop in front of The Lady Morgana public house. There was a town square, of sorts, though it would have been more accurate to call it a muddy patch in the middle of a few untidy buildings. And yet, in the centre of everything, one impressive edifice stood tall.

I got out to make sense of the towering structure which dominated the town. It was now clear to me why the place had such a strange name. We had located the folly, and it was a dramatic sight to behold. One gigantic stone tower soared out of the earth, and there were lower levels built onto it on either side. At first, I'd assumed it was a ruin destroyed in battle. I couldn't say which one. The Hundred Years' War perhaps? Where did that take place?

Well, as I was saying, at first, I assumed that parts of the castle-ish structure had been destroyed, but as I walked closer, I got the definite sense that the building had never been completed.

"That's the Wyndhams' doing, in case you were wondering."

I hadn't spotted him at first, but a huge muscly chap with a smith's hammer in one hand walked over to stand beside us. He was shirtless, and I noticed a snake in black ink curling around his arm.

He soon continued his tale. "Back when Lady Morgana was promised to the old earl, my ancestors hoped to expand the existing tower. They set to work, spending the money promised in the betrothal, but she died before she was married. The Wyndhams broke their promise, and it left us Mordaunts penniless. They knew what they were doing. They'd always looked down on us." It was impressive how he spoke of these ancient events as though they had only just occurred.

There was something rather wolf-like about him. He had shaggy black hair that looked as though it had been shorn with school scissors. A matching beard covered the lower half of his face, and the smell of sweat mingled with the fumes from the forge behind him. There was another man working in the shadows inside, but he did not come out to talk to us.

"I take it you are Jimmy Mordaunt?" Grandfather assumed somewhat precipitously, and the hulking figure shook his head.

"Jimmy's m' brother. I'm Cliff Mordaunt."

Grandfather turned from the monstrous construction to look at our new acquaintance. "Well, I'd like to speak to him."

Despite his rough appearance, there was a fire in Cliff's eyes that suggested a keen intellect. "What's happened? Where've you two toffs come from?"

I feel I should point out that, as I was still a mere adolescent, I didn't consider myself a fully fledged toff. If anything, I was a toff in training. Of course, I didn't dare contradict him. I was entirely petrified by this mountain of a man.

"I'm sure you can imagine whence we've come. We bear sad–" Before Grandfather could finish this sentence, another welcoming party arrived.

A group of figures emerged from the folly and walked over to us in a line. It reminded me of our reception at the castle the day before, and it didn't require any great rumination on my part to realise that we were about to meet the mayor of Scowles Folly.

"Hello there, both." The limping chap at the front of the line sent a wave in our direction. "Welcome to our town. New visitors are always warmly received." He had a reedy, sing-song voice and, though I understood him to be the lycanthrope's brother, the two siblings were in stark contrast. The new arrival was stick thin and, perhaps to disguise his impediment, walked almost on tiptoes. He was followed by a woman and three girls, who would not say a word the whole time we were there.

"So you're Jimmy Mordaunt?" Grandfather asked and put his hand out for the man to shake. "You're the mayor of Scowles Folly?"

"That I am, sir. For my sins, that I am." He grinned a gap-toothed grin and, thanks to the wild-eyed stare he displayed, I would sooner have thought him the village idiot than its mayor.

"I come from Clearwell bearing bad news. A young woman by the name of Florence Keyse has been murdered. She was the landlady of The Wyndham Arms."

I studied the reactions of Jimmy and his family but learnt nothing. The three girls had messy faces and grubby fingers and looked quite unaware of the weight of my grandfather's words. Perhaps more tellingly, though I thought nothing of it at the time, there was the sound of falling tools from within the blacksmith's forge.

"Sad tidings, indeed," Jimmy said, without feeling. "I don't see why you thought that would interest us, though, Mr...?"

"Lord." Grandfather said this with such force that it felt as though he'd revealed the identity of the killer. "I am the Marquess of Edgington. Perhaps you've heard of me."

Cliff stepped around us to stand shoulder to shoulder with his skinny brother. "You're that policeman, ain't you? I've read about you in the papers."

Jimmy still wore his fatuous grin. "That doesn't change anything. The death of a woman in that pit of a town has nothing to do with us here."

I thought this rather a rich criticism of Clearwell considering the state in which we found their muddy stain on the landscape. I took a moment to look about and noticed a set of stocks on what might generously be described as the green. There was a sort of scarecrow trapped within the heavy wooden contraption. It was dressed in a medieval leather jerkin and had horsehair stuck to its head to make it look like Algar Wyndham. Two barefoot boys were throwing old vegetables at the poor helpless dummy, and the scene turned my stomach.

This was not the only sign that we had visited at a time of festivity. A circle of ashes suggested a bonfire had been enjoyed the night before. I had to think that the fake Algar had been lucky to suffer such a minor punishment. He certainly looked the type to end up on a pyre.

"I'm afraid I must disagree," the esteemed detective continued. "They were your people, were they not, who launched a raid on Clearwell yesterday? You were the ones who doused the place in blood and fire?"

"They spilled the first blood, M'Lord." Though he spoke politely enough, it was hard to tell whether Jimmy's obsequiousness was genuine. "And all of that yesterday was just a game. We don't want them Clearwellians thinking we've forgotten the past, but we're peaceful people here in Scowles Folly. You'll find no murderer here."

"I knew Florence," Cliff confessed, and I noticed he looked a touch sadder than the rest of the family. "I did some work for her parents some years back, and she was a nice girl. But my brother's right. No one here would have touched her. What good would it do us?"

I could see that there was another game at play. Grandfather tilted his head appreciatively, but then his hand shot out in the direction of the gloomy workshop. "And what about your son? What about the only inhabitant of this village who regularly goes to Clearwell to drink in the pub where Florence worked?"

Jimmy looked puzzled by this description and his gaze strayed over to the forge. I can only imagine that Grandfather's vision was a darn sight better than mine, as I couldn't tell the figure in the shadows from Adam's Auntie Nora.

"My nephew?" the skinny mayor continued. "You're saying that Cliff's boy has been spending time in Clearwell?" It seemed this news came as something of a surprise, and he barked out a command. "Sam Mordaunt! You get over here this instant."

There was some more clanking, but 'The Infiltrator' whom we'd seen the night before did not emerge.

"Boy," his father said, and I saw more evidence of Cliff's impressive temper. "You come here this minute, or I'll be in there

84

with my hammer to knock you about until there's no sense left in your head."

I wondered whether the young man would try to escape then, as his hazy movements in the shadows became more panicked. The question was, why did he need to run in the first place? Was it the police – in elderly lord form at least – his jejune uncle or his ferocious father whom he feared most?

Sam finally walked into the light, and I was staggered at just how brawny that otherwise timid fellow was. Apparently, the men in his family had no interest in shirts; the muscles on his chest were like two ladders laid side by side. I could only imagine what Cliff's wife looked like. Perhaps she was a bear.

I hadn't had the opportunity to see Sam Mordaunt at close quarters the night before, but he had a cheerful face, closer to his grinning uncle's than his monstrous father's. His pale eyes were set deep and he had a pleasingly large nose. He was younger than I had first thought and couldn't have been much older than my brother.

"The gentleman is here to talk to you about what you did or *did not* see last night in Clearwell," his father explained with some emphasis placed on the negative option.

Sam peeked at his uncle then, and I was curious once more about who held the power in this strange community. Big Cliff would have seemed the obvious strong-man leader, and yet Jimmy was the mayor and seemingly held sway over his nephew's actions.

"It ain't a crime to go for a drink in a public house. That's why they calls them *public*."

This insolence earned him a slap around the back of his head from the blacksmith. "Enough cheek, boy. Just answer the man's questions."

"He ain't even asked me nothing." Sam turned to my grandfather for the first time, and something evidently registered in his brain. "You were there, M'Lord. You saw me leave without causing no trouble. So what's this about?"

Grandfather narrowed his eyes and performed a three-second bout of silent analysis. "I believe you've already heard the reason we are here. Florence Keyse is dead. She was murdered at…"

My mentor pointed at me then. I'd barely had the time to consider the question but managed to stutter out a response. "At… at just after

85

closing time last night. She was disturbed in the middle of tidying."

"Precisely." Grandfather offered me an appreciative nod, which I happily accepted. "And the fact that you left the pub before that moment proves nothing. Why did you go to Clearwell? Why have you been drinking on enemy territory, so to speak?"

"That's something I'd like to know," Jimmy agreed.

Sam no longer had the courage to look at his relatives but kept his eyes focused on the two of us. "I don't reckon they're our enemies. I think this whole situation is plain daft."

He gestured towards the pub sign – a painting of a bejewelled woman in repose – and then the stocks and blood that was splashed about the village. I must say the overall effect was a macabre one. I could only assume from the fervour with which the pair of youths were sending cabbages at the effigy of Algar that Sam's opinion was not shared by many there.

When Grandfather's next question shot from his mouth, it landed with great force. "Were you in love with the deceased?"

Sam stood his ground, but I could see the impact the accusation had made. "In love with her? I barely knew the woman. I've spoken five words to her, fifty or so times. And those words were 'Pint of Shires, please, love.'"

"Fifty times?" Cliff's fingers wrapped more tightly around the impressively large hammer in his impressively large hand. For a moment, he reminded me of the Norwegian god of thunder. Or do I mean the Swedish god of thunder? Well, he reminded me of Thor either way. "I knew you'd been over there; I didn't realise you'd set up camp."

The mayor of Scowles Folly had been taking in this conversation without comment but now straightened to his full, flimsy height. "Why would you have gone to Clearwell in the first place? We've got a perfectly good pub here and better ale to boot."

He wouldn't meet the man's gaze. "Funnily enough, Uncle, I don't plan to spend my life in this hamlet. Unless I plan on marrying one of my many cousins, I'll have to set out on my own one day."

The eldest of the three girls (who looked approximately twelve) did not seem to mind the idea of marrying her older cousin, but then she'd also been looking at me like I was a bowl of chocolate mousse. It made me feel most uncomfortable. Fortunately, her father soon shooed the three of them away, and they went to join the other children in their game.

"There are plenty of other villages around," he said with disappointment in his voice. "You didn't have to betray your family by mixing with the Wyndhams and their despicable clan."

Sam's gaze finally locked onto his uncle's, and he held it for several seconds without saying a word. "I don't care about the past. When will you see that? It's the twentieth century. There are no such things as clans or curses. We live in the age of automobiles and aeroplanes – not that anyone'd think it living here. I know you want us to pretend it's still 1726, but what good does it do?"

I thought for a moment that his father betrayed a touch of sympathy for his son's position but, instead of supporting him, he gave Sam a thwack around the back of his skull. "Don't talk like that in front of your elders. What would your mother think if she heard you spouting such rubbish?"

This did raise the question of where the presumably gigantic mother was. I also had to wonder why Jimmy's wife had been there the whole time without saying anything. Were women not allowed to speak in Scowles Folly? Was it some form of outdated community where only the men had any say in things? I jolly well hoped not!

"The boy's answered your questions," Jimmy said in that vacuous tone of his before placing his skinny arm around my grandfather's shoulders.

I realised in that moment that I had seen him in Clearwell the day before. There was something in his slow, jerking gait that was frankly unique, and I was sure he'd been the one reading out the charges against the Wyndham family.

"If there's anything else you want to know, I'll be only too happy to answer your questions. In fact, I'd like to invite you to a pint of our local bitter if you have the time. It's a family recipe, goes back generations."

Grandfather didn't appear to know how to view this offer. While clearly no great thinker, Jimmy Mordaunt was not the odious sort I had imagined from the way the Clearwell locals had spoken of him. He had a light, cheerful manner. Even when discussing the never-ending rivalry between the two villages, he had seemed faintly amused by the whole thing, as though he were playing someone else's game.

Was this a clever disguise or the real man we were seeing? And what of his burly brother? Jimmy clearly held sway in the village, but Cliff had the quick temper and the strength to squeeze the life out of another man. Assuming that no other complications arose, I was fairly certain that I'd narrowed down our field of suspects to a mere two names.

Gosh! That was easy for once.

CHAPTER THIRTEEN

It was clear there was a lot more my grandfather would have liked to ask the younger Mordaunt, but Sam returned to the forge, and we were packed off towards the scruffy pub.

While The Wyndham Arms had rustic charm by the barrowful, The Lady Morgana was a tatty mess. The floor was made of cold, clay tiles with straw strewn across them. There was plaster coming off the walls, as though someone had been throwing a large, heavy brick about the place. One of the beams was broken and, beside it, you could see through a hole in the ceiling to the derelict floor above. It might once have been a cosy spot for a ploughman's lunch or a glass of cider, but neglect and the never-relenting march of Old Father Time had turned it into a pub it would be best to avoid.

"What will you have, Lord Edgington?" Jimmy asked, and his brother loitered menacingly in the doorway as though worried we might escape.

The only other customers were two old drunks who had passed out on a bench in the corner. I could smell them as soon as we'd entered, and they certainly weren't the type to add character to the place.

"The bitter you mentioned sounded wonderful." Grandfather rubbed his hands together, and we sat down on stools by the bar. "My grandson here will have a glass of water."

Thank goodness. I couldn't imagine drinking a substance with such an unappealing title. *Bitter*? It sounded just as tempting as *sour* or *brackish*. Couldn't someone have thought of a better name than *bitter*?

You can't go wrong with a nice glass of water, straight from the tap. I thanked the mayor for my refreshment and tipped it down my throat, only to discover that you very much can go wrong with a glass of water. It tasted like mud. It was not my lucky week.

"Delicious!" Grandfather drained half the large mug and slammed it down on the bar. "There's nothing like country ale. I should drink it more often."

"I've known folk around here live to ninety!" Jimmy revealed as he placed his weight on one arm on the bar. "I reckon it's the beer what keeps us young."

"That may well be." Considering the purpose of our visit, Grandfather was in a shockingly agreeable mood. "But I'm afraid I have more contentious matters to discuss." He paused to prepare his next comment, and Jimmy was clearly interested in what he had to say. "I believe that it would be in the killer's interest to make it look as though you, or one of your fellow villagers, were responsible for the murder last night. And so I must ask what you can tell me to rule out your family's involvement in the crime."

I was amazed at his transparency. He normally kept his theories more closely guarded than the Crown Jewels, but here he was, revealing his thoughts to our top suspect.

The mayor allowed a variety of expressions to ripple across his phiz. "I appreciate the question, Lord Edgington. And I can see why you'd ask, but I can't disprove the possibility altogether." He had to stop speaking to pour himself a drink, and it was clear that he needed it. Though he never lost his gormless smile, I could tell just how much the news had disturbed him. "You already know I were in Clearwell last night. But this is the only weekend of the year I set foot in the damned place."

Grandfather nodded mutely and waited for the man to continue.

"To an outsider, our customs might seem strange. But the blood and the demonic rig-outs are all part of the traditions that our ancestors conceived, and I have taken it upon myself as mayor to revive. We're merely following their example, and I can assure you that, in the two hundred years since Lady Morgana were murdered, no one from Scowles Folly has done anything so wicked in revenge."

I could see that Jimmy's simple manner had successfully won over my grandfather. It wasn't so much the words he used as the rather sincere way in which he said them. He was a rare character in whom I could detect no artifice. To be perfectly honest, he didn't seem smart enough to pull the wool over our eyes.

Still staring at our suspect, Grandfather took another sip of beer. I had drunk quite enough water and decided to forego my earthy libation.

"Perhaps what I really wanted to achieve by coming here is to discover your side of the story." He weighed his words for a moment and then added another thought. "Not just from last night, but all those decades ago. I have heard one version of Lady Morgana's tale, and now I'd like to know the one you learnt as children."

Jimmy lost his smile for a moment and nodded thoughtfully. "Again, it's good o' you to ask, Lord Edgington. I always says it's important to hear both sides of any story and form your own conclusions."

I had assumed that Cliff would tire of listening and return to his work, but he remained right there at his post in the doorway as his brother recounted the legend.

"The Wyndhams and the Mordaunts had long been rivals by the year of 1726 when Morgana died. They say that, centuries earlier, we all came from the same village, but a feud split our fortunes. The Wyndhams left Gloucestershire for Wales and returned here years later, richer and more arrogant than before." He halted the story to provide some context to this claim. "We don't have many documents here in Scowles Folly, but there'd be proof of all I'm saying over in Clearwell."

He began to polish a row of washed glasses, and I had to wonder whether he was the barkeeper as well as the mayor. "The rivalry were reignited when the current Earl of Dunraven's ancestors moved back to Clearwell and made plans to rebuild the manor. It was called Clower-Wall Court back in them days, but the old lord at the time, Thomas Wyndham his name was, wanted a castle. That wasn't all he wanted, neither. You see, he passed through the village here one day and spotted a diamond. Us Mordaunts made our living from the mines around here, so we knew a precious element when we saw one, and Lady Morgana were priceless."

He nodded towards the end of the bar, and I turned to see a cracked and faded portrait.

"That were done the year before she died. Have you ever seen such a stunner?" While it was true that her face was obscured by the poor condition of the painting, there was something about the way the artist had captured her perfectly oval eyes that struck me. I couldn't look away from the painting, as though her very gaze had hypnotised me. It was hard to say whether it was the original woman's charm or the skill of the hand who had painted her, but I was quite smitten.

"The boy can see it," Jimmy said, smirking a little as he patted me on the shoulder. "And so could Thomas Wyndham. He'd been married once before but was in want of a new wife after the first died – in suspicious circumstances, some say, though I couldn't possibly comment."

Grandfather inhaled loudly, eager to hear the next part of the story.

"What of the rivalry? Why would the Mordaunts have accepted the alliance if so much bad blood had passed between the two families?"

"Why do you think?" He didn't make us wait long to reveal the answer, which was lucky as my first thought was some way off the mark. "Money, of course." Yes, it had nothing to do with the secret lovechild of Queen Anne, and I cursed my imagination for getting the better of me.

"The Mordaunts wanted to finish the tower that you see outside and turn it into a true castle of their own. Wyndham promised them the funds if Morgana agreed to marry him. Her parents objected, but they weren't the ones with power around here and her uncle made a deal."

I had to swallow then as, whether she was an aristocrat or a peasant, I couldn't stand the thought of a woman changing hands for silver. I saw very little difference between Lady Morgana's fate and that of poor Susan in Thomas Hardy's 'The Mayor of Casterbridge' of which I had admittedly only read the first few chapters, but I was determined to finish it soon.

"That all sounds fairly typical for the time. What went wrong?" Grandfather was wrapped up in the story, much like a man who hears of an untapped goldmine.

Jimmy leaned closer over the bar and his voice fell to a whisper. "Like everything the Wyndhams stick their fingers into, there was a catch to the bargain. Our Morgana was only nineteen at the time she was bartered away, and she couldn't marry without her parents' consent. Wyndham wanted to protect his investment, so he made her stay at Clearwell until she turned twenty-one and they could wed."

The story was really getting interesting now, and neither my grandfather nor I had any wish to interrupt. "Two years passed with her stashed in the old manor house, while Wyndham planned his castle. But just days before the wedding, she was murdered."

He had gone into such detail until now that I expected some substantial evidence for this key element of his tale.

Grandfather could take the suspense no longer. "Well?"

"Well, what?" Jimmy pulled his head in, bemused.

"Well, how do you know she was murdered?"

He had finished polishing the tankards and set each one on a tray at the back of the bar. "It's obvious, isn't it?"

"No, of course it isn't!" Whoops, I may have been the one to bark this angry rebuttal. I didn't mean to scream at the fellow, but I do hate not knowing how a story ends.

"All right, all right. Keep your shirt on, young'un. I'll tell you what happened." He took an inordinately long time lifting a box of empty bottles from a shelf. "One of my ancestors was a maid at the big house before she was given her marching orders, and she said that Lady Morgana were pregnant. Few people knew anything about it, of course, as that kind of thing was frowned on out of wedlock in them days."

"It's frowned upon now," Grandfather added a little snootily.

"There you go, then. Well, it's obvious what happened. Thomas Wyndham killed her to hide his indiscretion. He denied it but couldn't explain why she died. All he'd say was that she'd fallen to her death from the tower of the old manor."

"So perhaps she didn't wish to marry him after all and jumped to her death."

Jimmy had another great smile on his lips. He was clearly holding back some final titbit to make the revelation all the more exciting. "Then why wouldn't he let them have her body?" He clucked his tongue, and I realised that there was something oddly hen-like about him. Though he was a skinny specimen, his movements were distinctly avian, and he never stayed still for long.

Evidently impressed by the tale, Grandfather sat up straighter. "Hmmm… that does add a frisson of intrigue to the proceedings."

"And that ain't all, neither." I noticed that Jimmy's voice sometimes plumbed the depths of the local dialect and sometimes sounded quite normal. In past cases, such shifting characteristics had sometimes implied a hidden identity that was peeking through to the surface. Perhaps he was the secret lovechild of–

Sorry. I'll stop myself there. I was getting carried away with my imagination again.

"Old Thomas Wyndham was engaged within a month of Morgana's death to one of the wealthiest women in the west of England. By the following year, they'd broken ground on the castle, and he reneged on the agreement he had with my family. He got his fancy estate, and we were left with a ruin in the middle of the forest."

"It's no surprise he didn't want to give them the money if they accused him of being a murderer." I thought this a fairly sensible point to make, but Grandfather frowned at my bluntness.

Jimmy didn't seem offended. "But that's not all. My great-great… I don't know how many greats-grandmother cursed the whole bloomin' lot of the Wyndham clan."

"With what?" Grandfather had such a sharp mind. I would never have thought to ask such an important, yet obvious, question.

Jimmy scratched his cheek and considered his answer. "Well, she didn't exactly specify what would happen. She just said, "I curse every last one of you for what you did to the good Lady Morgana.' And, ever since then, no female member of the Clearwell Wyndhams has survived to adulthood. Not one of 'em!"

"How terribly sad." Despite the light tone in which the story had been told, I couldn't help feeling despondent. "If what you say's true and countless girls over the years have died because of the curse that your family placed on your enemies, don't you think they've suffered enough?"

Jimmy Mordaunt looked at my grandfather then, as he clearly didn't have an answer for me.

"All this rivalry and hatred for two hundred years and now another woman has died. Why can't you forget the whole thing?"

It was the first time I'd seen the mayor look truly serious since we'd arrived in their town. The natural smile to his lips evened out, and he could not answer. So that task fell to his brother.

"We wouldn't expect an outsider to understand what we've been through over the years." Cliff took a few steps into the pub and seemed to fill the space around him so that the air suddenly felt thinner. "We've suffered failed harvests, failed businesses and dashed hopes for two centuries, and it all goes back to Lady Morgana. That was when the scales tipped. That was when our luck changed." Despite the confidence of his message, there was a reluctance to his tone.

"That's right," Jimmy finally asserted. "We've done nothing they haven't deserved. This weekend is the anniversary of her death, and we'll mark it as we see fit."

The two brothers stood alongside one another then. One was skinny, one immense – one jolly, one morose – and I still couldn't say whether either of them was responsible for Florence Keyse's death.

CHAPTER FOURTEEN

As we walked back to the car, I spotted Sam working away in front of the forge. He had a molten-hot blade and was hammering it into shape on the surface of an anvil. It was quite remarkable how such brute force could fashion something so elegant. What concerned me most, though, was the reason he was making a sword in the first place.

Grandfather and I had one last look around the village. The place was busier now, and all sorts of people had emerged from their homes. I suppose they must have been preparing for the celebrations – if that's the word for a weekend given over to taunting neighbours and mourning a long-dead noblewoman. Tables had been set up in the muddy square, and Jimmy's three girls were bringing piles of plates out from the folly for the impending feast.

The men who were present came forward to see us. They stood in a semi-circle around their mayor, as if they were the knights of the round table and he was King Arthur. I could sense the unity that they shared and, though I wasn't sure how I ultimately regarded their odd little society in the trees, it was rather stirring to see the loyalty they felt for their leader.

And yet, it was half-human Cliff who would send us off. He walked past the gang to offer some parting words. "Remember the welcome that you got here in Scowles Folly, and don't believe everything that them Clearwellians say about us." He nodded three times, as if to endorse his own statement, then turned back to his fellow villagers.

Grandfather went to reunite with his hound, car and chauffeur, but I needed one more minute to make sense of the place. I hadn't noticed before quite how oppressive the woods were around the village. I could only see a few yards through the trees as their trunks were so thick and their numbers so great. It was not so much that a space had been cleared to make way for the settlement as that the forest had granted permission and could reclaim its land at any moment.

It was difficult to know whether Scowles Folly was a prison or a sanctuary, though I suppose such questions are often open to interpretation. Going by what I'd heard from young Sam Mordaunt, it was clear that he felt trapped there, whereas his father and especially his uncle saw their home as something worth defending.

I had never felt very connected to one single place and struggled to understand their strength of emotion. I'd barely been to my own family home at Kilston Down in the last year. My place at school had always seemed temporary, and so my grandfather's house was the one place I felt that I belonged. That was surely down to the people who inhabited it, though, rather than the bricks and beams with which it had been constructed.

I got back into the Rolls Royce and fell silent. It took me a few minutes to realise that Grandfather had done the exact same thing. Delilah sat on the seat between us, looking a little lonely, and I tried to piece together all that had happened since we'd arrived in the Forest of Dean. There'd been a murder – that was common enough by our standards – but it was almost as though we had to look past Florence Keyse's death in order to get to the truth of the situation.

There were ancient curses, warring tribes, broken hearts and broken promises, but what did any of it really mean? Would the mystery of Lady Morgana set us on the path to finding a killer all this time later? And what of Young Cole Watkins? How did he fit into the mismatched tapestry my grandfather was busy weaving? We didn't know the first thing about who Cole was or why he might have been killed. All I could say for certain was that he'd fallen down a well. Now that I thought of it, we hadn't learnt much more about Florence either. If my distinguished companion had asked me to summarise everything I knew about the tragic figure, I would have told him that she had pretty brown eyes and was now dead.

I was just about to open my mouth to point out this failing when my grandfather beat me to it.

"We've gone about this all wrong, haven't we?" He had that oddly distant look on his face, even as his eyes locked onto mine. "I believed too readily in the Lieutenant-Colonel's story that Florence Keyse's death was connected to the Mordaunts. What if the killer was relying on the fact that we'd get distracted by the historical feud? Or perhaps it was just a coincidence. Perhaps she would have been murdered this weekend even if it hadn't fallen on the anniversary of Lady Morgana's death."

Though I'd considered such points myself, I was unable to determine what had upset the old fellow so. He was acting as though he were the agent of some terrible injustice rather than simply having wasted an hour or two on the wrong suspects. The only explanation I could think of was that this was a test, and he was attempting to throw my suspicions off the real culprit. Well, it wouldn't work.

"My money's on Cliff Mordaunt," I said, perhaps a little too confidently. "Did you see the monstrous chap? He would have had no trouble strangling Florence, that's for certain. He even confessed to knowing her."

For once, Grandfather did not seem interested in one of my theories. "It's a little premature to decide who the killer is before we know why Florence and Cole were murdered."

I tried to hide just how much this comment excited me. I hadn't previously known whether he thought the two deaths could be connected. He'd asked the Lieutenant-Colonel about Cole, of course, but considering how tricky the old detective could be, it was difficult to know whether he meant a word he said in front of our suspects.

"So you do believe that Cole was murdered?" These words came out in one long gasp, and I failed to hide my interest after all.

He paused and tapped one finger along the line of his jaw. "I've told you Christopher; we're getting ahead of ourselves. I believe that Cole was murdered just as much as I think it's raining in the Outer Hebrides at this moment. Without further investigation, we can't possibly say for certain."

This was typical of my grandfather. Whenever he fancied a bout of speculation, it was just the thing to do. But as soon as I decided to forego evidence and state a nice old-fashioned hunch, he claimed I was being precipitous.

"What's our next step, then?" I didn't see how he could disapprove of such a simple question. And, to give him his due, he did not. But neither did he answer it.

"I'm feeling hungry." I agreed whole heartedly with his statement but didn't see how this would help us find a killer. He leaned closer to our driver and issued a command. "Back to the castle, Todd. I imagine that lunch will already be served."

He folded his arms, sat back in his seat and wouldn't say another word until we reached our home for the weekend. He really was a most perplexing fellow. I loved him with all my heart and more, but he could be a troublesome old goat.

He seemed thoroughly dejected throughout the journey, and I wondered if he'd finally reached his quota of dead bodies. The first few hundred of his detective career hadn't fazed him, but perhaps a murdered landlady in a small village would be the death that finally broke his spirit.

We drove through the Clearwell gatehouse, where Dorie and a footman were still on the lookout for trouble. Being a thorough type, she made Todd open the boot of the car before allowing us through.

"Sorry for the inconvenience, Mr Lord Marquess Edgington, your worship. But you can never be too careful."

Grandfather had already descended from the Rolls and offered the oversized domestic a wave. "Jolly good work, Dorie. I'm proud of you!"

She blushed accordingly.

He was right in his prediction, about lunch at least. When I scampered after him into the castle, a maid directed us towards the back of the building. We navigated a dark, stone corridor and cut through an airy salon to reach the incredibly long ballroom that made up the rear wing of the building. It really wasn't like the castles I'd read about in history books and was a pleasant mix of the ancient and modern. In fact, a simple lean-to structure had been attached to the exterior of this protruding room, and the Wyndham family had gathered there to eat.

"My apologies, old chap," Algar said, his usual smile notable for its absence. "We would have waited for you, but I know what happens when you get on a scent. You're just like my dogs after a fox."

Cressida was slightly less polite in her greeting. "So it's true then? The tavern wench has really been murdered?" She did not wait for an answer but ploughed on with her own line of condemnation. "It's hardly surprising, considering the way that woman strutted about the place as though she were queen of the village. I certainly never saw her at church on Sundays, which is all you need to know about–"

"Mother!" I was surprised to hear Dante complain. "The poor girl is dead, and you're looking to blame her for all the sins of the world."

His sister looked at him quite fondly, but their father's eyes fell to the floor as he shook his head in the grip of a sudden depression. The silence that followed was too much for me to bear and, as we took our seats at the round table, I had to say something to fill the awkward hush.

"I obviously didn't know her very well, but it was quite apparent that Florence Keyse was a terribly nice person who was beloved here in Clearwell. The faces of the townsfolk this morning were quite distraught, and that isn't always the case in our investigations."

"Investigations?" Dante asked, his tone curious.

I would most likely have tooted my own horn just then, but Grandfather did it on my behalf. "I have been training Christopher in the art of detection. Together, we have already identified several unscrupulous characters, and I have no doubt he will assist me in finding the current ghoul who is haunting the village."

At the mention of the supernatural, a shiver passed over the lady of the house. "Then you've heard about the ghost that walks the halls of the castle? I've seen her late at night when everyone is abed. I believe it is Lady Morgana herself. She has returned to remind us of our shame."

"I was speaking metaphorically, Cressida." Grandfather clearly felt some concern for our sensitive companion. "You must not trouble yourself with that which is not of this earth. There are worries enough in our own realm."

"Hear, hear," Algar said a little half-heartedly, and I was forced to wonder what part this peculiar family might have played in the murders.

We had reached another impasse in the discussion, and so it was lucky that our first course was about to be delivered. I recognised the dish as one of our cook's specialities. It was steamed herring with chives – a particular favourite of Lord Edgington's.

"You didn't force Henrietta onto our hosts, did you, Grandfather?" There was more than a touch of disapproval in my voice.

"No, of course I didn't." He huffed out an affronted breath. "I merely suggested to Algar that he might enjoy sampling some of her food."

"It's delicious," the tubby chap replied, having already finished his plate before we sat down.

"You can really taste the chives," Gertrude added.

There's nothing like a lull in a conversation to put one at ease. I was ever so close to discussing my knowledge of beer production again when my grandfather saved me.

"Perhaps this is not the best moment to discuss such matters, but

I'm afraid that I will have to ask for your impressions of what has been happening in the village this last month. Not just to the landlady of The Wyndham Arms, but Young Cole Watkins, too."

Now, this was more like it! I wouldn't have had the courage to haul our distant relatives over the coals, but my prestigious colleague thought only of justice and had no such qualms. It was fascinating to watch the reactions around that table as the implication of his words came to be understood.

"Cole Watkins? Are you saying that he was murdered?" Cressida was clearly shocked by the idea, but it was her husband's face that had turned as white as a rabbit's tail.

"I'm saying that I have reason to believe that someone may have wanted him dead and, if so, it might yet explain last night's attack." Grandfather spoke between tiny bites of his fish. I'd honestly never met such a polite eater. "But, for the moment, I have no evidence to prove my theory."

I had expected the parents to be the most vocal of the group, but Algar was unable to produce a sound. In many ways, he was the monarch of the village, and he evidently couldn't bear to see his subjects endangered.

"Why would anyone have hurt that jolly drunk?" Dante asked. "And, for that matter, why would anyone have wanted to kill poor Florence?"

All eyes were fixed on my grandfather. "Those are two very good questions, the answers to which I will do my best to ascertain. Did you know Cole, Dante? What did you make of him?"

It wasn't my new friend who answered. "Cole Watkins was a feckless scoundrel. He brought the good name of this town into disrepute." Guess who said this. Go on. Have a go. I'll give you a clue; it wasn't Dante, Gertrude, Algar, me or my grandfather.

"Really, Mother!" Cressida's daughter took her turn to object to one of her fiery declarations. "I thought Christianity required a degree of compassion and forgiveness. You sound as though you're happy the man's dead."

"It's certainly not the worst thing that has happened to Clearwell this century." The matriarch of the family was in no way chastened by the response to her vitriol.

"I am not trying to cause you any problems." My grandfather attempted a conciliatory tone. "I simply wish to know why someone would have wanted to murder him – if, in fact, he was murdered, which is still an open question."

"Perhaps he stumbled across a secret," Dante suggested with a little mischief in his voice. "Young Cole liked to believe he knew more about the town than anyone else. He had all our old books and papers in his house and even liked to note down the daily happenings as though he were Samuel Pepys or some such fellow."

"That's interesting, don't you think, Grandfather?" It had been a few minutes since I'd said anything, so I decided I should contribute some new inanity. "If Cole had seen something that someone else didn't want someone to know about, something bad could have happened... to someone."

He pursed his lips before responding. "Yes, I did wonder – in slightly more precise terms – whether that could be the reason our killer pushed the chap down the well." He allowed his brain to work through certain possibilities before turning his gaze back to his old friend. "The other explanation I entertained was his connection to you, Algar."

"To me?" The Earl of Dunraven finally spoke, but he looked just as bewildered as when the conversation had begun.

"Well, your ancestors, at least. I heard that Cole claimed he was related to you some generations back."

Cressida was quick to answer. "That was just gossip. We've never seen any evidence that the cretinous peasant was in any way related to the bastard offspring of some long-dead Wyndham. By all reports, the man was drunk most nights; why would anyone believe a word he said?"

I was interested to note that Gertrude was eyeing her mother with just as much suspicion as the celebrated detective at this moment. It appeared that she was about to express a thought of her own, but Cressida had another question.

"And more to the point, the fool fell down a well. Why would you ever imagine he was murdered?"

"The diameter of the well, for one thing." Grandfather had sharpened his tone to a fierce point and propelled this comment across the table. "If Cole had merely leaned too far backwards, he would have hit the wall behind him and been able to brace himself. The fact he reached the bottom suggests that someone made sure of his fall."

Dante turned his head to look at me then, and I could tell he was full of excitement. I had probably felt the same when investigating my first murder. But I was an old hand by this point and failed to summon the same giddy enthusiasm as my novice friend.

"I don't mind telling you that I knew Cole rather well," he revealed. "Everyone liked the chap. Wherever he went became a true celebration. Wherever you saw him, there'd be singing, laughter and, most likely, a few jugs of cider. He wasn't as dim witted as people liked to say, but I doubt he'd discovered anything particularly revelatory about this place."

Grandfather only seemed more confused by this account. "So, what did he do with his life? He can't just have got drunk and sung old songs. He couldn't have afforded the drink for one thing."

Dante smiled a little more broadly. I thought he would make a joke then, but his father intervened. "We let him keep the old family files in his house and paid him–"

"Algar!" Cressida interrupted in a harsh whisper.

"There's no point denying it, darling. Everyone in town knows." He waited a few seconds to ensure he had convinced her of this argument, then turned back to their inquisitor. "My father had taken pity on Cole's family. They were a sorry lot and would have made a much bigger fuss about their connection to us if we'd ignored them. So, around the time Cole was born, we found a way to explain the payments. We'd had our library redecorated, so we moved some musty old books to one of the cottages we own and settled the Watkins there. I was a young bachelor at the time, and Daddy gave Cole's father the title of chief records keeper for the Wyndham family. The books would only have been thrown away otherwise. When Old Cole died, Young Cole took over."

I needed a few moments to realise that father and son must have shared the same name.

Grandfather examined our companions' contrasting expressions as the footman delivered our second course. This being Henrietta's dish, I'd predicted that the pheasant would be stuffed with herring, liver and Spanish broccoli – or some such disaster. To my pleasure and surprise, it turned out to be a nice traditional rosemary and sage filling, and I enjoyed it immensely.

Ever since we'd left the rival village, my grandfather had not seemed like himself. I thought he would continue drilling into our suspects until we discovered exactly what sort of materials had been placed in Young Cole's care. Instead, he peered out of the misty glass that looked onto the neat lawn at the side of the castle. I could see the poorly defined shape of the forest beyond the walls and once again had the sensation that those vast trees were the real stewards of this land. The humans who'd made their home there were little more than temporary guests.

A thought came to me at just the right moment. "Isn't it possible that Young Cole discovered something in your family documents about which the killer didn't want the rest of the village to know?"

"This is becoming ridiculous." Cressida only grew angrier as the discussion unfolded. "There was no secret to discover, and Cole Watkins was not murdered. A young boy with too much imagination and an old man with time on his hands aren't going to solve a crime that doesn't exist."

I thought that Grandfather would take exception to this characterisation. Well... to his half of it, at least. Instead, he fell back into the conversation and picked up a new thread.

"I have another question for you." He had the voice of a world-weary policeman. "The Mordaunt brothers told me of the Clearwell curse."

"You've been to Scowles Folly?" Algar remained alarmed by every new revelation.

Grandfather gave a curt nod. "Of course I have. I'm investigating at least one murder and, should a real police officer ever turn up to assist me, I will pass on everything I have learnt. Now, who will tell me about the curse? Is it true that no female offspring of the Clearwell Wyndhams has made it to adulthood in the last two centuries?"

Even Dante looked hesitant to answer such a sombre query and so it fell to his sister to reply. "That's right. Some generations were lucky enough to only have boys, and the others saw their daughters die at a young age." Her voice became more hesitant, and I could see that her hand was shaking as she picked up a fork to move some food around her plate. "As it happens, I believe I am the first girl in the family to live as long as I have since Lady Morgana died."

Grandfather moved his hand across the table, as though to comfort her, but stopped halfway. "When is your twenty-first birthday, child?"

Having stared at the chunk of poultry on her plate for some seconds, she finally looked back up at him. "The day after tomorrow."

CHAPTER FIFTEEN

The meal continued in just such a fashion for some time. There was no joy or spirit to the occasion and, no matter how hard Dante tried to lighten the mood, the initial discussion in which we had engaged overwhelmed all that followed. It would be easy to conclude that Florence's violent death had permanently dampened our stay there at Clearwell, but that would overlook the unusual atmosphere that had greeted us on arrival.

I couldn't get beyond the idea that the Wyndhams were shadows of the people they should have been. I just wished I'd known how much of this was due to everyday family problems and how much the murders had changed things. Or perhaps it was the curse. Perhaps living with two centuries' worth of guilt, shame and pain had left its mark upon them.

I was frankly quite relieved when the main part of the meal was over, and Henrietta's Devonshire Splits had been served. The Wyndhams–

Sorry, I won't be a moment.

We'll get straight back to the tense atmosphere there just as soon as I've described how delicious those airy mouthfuls of pastry were. The bun-shaped cakes weighed less than a baby bird in the hand – and so I ate five of them to make up for it. But what delights! Filled with fruits of the forest preserve and clotted cream, the rich intermingling of flavours exploded in my mouth as I devoured them. My dining companions must have been talking about… something, while I was inserting those heavenly bites into my mouth, but I can't tell you what.

Now, where was I?

Ah, yes. I remember! The Wyndhams truly were a queer flock. Lunching with Cressida was as much fun as taking tea with an executioner – and a particularly judgemental one at that. It was a genuine relief when the meal was over, and she bustled off to the church for a good old pray. I like a chin-wag with the Man upstairs as much as the next boy, but I could only conclude that Cressida bothered the poor omniscient Chap so often that He had stopped listening.

Gertrude brightened a touch once her mother had left but could not be persuaded to go for a walk with us in the forest. Instead, she floated back through the castle like the ethereal nymph that she was. I must say it was terribly difficult not to fall madly in love with the beautiful girl, but I just about managed it – if for no other reason than the moment when we would have to tell our grandchildren how we'd met.

Well, I was investigating a string of murders with your great-great-grandfather and, oh yes, your grandmother is my third cousin!

Algar remained nervy even as he ushered us out of the small conservatory. Unlike most of the grand houses I'd visited over the previous year, and throughout my life, in fact, Clearwell had no vast formal gardens laid out around its perimeter. Beyond a few lines of rose bushes and the lawns on two sides of the castle, mother nature had been left to her own devices. We followed a path that led us to a door in the high stone wall which surrounded the property. On the other side, the dense forest stood firm, like an invading army, waiting for the call to attack. I was even more impressed by its eerie beauty during the daytime than I had been the night before. The colours of the ferns and leaves were just so vivid that it was hard to believe someone hadn't painted them by hand.

Grandfather was deep in conversation with Algar as we walked along. Sadly, they spoke in murmurs, and I was unable to catch much of what they said.

"Chrissy, there's something I want to show you," Dante proclaimed before shooting along the path at speed. I glanced back at the old folk we were accompanying, and Grandfather waved me off as though I were departing on a trans-Atlantic voyage. I just had to hope it was not the Titanic I was boarding. Either way, I feared I would not see him again for some time.

The part of the forest we eventually reached was rather unique. It was more like an alien world than a rural patch of Gloucestershire. Every surface was covered in thick green moss that looked like the skin of some oddly fluorescent bear. As I ran after Dante, I stuck my hand out to feel the soft texture against my fingers.

The path we were on dropped down into a valley that was carpeted with dead leaves and detritus from the previous autumn. With the sun behind the trees, their bright foliage stood out against the oranges and muddy browns.

There were huge boulders about the place, which were similarly cloaked in green. They protruded from the ground like the dolmens at Stonehenge – only more jagged and haphazardly arranged. It wasn't until I caught up with Dante in the next hollow that I realised that not everything I was seeing was entirely natural. I climbed up the steep bank and immediately stopped in my tracks.

"Isn't it wonderful?" He spun around to appreciate the sight he must have seen a thousand times before.

Rarely in my life had I beheld such a complicated view – neither looking across the rooftops of London nor falling to earth from a balloon. It's hard to put into words the sight that was before me, but perhaps the best I can say is that I'd come face to face with an exquisite mess. On the verdant forest floor, countless fallen branches lay in piles between the immense rocks. English oaks, clothed in a suit of lichen, reached up to the distant sky like fingers from a grave, as red squirrels jumped between them without fear.

I navigated a short corridor of towering stone which led down to my friend. The walkway was bordered by intricately constructed handrails made of knotty branches, but they had been there so long I'd mistaken them for natural features of the strange landscape. It was only after I'd spotted a cabin concealed in the roots of a high tree that it became clear to me that this whole environment had been cultivated in some respect.

"One of our ancestors laid out the paths and built all sorts of magical features," Dante explained. "I suppose it was a kind of playground for the family back then, but my parents and sister don't like coming out here. They say it's quite unearthly, and so I've always had it to myself."

I had come to appreciate my cousin for the wide-eyed optimism that he managed to communicate at nearly every moment. He glanced about the scene once more, not just proud to show me his private getaway, but excited to see it for himself.

"It's wonderful," I said, shaking my head, as I'd never imagined anywhere quite like it before. Even now, it's hard to believe that I visited such an extraordinary place. It reminded me of some forgotten land in the Grecian underworld - the Asphodel Meadows, or perhaps the Fields of Mourning. A musty, mildewed place – both natural and refined - in which nature was the only monarch and night the only threat.

"You'll like this," Dante predicted, and, walking over to his cabin, opened a wooden door that was nearly falling off its hinges.

I followed him inside, expecting it to be dark and dismal. To my joy, there were holes cut into the earthen roof of the structure, which allowed spears of sunlight to cut through to us beyond the tendrils of the tree's roots.

"You lucky thing," I said, looking about at the surprisingly comfortable interior. "I wish I'd had somewhere like this at boarding school. I could have escaped from nefarious teachers whenever they gave me too much work."

There was a small, round table and chairs formed from tree stumps. The cosy cavern we had entered had been made by cutting directly into the earth. It was an impressive endeavour, and I wondered how long ago the whole place had been designed. It didn't seem like the kind of project most adults would have undertaken, so I had to assume that Dante – and, by that reckoning, I myself – had some interesting ancestors.

"I come here when I don't want to talk to anyone... when I wish to feel like the last person on the planet." Though this sentence started just as cheerily as any other, I think he realised that he couldn't hide the sadness at its core.

"Do you often feel that way then?"

He shrugged and sat down on one of the two stumps. It had been hollowed out and reminded me of the dickey seat in the back of Grandfather's Aston Martin.

"I suppose I do, actually. And more than ever since..." He wouldn't finish the thought and I didn't find the courage to make him.

"The woods at Cranley Hall aren't nearly so spectacular as this place," I said, so that I didn't have to put my foot any deeper into my mouth than I already had.

Of course, what I really wanted to ask him was why his mother acted like a banshee. I wished to know why his sister seemed so tragically unhappy whenever her parents were near and whether his father was to blame for any of it. Those topics being off the menu, I plumped for the far more diplomatic discussion of a murdered noblewoman and a supernatural hex.

"Does your family actually believe in the curse of Lady Morgana?"

He'd lost his vim, and it took him some time to reply. "Yes, I think we probably do. After all, what are the chances of not one single girl making it to adulthood in a family in all that time? Then there are the sightings of Morgana's ghost. And, if I'm perfectly honest, I don't see any reason to think that old Thomas Wyndham was innocent. I mean, just because we're descended from him, that doesn't mean we owe him any loyalty, does it?"

"No, I suppose you're right." I considered the passion with which the two villages defended this ancient story as though they had lived through it themselves. It all seemed rather silly. "I must confess, the Mordaunts are adamant that someone in your family was responsible for Morgana's death. They say she was pregnant at the time and that Thomas Wyndham murdered her to kill the child. They say that one of Morgana's maids was a Mordaunt and told everyone what she'd seen."

He looked down at his hands as though he himself were responsible for the poor woman's death. "Perhaps that's why she still haunts us. She must wander the halls looking for her lost child."

"Whoever's to blame, it's a tragic story," I muttered, before finally summoning a dash of my grandfather's courage and asking a significant question. "As is the tale of poor Florence. I don't suppose... Well, I don't suppose you have any idea who wanted her dead? She seemed such a dear person in the pub last night. It's hard to imagine anyone would want to hurt her."

Not for the first time that afternoon, he couldn't look at me but glanced at the sky through the holes in the muddy ceiling. "She was very kind, it's true." His words started quietly and fell to near silence, but then a new sentence burst out of him. "I saw something in town a few weeks ago, but I don't know whether I should tell you about it."

I summoned a particularly clever reply to this. I said simply, "Oh."

"I don't imagine it means anything." He became more nervous the longer he spoke but waved one arm through the air, as though what he was saying was entirely transparent. "In fact, I'm sure it's got nothing to do with her death. I'm probably being a bit silly."

"You can tell me." I spoke in calm tones, for his sake.

He looked up at last and his gaze stabbed into me like a... well, a blade, obviously. What else can stab?

"Yes but, Chrissy…"

"I mean it, Dante. You can trust me."

"No, Chrissy, listen." He was shouting by now, his hand outstretched, and I knew it was my job to reassure him.

"Not just because of the work I've been doing with my grandfather; you're my cousin, and I would never–"

"Chrissy, there's a snake!"

It wasn't me he was pointing at. It was the grey, green and black monstrosity that was peering down at me from its perch on the wall. The coiled creature had been having a nice doze there until two silly humans came along and disturbed him. I can't say that his somnolence was my first worry, though, as I found myself eye-to-eye with the hissing, tongue-flicking creature.

It had a collar the colour of sulphur and was moving its head from side to side as it considered its next move. I'd always thought it ridiculous that my biology teacher at Oakton Academy had taught such things as the difference between venomous and non-venomous snake markings. I now wished I'd paid more attention in class. It had bars all along its side. Did that mean it was an adder and was about to kill me or that I could go about my business without fear?

"What should I do?" I thought this a reasonable question, in the circumstances.

"Just step backwards so that you're out of its reach before–" Dante never finished this sentence but not because a snake bit him. No, that was my good fortune.

"Errrrrrrrrr!" I can't say for certain what noise I made as the beast sprang forward to attach itself to my nose, but it was something along these lines.

"Stop moving so much." My friend was far too insouciant about the fact a serpent was dangling from my face. "If you calm down, I'll be able to tell what kind of snake it is."

"How do you expect me to be calm when–" It was my turn to leave something unsaid as I kicked open the crumbling door and ran outside in the hope that the fresh air might encourage the beast to relinquish his grip.

Following me into the light, Dante started laughing. "Oh, there's nothing to worry about. I can see now that it's just a grass snake. They're quite remarkable, really. They can change the shape of their heads to look more like their poisonous brethren. I thought perhaps an adder had got you. I shouldn't have worried."

"For some reason, that doesn't make me feel a lot better." I hope it doesn't sound as though I was overreacting, but I was rather alarmed by the fact that the writhing creature's jaws were still attached to me. "For goodness' sake. Just get it off my face!"

CHAPTER SIXTEEN

"Chrissy!" I heard my grandfather call from the next glen.

"It's got me, Grandfather. Send for an ambulance. Call the nearest hospital. It's got me, and it's not letting go."

He must have followed the sound of my panic, as he soon appeared through the corridor of rocks and came stumbling down the slope towards us.

"I told you, Chrissy. You just have to stay still," Dante was persisting with this trivial demand, as though my kinetic disposition was the reason that the wicked creature wouldn't release me.

Grandfather reached the spot where I was spinning around in circles and took hold of me by both shoulders. "Why on earth are you fussing, boy? It's merely a grass snake."

"It may be a grass snake, but it's trying to eat me." I finally stopped bucking about at this moment. I couldn't believe how nonchalant they both were.

My stunned reaction gave Dante the opportunity he required. He stepped closer to lift the snake's fangs up and away from my skin. "I needed you to stop moving so that I could remove the poor thing without hurting him."

"Hurting him? He thought nothing of hurting me!"

"He was only scared." Instead of casting the beast back whence it had come, he held it in his hand as though it were a kitten. He even gave it a gentle stroke, and I was amazed to see that the snake thoroughly enjoyed it. I couldn't fathom why he had taken against me. Perhaps I have the kind of face that snakes like to bite.

As though Dante were some kind of expert herpetologist – oh, gosh! I did remember one thing from my biology classes after all – the creature spiralled around his arm before leaping to the floor to disappear beneath a pile of logs.

"Must you insist on making a drama out of the slightest thing, Christopher?" my grandfather chastised me. "When I heard you screaming like that, I thought there was something wrong."

I was carefully prodding my nose to check for swelling and came away with a spot of blood on my finger. "There was something wrong.

I could have been nipped to death by that devilish beast. I had every right to express my agony."

My complaints would have continued in this vein for some time had Dante not interrupted me.

"What was that?" He walked along the path and stood with his hand to his eyes to shield himself from an errant ray of sunlight. "I saw something, I'm sure of it."

"I'm sorry. I was too busy being assaulted by a reptile to notice the trees swaying in the breeze." Very well. I was possibly overreacting by now, but when everyone absolutely refuses to offer any sympathy, what is a boy to do?

"Not the trees," Dante said with a hiss in his voice that I could only imagine his reptilian friend had inspired. "I saw a figure. I'm sure I–" His eyes widened just then, and he reached out to trace a movement through the branches on the higher ground. "Yes, he's right there."

Grandfather hurried along to see what was happening. "Up by the old oak? Where the path curves?"

"That's right."

They kept their eyes fixed on the same point, but I could make no sense of Grandfather's description.

"I'm not sure that I saw anyone," he finally concluded, but Dante was more confident.

"I did. I'm certain that someone was watching us. He must have heard Chrissy shrieking and–"

"Oh, come along," I interrupted. "It was hardly a shriek. If anything, it was more of a wail… or perhaps a cry. It was most definitely not a shriek."

I noticed that Lord Edgington turned his critical gaze on my cousin just then. Dante must have realised that he was being judged as he responded with a frustrated, "I'm telling the truth. There was a chap up there in a long black cloak with a hood. He ran away as soon as he saw I was watching him."

"So you didn't see his face?"

"The sun was behind him; it was hard to make out his features." Dante suddenly sounded less sure of himself.

I decided that it was probably time to move on from my experience with the scaly monster that had assailed me, and so I asked a question of my own. "Are you sure it wasn't a deer?" I didn't say it was a sensible question.

"No, Christopher, it wasn't a deer. Well, not unless the animals in the forest have opted for a more contemporary wardrobe this season."

Grandfather pulled back from us, as though he had some thoughts of his own to compute. "But you're sure that it was a man you saw? Or rather, you're certain it wasn't a woman?"

My cousin looked between the pair of us and tried to recall exactly what he had seen. "I think... Yes, from his profile and height, I'd definitely say so. He was far broader than most of the women in Clearwell – except for Bessie, the farm hand, of course. She's bigger than my father!"

"Where does this path lead?" Now, this was something worth asking. I was quite proud of myself.

"It turns into a game path after a mile, but that would lead you northwest, right through the forest."

"All the way to Scowles Folly?" Grandfather was quicker than me and neatly fitted the pieces of this puzzle together.

"That's right." A look of anger crossed Dante's face.

Algar appeared beside the boulders at that moment and called down to us. "Is all well? What was all that commotion?"

"Oh, it was nothing of any importance." I produced a carefree laugh to express just how little my brush with death had fazed me.

Despite being some years younger than my grandfather, the Earl of Dunraven was no athlete and was clearly out of breath from the climb. His son made good progress up the hill to him, but I loitered behind.

Grandfather watched as the young chap explained what had occurred to his father but said nothing until he was sure they were out of earshot. "Just like you, Christopher, I saw no one in the trees. I wonder what it could mean."

We meandered back along the labyrinthine trail of paths that previous generations of the Wyndham family had constructed. I noticed a number of natural caves about the place and grandfather informed me that the land around – or rather beneath – Clearwell had been mined for thousands of years for its deposits of iron and ochre.

I found the whole place enchanting and could quite happily have spent a week exploring. This made me consider all the fun we would have had if Florence Keyse hadn't been murdered. Of all the ill effects of that crime, the impact on my holiday was possibly the least sinister, but that didn't make me feel any better about the larks I would not be having there with Dante, or the tree houses we would not be constructing. Which I suppose must make me a very selfish cove indeed.

It was a slow walk home. Algar was an absolute barrel of a man and whatever speed he had called upon to catch up with us had left him quite exhausted. In fact, like a cooper delivering wares, we should probably have rolled him back to the castle.

When we finally reached the Clearwell estate, Dante unlocked the rear gate, and we passed through the perimeter wall. I wondered whether someone nefarious soul could climb a tree to gain access. On closer inspection, I realised that the thick-trunked spruces and elms had been pruned of their lower branches and could only conclude that you would require ropes and perhaps a harness to get inside without the key.

"What should we do now, Grandfather?" I asked once we were alone in his grand medieval bedroom. I was hoping the answer would be *Let's forget about this far-fetched investigation and have afternoon tea,* but I knew the chances were low.

"Let's have afternoon tea." The old chap was full of surprises.

"Fantastic! I'll run and find a footman to tell the kitchen."

He interrupted me before I could dash from the room. "Not here, my boy. We'll walk into Clearwell village to gauge the mood of the local population."

It was hard to know whether to be excited or disappointed by this announcement, as I was not convinced we would actually end up eating anything. Too many times over the last year, the promise of a tasty meal had been the carrot which he dangled before his donkey of a grandson to get his own way. This time, if he decided to withhold my victuals, I would simply go on strike. He'd get no observations on the case from me (insightful or otherwise). No helpful conclusions or subtle theories. We'd see just how good a detective he really was without me prattling away at his side.

116

CHAPTER SEVENTEEN

Leaving word with our staff that we would be absent for the afternoon, we prepared to leave the castle. I didn't see Dante or his parents, but Gertrude was in the ballroom, sitting in a bay window with the sun shining as though just for her. She had a book in her hand and looked like a woman in need of a saviour – which is no doubt a highly ignorant view to take on the matter. Perhaps she just required a little solitude and some time to read, but I couldn't help thinking of her as a sad character. Half-human, half-spirit, she was like some supernal heroine from Spenser's 'The Faerie Queene'.

Delilah always knew what her master had in mind and was sitting on the steps to the castle, waiting for her afternoon walk. She'd been well looked after by the staff there. I'd rarely seen her looking so round, but she jumped up as we exited the building and was full of energy as she shot along the path towards the village.

Dorie and a couple of the footmen were still on duty at the gatehouse, though any initial excitement at their task had clearly dissipated. They were standing with Todd, playing a hand of cards over the bonnet of the Rolls.

"Don't trust my maid, gentlemen. She may not show it, but she is quite the sharpest card player I've encountered."

The three chaps immediately brought their cards closer to their chests.

"I can't help it if I'm good at the game, Your Lord Highness."

"No, Dorie. But you can help cheating. Have a nice afternoon, everyone." He tipped his hat to them, and we strolled off the grounds.

"Grandfather, can you tell me what you discussed with Algar on our walk?"

He once more waited until he was certain we were alone before revealing what had taken place between them. "I have had the unshakeable feeling since our arrival that all is not right here at Clearwell. I do not refer to the murders. They are evidently most troubling, but there is something rotten at the heart of the family."

"I've been thinking the very same thing," I said quite truthfully, while hoping he might approve of my skills of observation.

"Of course you have. I've taught you extremely well." So much for his high opinion! "However, I have an advantage over you in that respect, as I have known the family for many years. Your grandmother adored Algar. Their two families were close when she was a young woman. She treated him like quite the little doll and, as he grew up, we made sure to keep an eye on him. He was something of a feckless youth, but upon marrying Cressida, he seemed to mature."

I was attempting to retain the information he disclosed, but it was hard enough keeping up with the pace of his walking.

"As a young couple, they were incredibly happy together and Cressida showed no signs of the zealotry we have witnessed this weekend. She was a sweet-hearted, carefree girl. She was always a little traditional in her ways, but she made our family feel most welcome."

"So what do you think has happened in the intervening years?"

He ground to a sudden halt, and Delilah sprinted back to us. "That is what I have been trying to discover. I have begun to wonder if it is connected to the fact that Algar is the head of this little community. You will have noticed that they have appointed no mayor in the village. I believe that is because of the role that the Wyndhams play here. Perhaps an imbalance in the royal family of Clearwell had caused ruptures in the area as a whole."

This was the kind of detecting that I expected from my favourite old fellow. He'd seemed distracted for much of the day, but I should never have doubted that his mind was busy with the calculations we required.

I took up the discussion. "What about the other members of the family? Gertrude is rather dolorous. Dante is forever trying to make the others happy, and Algar looks perpetually alarmed, as though some tragic incident could come to pass at any moment."

He recommenced his purposeful strolling. "It is very hard to say whether their behaviour is due to the change in Cressida, or vice versa. If you're asking me whether I suspect their involvement in the murders, I simply have no answer. All I can say is that there are secrets in Clearwell we have not yet discovered, which is why we're on our way to talk to the real villagers and find out what they know."

I thought it unusual for a lord to consider workers and everyday folk to be more authentic than his aristocratic brethren, but I was curious about another point that he had failed to address. "You didn't tell me what you discussed with Algar in the forest."

Grandfather smiled. "Well, I tried to be subtle in my enquiries. He has no reason to tell me the truth, no reason to even tolerate our presence in his house, and I did not wish to unnerve him."

"He must have said something?"

We had reached the village school, which the former Countess of Dunraven had established in the previous century. It being a Saturday, the quaint schoolhouse was deserted.

"We talked about the management of our estates, his children and you, of course." My mentor's eyebrows performed a brief dance. "But whenever I tried to shift the conversation to more sensitive matters, he became evasive."

"Might that not be a sign of guilt?"

He flexed his moustache as though it were a muscle. "It might well be, though I'm sure I don't need to tell you that–"

"The fact a suspect hides a secret is no guarantee he is a murderer." As though it were a quote from some great poet, I repeated this phrase he'd told me any number of times.

"Precisely, Christopher. You've been paying attention."

I might have blushed a little then. "I do my best."

"I can't say that Algar is the same man I knew all those years ago, but time changes people. More importantly, we've yet to discover any evidence to suggest that one of the Wyndhams chose to exterminate two villagers."

I considered this point before responding. "You said it yourself when we returned from Scowles Folly; we haven't gone about this investigation in the most logical order. In one sense, we're starting from the beginning right now." I didn't like to say that we were behind schedule, but it certainly felt that way.

He smiled to himself and increased his speed along the road. "A little method, that's what we've been lacking. Perhaps I'm getting old–" he considered the possibility for approximately two and a half seconds before ruling it out. "No, that can't be it. But it's not like me to run half-cocked from the scene of a crime on the basis of such flimsy evidence as a local rivalry."

"So you really don't think the Mordaunts are to blame?"

"I cannot say that. However, we've no reason to suspect them more than anyone else we've encountered."

"What about the figure Dante saw in the forest? His attire and the direction from which he came would suggest he was one of them. The theatrical procession that we saw upon arriving in Clearwell was carried out in just such garb."

It was another point for him to consider, and he ran his fingers through his steel-wire hair as he did so. "Yes, but we cannot say for certain what Dante really saw. Or even whether–"

He did not finish this thought, as we had reached the old stone cross that marked the meeting point of Church Road and High Street. Instead of turning left to The Wyndham Arms as I'd expected, Grandfather took us to a part of the village we had yet to explore. To my surprise, there was another pub set in a row of nondescript brick cottages, which kissed the edge of the road.

"I thought we were going for afternoon tea." The disappointment was plain in my voice. "If someone tries to make me drink beer or cider or scrumpy again, I'll refuse point blank."

"Scrumpy is a type of cider. And you shouldn't expect the same things wherever you go. Life would be really very dull if everywhere on earth served identical food and libations." He gave a definitive nod and marched into The Butcher's Arms.

Though reluctant to follow him, I must admit I was curious to discover what would pass for an afternoon snack in a Gloucestershire pub. And would you believe it? It surpassed my expectations.

"Cake!" I said with great glee as I saw what the cheery man behind the bar had delivered in place of neatly triangled sandwiches and cups of tea. "Apple cake!" This was as much of a reaction as I could produce, as I set to work devouring the iced sponge cake that was filled with stewed apple and a slightly tart flavour I couldn't place.

"It's cider," Grandfather explained without me having to ask. He looked more than a little smug. "A common ingredient in West Country Apple Cake."

"I never said that I wouldn't consume cider in cake form. In fact, there are few ingredients that wouldn't taste better baked in a cake."

Unsurprisingly, he doubted the truth of my statement. "I once investigated the case of a woman who had murdered her husband with a Victoria Sponge laced with cyanide."

"Yes, and I bet it was a darn sight more delicious than if she'd given it to him in his tea!"

He gave me a look then which said, *Christopher, you are a very strange boy indeed.* But I didn't mind. I had cake! I emitted a rather satisfied sigh as several of the pub's regulars peered grumpily over their drinks in my direction. I suppose they were still getting used to that morning's bad news and didn't want outsiders intruding upon their quietude.

Grandfather hadn't ordered anything for himself and surprised me by suddenly getting to his feet to gaze around the dark bar. It really wasn't so different from the pub across the road. There were low beams on the ceiling and the tobacco smoke was thick in the air, but the naked stone walls gave the place a more ancient feel.

"Who can tell me something about Cole Watkins?" He spoke with great confidence, as ever, but there was a touch of aggression in his voice, as though he expected opposition.

A murmur of interest travelled from table to table before a man in the corner stood up. "What be you wanting to know about Young Cole for? He never did no one no harm."

Lord Edgington straightened his black silk cravat before speaking. "I'd like to know what happened on the weekend that he fell down the well."

"Yerp," the haggard drinker continued – presumably in the affirmative. "But why do you wanta know?"

The old detective was a natural communicator. I'd seen him rub shoulders with folk from every corner of our country – from beggars to dukes – but, for a moment, I genuinely believed he had bitten off more than he could chew with the people of Clearwell. Of course, whenever I thought such a thing, he inevitably disproved the theory.

"I have reason to believe that Cole's death could be connected to the violent act perpetrated last night in The Wyndham Arms. So, I'll repeat my question. Who can tell me what I need to know about Cole Watkins?"

There was another figure sitting in the shadows by the door. I hadn't noticed him when we entered but, as he stood up, I had a feeling he would turn out to be someone vital to the investigation. Perhaps this was the shady figure who had witnessed something ever so important, or even the killer himself!

I was wrong, of course. He was just an old drunk in a pub.

"Talk to Jed Gibson at the petrol station. That's what I'd do. Them two were like peas in a pod." He said his piece and sat back down to finish his pint.

"We should probably have thought of that ourselves," I said and, presumably just to spite me, Grandfather made for the door before I could finish my cake.

I had the last laugh, though. I stuffed the whole thing in my mouth and gave him another chance to look disapprovingly at me. Before he could duck out of the door to the bright world outside, a new customer walked through it.

"You're not welcome here," yet another hidden figure in a dark corner declared.

The newcomer stood dumbfounded, and I recognised him as Sam Mordaunt, the young blacksmith who'd been in The Wyndham Arms the night before.

The angry voice materialised into a person and there was Lieutenant-Colonel Stroud, still in his immaculate blazer, pointing his finger across the pub at Sam. "Did you hear me, Mordaunt? You're not welcome in this village."

Sam looked just as nervous as when the great Lord Edgington had arrived on a mission to speak to his family that morning. He stuttered out an incomprehensible reply before steadying himself and saying, "I only want to put things right between our villages. I didn't have nothing to do with the poor girl's death. I've come here to make peace."

"You would say that, wouldn't you?" The old soldier stepped into the light that was cutting through a small leaded window at the end of the bar. More of the locals came to join him, so that we ended up with a gang of ageing drinkers, standing their ground before a muscle-bound youngster. "Now, get out!"

Grandfather seized Sam's arm before matters could deteriorate and, a few seconds later, the three of us had escaped into the fresh air.

"The old chap didn't seem to mind me so much in the pub last night," Sam said with a sad laugh.

"I think you've done remarkably well to be accepted here for as long as you have," Grandfather consoled him. "If the Lieutenant-Colonel is anything to go by, people in Clearwell are unforgiving sorts."

The man who had earned his nickname as The Infiltrator sat on the rough stone wall outside the pub. He stared down at the ground as he released a mournful lament. "I just wanted t' put things right, you know? I just wanted t' make life better for everyone."

The sorry chap wore a woollen waistcoat that made his impressively massive arms stand out even more. He wore a knapsack on his back and reached inside in search of a flat cap to keep the sun off his face. He cut a sad figure, and Delilah must have felt some sympathy for him as she came out from her spot under a bench to lick his hands.

Sam seemed quite enthused by the affection she showed him. He ruffled the soft hair on the top of her head and patted her flank. It was hard to think that this friendly young fellow could be responsible for a murder, even when considering his family's hatred for Clearwell and the incredible strength he possessed in his workman's hands.

No, no. I'm fully aware that I'd been taken in by innocent-seeming characters before, but I was quite certain that Sam Mordaunt could not, in any way, shape or form, be the killer. I (honestly) promise.

This didn't stop Grandfather taking him to task. "Did you really think you could change anything by coming here? If you want to make things better, you should stop your uncle and his gang of troublemakers from coming to Clearwell in the first place."

Sam's face fell once more. "I can't talk to Uncle Jimmy. All he cares about is this miserable celebration. He's had everyone in the village planning it for months. Without Lady Morgana, he'd never have been made mayor. There's no doubt about that."

Delilah offered a rising whimper to comfort him, and he bent down to put his head next to hers. See! More incontrovertible proof of his gentle soul.

The ever-wise Lord Edgington evidently believed we had bigger fish to grill as he tapped me on the shoulder at this point and issued an order. "Come along, Christopher. We have to see a man about… well, another man, I suppose. To the petroleum station we go."

He turned on the spot and veritably marched off along the pavement. I felt a little sore for poor Sam – the innocent sort who, I repeat, was definitely not the killer. Delilah nuzzled him one last time to say farewell, before bounding after her master.

"Goodbye," I said and, when nothing else came to mind, added, "Have a lovely afternoon."

CHAPTER EIGHTEEN

Jed Gibson's place of business was not far away. We swiftly arrived at the garage forecourt, where he was sitting in front of a small grocery shop.

He stood up as Grandfather turned off the road to greet him. "Hello there, Jed. I was hoping you could help us."

"Afternoon M'Lord. And to what does I owe the pleasure?"

The ex-superintendent looked a little confused as he had already provided the answer to this question and could only repeat his previous phrase back to him. "I was hoping you could help us."

"Right you are."

My grandfather's eyes scanned the scene, and I had the definite feeling he was improvising his response. "I'd like to... buy something... in your... shop."

"Now, *that* I can certainly help you with. What would you be in the market for?"

Grandfather could not divine the answer to this question, no matter how long he stared through the shop window. "I'm afraid I cannot say until I've had a good look around inside. I'm what you might call an impulsive shopper."

Jed chewed on the piece of grass that was sticking from his mouth but pointed us toward the green wooden door to the grocer's.

"What a lovely selection," Grandfather exclaimed, sounding like a man who had never been inside a shop before – which, thinking about it now, he probably hadn't for some years. "You've got everything one might need. Fruit, vegetables, canned goods, car... things."

The space was divided into two areas. Most was given over to food, except for a few shelves of products for the maintenance of automobiles.

"So, what will it be, guv'nor? What takes your fancy?"

Grandfather glanced around the rectangular room one last time. "I'll have... yes, I'd like three tins of your best snuff and a bottle of motor oil."

"Wonderful." Jed seemed pleased with the order and darted about to retrieve the items.

"Oh, and, while we're here, I wonder if you might be able to tell me something about Young Cole Watkins. I heard the two of you were friends?"

For all his previous agility, this remark brought Jed to a sudden halt. "Ahh, Cole. Good old Young Cole. He really was one in a million. The salt of the earth. A lord among–"

"Yes, that's the chap." Grandfather was no fan of grandiloquence (in other people, at least). "Now, could you possibly tell me what happened on the day he died?"

Jed clutched the bottle of oil to his chest as though it were his own baby then gazed up at the ceiling with a nostalgic look on his face. "Well, the day after he died was the village fete. Reverend Clarke won the biggest marrow competition – his entry was over two feet long! And Mrs Breakwell, from Millend House, was judging on account of her–"

It was time for Grandfather to interrupt again. In actual fact, it was long overdue. "How fascinating," he lied. "And what of Cole himself? Seeing as he would have been dead by the time the fete began, I was more interested in what happened to him the day before."

"Right you are." Jed ran his fingers over his weathered cheek as though he planned to sketch out his wrinkles on canvas. "Well, we went for breakfast together in The Butcher's Arms, as always. Then I had a break for lunch at around one o'clock, and we went to The Wyndham Arms."

"But there are only two pubs in the village," I pointed out. "Where did you go for dinner?"

He looked at me as though I were quite the dunce. "We went home, of course." He laughed rather merrily. "My dear wife would be up in arms if I din't go home for dinner. Who's ever heard of dinner in a pub?"

Grandfather took this moment to ask a more significant question "So Cole had no job of his own? He spent most of his time drinking?"

The grocer-cum-mechanic-cum-accordionist's face scrunched together in apprehension. "Now, I never said that, did I? Cole din't have a regular job like me or..." He looked the two of us up and down before coming to the right conclusion. "...well, me. But he did the odd job here and there. He sold bits and pieces if they happened to come his way, but then he had his stipend from the Wyndhams, so he didn't need for nothing. In fact, he were the favourite to win the marrow competition at the village fete and would have used his acceptance speech to–"

"Did he live alone?" I interrupted before he got carried away with unrelated stories again.

"Aye."

That didn't lead us anywhere but, luckily, my grandfather... Well, that says it all really; luckily: my grandfather!

"Do you have any reason to believe that someone wanted him dead?"

Jed walked back to the counter where a selection of meats and cheeses was displayed behind a pane of glass. "Not as far as I'm aware."

It was, again, good fortune that I wasn't the one conducting the interview. I would have taken this statement at face value, shaken his hand and wandered away.

"And what exactly happened on the night he died?"

"Oh, that was a fine night indeed... except for the sad ending, of course. You see, Young Cole Watkins was a cheerful drunk..."

Jed became most animated as he told us his tale. He interspersed the events of Cole's last night on Earth with the occasional verse of a song the dead man used to sing. In fact, we probably learnt more about Cole's musical repertoire than what went on that night. It was a good thing Jed didn't have his accordion to hand or I'm fairly sure it would have turned into a full-blown concert.

When we finally got to the part where Cole was pushed down the well, Grandfather delivered a response. "Thank you kindly for such a complete answer, and for all the verses of the song you performed with quite such aplomb. But is there anything else that occurred that weekend that you think may be of importance?"

The shopkeeper (etc.) had pulled down the tins of snuff but froze with them in his lined hands. "That's what I've been trying to tell you from the beginning. If Cole'd won the marrow competition – or, let's be honest, even if he hadn't – he would have got up in front of everyone and revealed the big secret he'd been keeping."

This sounded like something a child would do, but Grandfather found the faintest spark of interest in it. "What big secret?"

Jed looked about the shop for eavesdroppers and, in a whisper, revealed, "I don't actually know."

"How helpful." Whoops! I was being sarcastic to a witness again. I really couldn't understand how my grandfather managed to hold his razor-sharp tongue when faced with such equivocation and – I have to say – down right ignorance. Though, now that I think of it, I had provided him with a fair amount of practice in that department.

"I believe what my grandson wishes to know is whether Cole made any allusion to what he was planning to reveal."

Apparently unoffended, Jed pointed his finger across the counter at us. "Now that you come to mention it, he said that he had discovered something that would change Clearwell as we knew it."

To his credit, Jed had stunned me. Surely this could tie so much of the case together, and yet Grandfather needed more convincing. "Did he give you any idea whether this 'big secret' referred to present-day events in the village or his interest in the past?"

"You mean them dusty old books he kept at Rosebank Cottage?" His laughter filled the shop, and I wondered how long it would be before he recovered from the hilarity of this suggestion. "I'll tell you something about them books. Not even the Wyndhams never spent no time reading 'em. So what fascinating facts do you reckon that Cole would have been able to extract?"

Grandfather looked a little dismayed by this response. "He did read them, at least?"

"Aye, he read them. He spent every Sund'y poring over them, religiously like. The only thing of interest he ever told me were a couple of recipes that my missus cooked for Christmas dinner last year. Cole was a kind-hearted, simple-headed sort, and he was certainly no scholar."

Grandfather glanced out of the long window, which was partially covered with hand-written notices and offers for discounted produce, and so I spoke for him.

"May I enquire whether there was any connection between Young Cole and Florence Keyse?" I thought it was worth asking.

"There certainly was." Jed's voice fell once more, and he had a conspiratorial glint in his eye. "She served the ciders, and he drinked 'em." I couldn't be certain whether I found his sense of humour endearing or tiresome. "Now, that'll be ten and sixpence, please, gentlemen. And I'll throw in the paper bags for free."

Gosh! Ten and sixpence for a few small purchases. It didn't seem so very long ago that you could have got all that and still had change from a guinea for a sumptuous lunch.

128

I accepted the items, but Grandfather had lost his voice for some reason. At this stage in my investigative career, I still hadn't been able to ascertain what such sullenness signified on his part. It was quite apparent, though, that the former superintendent had either just discovered a vital clue and was allowing its ramifications to parade through his head, or he was miffed not to have learnt anything useful in the slightest.

He paid the man, and we moved to the door. With Grandfather's hand on the handle, a thought occurred to him, and he broke his silence. "What of Florence? Do you know anything useful about her?"

Jed's laughter died and, in a second, he had transformed. I suppose that the undeniable violence of Florence's death was a very different matter from the possibility that someone had killed his friend Cole.

"Not really, M'Lord. She was a lovely young woman, but I didn't know much more about her." He sighed a truly hollow sigh and his shoulders re-slumped themselves. "I spent so many nights in the pub with her, and yet I never knew nowt about what she'd done with her life before moving here. 'S ever so sad when you think about it."

Grandfather clearly felt the man's pain and nodded a few times with his lips pursed. "I'm afraid that is sometimes the way of things. I have had servants at my house at Cranley about whom I could write a biography, and others whose names I would struggle to remember though they worked there twenty years." The two men indulged in some silent lamenting before Grandfather finally opened the door. "I appreciate your help. We will keep you informed if we learn anything more."

We were about to leave when the shopkeeper (etc.) offered one last piece of information. "If it's Florence you want to know about, then I'd recommend Mrs Yarworth in the butcher's. The two of them were thick as thieves before the gallows. If there's anyone what knows anything about our poor fallen landlady, it'll be her."

"Thank you, Jed." I thought I should at least try to make up for being short with him. "You've been a great help."

I waited until we'd walked past the two rusty petrol pumps and off the forecourt before dropping the bag onto a bench and asking my first burning question. "Grandfather, isn't it possible that Jed Gibson is to blame for the killings? Perhaps he was only pretending to be ignorant in order to throw us off the trail."

His expression was incredulous. "Christopher, there's absolutely nothing to connect him to either of the murders."

"Exactly. What better way to hide one's guilt than to avoid leaving behind the tiniest scrap of evidence?

"That is a truly beautiful sentiment, boy. You are quite the modern poet." Though this sounded like a compliment, I knew for a fact that Grandfather remained singularly unimpressed by twentieth-century poesy. "But I am close to certain that Jed Gibson had no hand in these crimes."

"Then what about the various staff at Clearwell? Or the farmers who were drinking in the pub last night? We haven't considered them as suspects."

"Is there anything to suggest their involvement?"

I considered the question, then ignored it and had another stab at guessing the identity of the killer. "Then the barman in The Butcher's Arms? Perhaps the real rivalry here is not between the neighbouring villages, but the two pubs that stand opposite one another."

"You're being ridiculous, Christopher. We have gathered no evidence on any of these people."

A flash of inspiration came to me. "That's right! Which only goes to prove that the real culprit is Reverend Clarke!"

He shook his head but couldn't resist asking. "Who the dickens is Reverend Clarke?"

I was growing into the idea and clicked my fingers in the air. "The vicar at St Peter's, of course. If you'd been paying attention, as I was, you'd know that Jed Gibson just provided us with the key piece of information we need to solve this case."

He actually huffed this time before bending to the pressure. "Which is?"

"The produce competition at the Clearwell fete!" A snap of the fingers wasn't nearly enough to express my satisfaction, so I gave a full-handed clap. "Young Cole Watkins was tipped to win the biggest marrow competition, but he suspiciously died the night before it took place. It wouldn't take a genius to conclude that the vicar killed Cole and made off with the winner's rosette."

"You're right, Christopher!" Don't worry, I didn't trust him for a second. "It would not take a genius to conclude such a thing. It would take someone of very limited intellect altogether. Now stop playing games and let us interview our next witness."

He marched off, and so I picked up the bag and hurried after him. "Fine, but I have another question for you." I paused to add a little tension. I don't think it worked. "For what reason could you possibly require a gallon of motor oil and three tins of snuff?"

Looking quite bemused, he watched me as we walked along the high street. "I have no interest whatsoever in a gallon of motor oil and three tins of snuff." Much like any number of the witnesses we'd spoken to that weekend, he could be irritatingly literal at times.

"Then why did you buy them?"

We had reached the white-fronted premises of 'Kate Yarworth & Sons, Butchers', and he stopped to reply. "I bought them because I needed Jed Gibson to talk to us. They were the most expensive items I could see in his shop."

"Oh, how clever." The bag was quite heavy, and I had to keep shifting my weight to support it. "In which case, can I leave them here on the pavement for someone else to find?"

He tutted loudly. "No, of course not. I paid good money for my purchases, and I'm sure we'll find a use for them at Cranley Hall. Now stop dawdling, Christopher. At this rate, our victims will be dust in their graves by the time we solve their murders."

Exhausted from the pace of our walk, the hot, scalding sun and the load I was bearing, I followed him into the shop, and the bell above the door gave an excited *ting-a-ling-a-ling.*

CHAPTER NINETEEN

There was a diminutive chap in a white apron, standing behind the counter, looking worried.

"Mr Yarworth, I presume?" my grandfather chimed.

The short, pale-featured chap opened his mouth to answer, just as an incredibly tall woman with arms like rolled-up carpets thundered over to him.

"That's right. Who's asking?"

Grandfather removed his top hat and offered an exceedingly respectful bow. "My name is Lord Edgington." He didn't even say, *perhaps you've heard of me.* "I've come here today as…" He perused the cuts of meat before selecting the most expensive. "I would like fifteen pounds of your best sirloin steak, please, madam."

She was overcome with emotion and turned into quite the blushing violet. "Fifteen pounds, M'Lord. Oh that's wonderful. We've five here and I'll get Mick to nip over to Milkwall in the car. M' sister runs the shop there, and they normally stock more than us."

Her mute husband stood staring at their dapper customers and didn't move, so Kate Yarworth decided to kick him up the derriere. "What are ya waiting for, ya silly man? Milkwall isn't going to come to you."

Finally shocked into action, her husband pulled his apron from around his neck, dashed around the counter and out of the shop. I considered asking whether I had heard the name correctly and there really was a town called Milkwall, but she spoke before I could.

"Sorry to keep you waiting, M'Lord. It won't be long."

"There's no hurry whatsoever, madam. We have all the time in the world, except for one small matter."

"Oh, yes?" She was still blushing like a… like a… what the devil blushes except for people? Do turtles blush? What about albatrosses? Anyway, she was blushing and had clearly fallen for his act.

"Perhaps you haven't heard, but my grandson and I have acquired some considerable experience in the field of criminal investigation."

"So Florence *was* murdered then?" It all got too much for the distressed butcher and she burst into tears. "My poor Flor was killed right here in Clearwell. What has become of the world?"

My grandfather attempted to comfort her with a ripple of his moustaches and a few well-chosen words. "What indeed, madam? What indeed?"

It was like watching a Victorian farce. I was not in the mood for such theatricality so turned the conversation to a more useful point. "We were told that you were good friends with the deceased. Is that correct?"

"She was like my sister!" Her words came out in one unbroken exclamation, but I believe that is what she said.

"Can you tell us a little about her?" Unlike his bullyragging assistant, Lord Edgington's manner seemed to soothe that distressed woman and she went fishing in her pocket for a somewhat bloodstained handkerchief. For a moment, I thought we'd found evidence of her part in the crime, but then I remembered she was a butcher.

She sniffed a little before replying. "I'll do my best." A touch more sniffing, a wiped eye, and she was ready to paint a picture of our second victim. "There was no one like Flor. I can tell you that for starters. I've been crying all day since I found out. I can't think of a single reason why someone would do such an awful thing."

Her voice faded away, and I was loath to hurry her along, but… well, I did it anyway. "I'm sorry, do you mean that literally? Only we were rather hoping that you might have some idea of why she was killed."

Grandfather elbowed me in the ribs when our suspect wasn't looking. Perhaps I had been a little insensitive, but I was only telling the truth.

"Honestly!" she separated up the syllables in the world in order to communicate her message more clearly. "Everyone loved Florence. Just everyone."

"Perhaps that was the problem." Ha! This might sound like the insensitive sort of thing that I would say, but it was actually my grandfather speaking. "Did she have many admirers?"

His question brought a few more tears to Kate Yarworth's eyes. The two blue orbs were quite the prettiest thing about her as, despite the fact she was blessed with dainty features, her bright red skin looked as though it had been treated with a butcher's mallet. "You're right. She had too many. And she weren't interested in most of 'em. Do you think that's what this is about? I always told her. I said, 'Flor, you're too pretty by half. You should marry the next man who asks you and put all them others out o' their misery.'"

"Did she receive many offers of marriage then?" I managed to ask a question without sounding rude, which was surely real progress.

"Did she! Half the men in this village would have had her. Everyone from Lieutenant-Colonel Stroud to the brewer's boy have thrown their hats into the ring at one time or another, but she wasn't interested. I could never work out why. I suppose she thought she could do better for some reason."

"And what about Cole Watkins? Was he one of them?"

She smiled for less than a second then breathed out a sorry note. "Young Cole? Oh, no. I don't think love was where his interests lay. I'd say he wasn't built for such things." She waited a moment to see whether we caught her meaning and, when it was clear that we hadn't, she clarified. "He was a simple sort. You know, a bit of a Peter Pan. It was as though he'd never grown up, poor lad."

"Was there one *special gentleman* in Florence's life?" Grandfather chose his words more carefully this time.

Mrs Yarworth looked uncertain of herself, and it was at this moment that her sons peeked in from a back room. They were younger than I had imagined from their prominent billing on the shopfront. The eldest couldn't have been more than ten, and it was clear they were suffering Florence's death as much as anyone else that day.

"Go back upstairs, boys," our witness said in a more tender voice than we'd yet heard. When the trio of little chaps wouldn't move, she threw a dirty apron in their direction, and that did the trick. She waited to hear their footsteps on the floor above us before answering Grandfather's question. "There was someone over this last month, but I never found out who he was. All I know is that he was an older man and, no matter how much I begged her to say his name, she wouldn't tell me."

I was once more certain we had found the piece of evidence that would send us hurtling towards our killer. That was until I realised that nearly every man whom we'd met in the Forest of Dean was older than lovely Florence. I suppose we could rule out Sam Mordaunt and my cousin Dante as her inamorati, but that didn't get us a great deal closer to discovering who it actually was.

"Did he treat her well?" Grandfather asked, a seriousness having now crept into his voice.

"Like I said, she wouldn't share much with me. All I can tell you is that she took the bus into Cinderford to see him. I found it strange, as eight miles is a long way to go for a man."

"Perhaps he was from over that way?" I suggested, and she hesitated before answering.

"No, I put that to her, and she just laughed." She needed another moment to consider the facts. Something about the spasming muscles in her temples made me think of the intensity with which my grandfather analysed the details of our cases. I could tell she had a quick mind behind her strangely chapped skin. "I got the impression that Florence didn't want anyone here knowing about her fancy man."

I always found it strange when my grandfather decided that a line of investigation had run its course and that it was time to change topic. This was one of those moments. "She wasn't from around here, was she?"

Mrs Yarworth shook her head. "No, her people were from the city."

"London?"

"Nooooo." She looked quite bemused by the idea. "Gloucester! But her parents bought the pub when she was still young. She were only twenty-one when they died."

"'In a tragic threshing accident'?" I asked, repeating what the Lieutenant-Colonel had told us that morning. Grandfather looked faintly impressed that I had remembered such a minute detail.

"That's right." The butcher shook her head again as she recalled the great misfortune.

"How very awful." I simply had to ask the question that my grandfather wouldn't. "If you don't mind me asking, how exactly were two people who owned a pub killed in an agricultural accident?"

"They were out for a walk near Stank Farm. Them poor folks never saw the thresher coming."

"Didn't they hear it?"

Before the tearful woman could reply, my grandfather attempted to brush over my insensitivity once more. "Those poor people. What a tragedy."

She sighed quite mournfully. "I did what I could for Florence after her folks died, but there was nothing that could have prevented this."

"So very true, Madam." Grandfather cleared his throat as though sorry he would have to inconvenience her with more questions. "May I ask whether there is anything else you recall that could help us understand what happened last night?"

She worried the buttons on her jacket and bit one side of her lip. "I wish there was. Like I said, everyone loved Flor. She never cheated no one and held no debts. Never stole nor cursed even. She was as good as she seemed and better. I don't understand any of it."

"Well, thank you." I believe that Lord Edgington would have put one hand on our witness's arm in sympathy for her loss had there not been a large cabinet and any number of meaty cuts in between them. "We greatly appreciate your help."

"You're very welcome, M'Lord. That'll be two pounds and ten for the beef." Her sorrow apparently having subsided, she held her hand out for the money, and Grandfather had to extract what he owed from a slim leather wallet that he kept in the inside pocket of his stubbornly un-summery coat.

It was at this moment that Mr Yarworth's old van screeched to a halt outside the shop. He came running towards us with the weighty piece of meat tucked under his arm like a rugby ball. I'd played rugby any number of times at school and had developed quite the knack for throwing the ball as far as possible whenever the opposing team came within ten yards of me. I'm sure that's the only reason I'd lived to (almost) adulthood.

Inevitably, once the two portions of sirloin had been united, I was the one charged with carrying them. I could see Delilah sitting outside, looking very excited for what she hoped was coming her way.

"There is one more question I'd like to put to you," Grandfather explained, still rooted to the spot in front of the counter. "Can you tell me whether there was any other connection between Florence and Cole Watkins?"

Mr Yarworth raised one finger to respond, but whatever he muttered was soon drowned out by his wife. "They both liked singing. Is that any help?"

"I was thinking more of their backgrounds. Did they have any family connections or business dealings?"

She had a good think, and it was clear by this point that her husband

137

would not even try to provide an answer. "Nothing comes to mind, I'm afraid. But then I never had much to do with Young Cole. You'd be better off asking old Mrs Fox in the bakery. She was something of an aunt to the lad. She's certainly the only other person in the village who gave a fig for them old books of his."

"Thank you, Madam. You've been extremely helpful." Grandfather bowed, and the woman blushed once again like a… like a… No, I still can't think of anything that blushes. An elephant, perhaps? Do elephants blush?

"I also have one last question," I said, though I didn't mean to sound so mysterious. "Would you happen to have any scraps for our dog? She's been watching us this whole time, and she won't leave us alone if we don't give her something."

CHAPTER TWENTY

"Are you sure they're not sending you from shop to shop as they know you'll end up spending money in each one?"

Grandfather looked both ways along the high street before crossing. It was an incredibly quiet road, and we would surely have heard a car approaching but, after that threshing story, I didn't blame him.

"Christopher, you must try not to be so excessively distrustful. These people are not suspects; they are witnesses. We are gathering general information about the circumstances which preceded the two murders, not infiltrating a criminal gang." There was a silent tut in every word he said.

"I'm not suggesting they're underhanded miscreants. I merely wondered if they saw an opportunity and made the most of it."

Grandfather let out a low note which I had long since realised meant *I despair of you, Christopher. I really do!*

We soon made it to the bakery which, by this time of day, was nearly empty of its goods.

"Good afternoon, madam. I take it you are Mrs Fox, the trusted friend of Young Cole Watkins."

She was an elderly woman with tightly curled hair and a suspicious look on her face. "I might be. And what of it?"

"I am here, madam as…" Grandfather had momentarily forgotten his own strategy from the previous shops and had to change tack. "…I would like to buy three cobber loaves, two currant buns, a wholemeal roll and that biscuit in the shape of a malformed child." His description really wasn't very clear, and so he pointed to explain better.

"That's a gingerbread man. Ain't ya never heard of a gingerbread man before?"

"Of course it is. Silly me. Oh, and if that fruit loaf behind you is for sale, I'll take that too."

Her cheeks puffed up as a smile transformed her features. "Williaaaaaaaaaaaaam!" She shouted through the door behind her. "Williaaaaaaaaaaaam! We've sold the last of the bread. We can lock up and go for a drink after this."

Grandfather's neat ploy had done the trick; she couldn't have looked happier.

"There is another matter I wish to discuss, Mrs Fox."

"Young Cole, I suppose?" Every word she now spoke was powered by her enthusiasm. "Tragic case it was. Tragic." I'd heard that word a lot since arriving in Clearwell… and, for that matter, since spending any time whatsoever with my grandfather. "I was friends with Old Cole, you see. When his wife died, I looked after the young'un as best I could. By the time Young Cole were fifteen, he were alone in the world. I were the only family he had."

"I would like to ask you two key questions." Grandfather had straightened his posture and, with our witness sufficiently charmed, he could concentrate on his task. "First, I would like to know whether Cole had any dealings with Florence Keyse outside of The Wyndham Arms?"

"No." Well, that was a resolute answer.

"Very well. And second, we heard tell that you shared Cole's interest in local history. I was rather hoping you might know what he planned to reveal at the village fete the day after he died."

She had placed Grandfather's order in a large paper bag, which she held by the corners and rotated through the air so that the ends furled in on themselves and the bag stayed sealed.

"Now, that's an interesting question." Her face expressed as much. "A very interesting question." It was unclear whether she had any plans to answer it, though. "Cole was particularly excited the week before the fete. I remember that. You see, he'd been working through the books from the Wyndham family library for nigh on ten years by the time he found a document hidden away within a large tome."

Grandfather took a step closer to the woman. "Do you know what it contained?"

"That's the funny thing. Young Cole and I used to enjoy reading about the big house and all them people what lived there. I taught the boy to read using them books – though the handwriting weren't always legible, and there was the odd page missing. We loved reading the gossip and about all the things what went on there. There was far too much detail on family succession and taxes, but Cole even enjoyed them dry bits."

"I'm sorry. You said there was something funny about it?" Even if my words were not the most polite, I certainly used a delicate tone to bring her to the point.

"That's right. The funny thing is, Cole wouldn't tell me what he'd found."

"Might it have pertained to his own connection to the family? Several people have told us of the rumour that he was descended from the Wyndhams."

She laughed then. "Oh, I doubt that. I always thought that were something his parents made up to get what they could out of the Wyndhams. I'd certainly never heard no one speak of such things before he were born."

Grandfather was grinding his teeth; it appeared that our interview would not deliver the essential clue we required. "So you've no idea what he planned to reveal at the fete?"

"No. He wouldn't tell me a thing. Just said that he'd found something extraordinary, and it would change the village for ever. Though I did have a bit of a feeling about it."

"Oh, yes?" I was the one who sounded excited now, whereas my grandfather glanced away. He had no time for feelings, presentiments or gut intuition if they could not be backed up with evidence.

"Yes. You see, he waved his find around the last time I was over there. I saw the handwriting, and I could tell it was very old. It looked to me that the pages'd been ripped out of a diary of some sort. Of course, back in them days, it were only you toffs what could read and write."

"When you say, 'them days'…" I could tell that my grandfather hated having to repeat this grammatical atrocity. "…to when exactly are you referring?"

"Well, the time of Lady Morgana, of course. What else could shake up the village if it weren't related to her?"

The esteemed detective and his gullible grandson were finally experiencing the same emotion. I suppose, just as a stopped clock is correct twice a day, it was inevitable we would align at some point. He looked at me with a stern, yet prescient glare, and I nodded.

"If only we could read the text he found," I said, in the unlikely hope this might spark some major development in the case.

Mrs Fox looked at me as though I was talking a brand-new kind of nonsense that no one had invented before. "Well, you could just go over to his house, I suppose."

Even Grandfather appeared confused by the simplicity of her suggestion. "How do you mean?"

"Unless Cole had it on him when he fell down the well, surely whatever he found would be there." Her words were met with shocked silence. "Jed Gibson must still have the key."

"You have been incredibly helpful, madam." Grandfather handed over another shilling, though he must have been overpaying by some margin.

On leaving the bakery, with my arms now full and aching dreadfully, I realised that Delilah was still over by the butcher's, enjoying her scrag ends. So much for her faithful devotion to our investigation.

"Jed," Grandfather called to the jack of all trades, who was back in his usual spot. "We require the key to Young Cole's house."

"Right you are, guv'nor. It's hanging inside. I kept a spare here because he was always losing his." He looked as though he would leap into action and provide us with what we needed, but he stopped himself to ask a question. "I don't suppose I can interest you in a pound of plums and some sparking plugs?"

CHAPTER TWENTY-ONE

Rosebank Cottage was a pretty sight. Unlike the other houses on the street, it was surrounded by a large garden with rows of cane pyramid structures with sweet peas growing up them. On either side of the front door, towering hollyhocks grew in a variety of colours from white to purple and every shade in between. The house itself was all that one could want in a cottage. Below a dense thatched roof, it had whitewashed walls, and glossy red paint on the window frames. Even Grandfather was impressed, and we stood before the wooden gate enjoying the serenity of that bucolic scene.

"What a peaceful property." He sighed, before returning to darker concerns. "Of course, it does beg the question of why the Wyndham family would keep a man to whom they deny any connection in such pretty surrounds."

"Are you saying you believe that Cole really was descended from the illegitimate heir of the former Earl of Dunraven?"

"No, of course not."

I was lost for words. I simply had no idea how I had added two and two together to make four, only to be told that the correct answer was a butter knife. Such complicated equations were beyond me.

"Come along, Christopher." Grandfather pushed the gate open with a resolute shove. The white paint seemed to have melted a little in the sun, which suggested that no one had been inside for some time.

I dropped everything we'd bought (except the bag from the bakery) onto a white metal love seat near the house. I could see the excitement in the old fellow's eyes as he held out the Jed Gibson's long brass key to insert it into the door. Perhaps it was the symbolism involved that had sparked this reaction. We were literally about to unlock the secrets of a man whose shadow had lain over the village since we arrived. I tried not to consider the symbolism of the fact that, on closer inspection, the lock was splintered. The door had been forced open and we would not need the key after all.

"Someone broke into the house," I said, as such simple deductions were within my range of expertise.

"Yes, and it matches what Florence Keyse told us at the pub last night."

I tried to remember the pertinent fact she had shared. I promise I did. All I could recall were her pretty eyes and the way I, Dante, and even Algar had looked dreamily at her as she poured pints. Oh, and her ideas on Cole's death of course! How could I have forgotten? She said that she thought he'd been murdered and–

"She'd seen smoke coming from the chimney!" Hurray! I did have a functioning memory after all.

"Correct." Grandfather took his gloves from his pocket and pushed the door with two fingers so that it swung open with a long, unnerving creak. "Which seems increasingly likely to be the reason she was murdered."

I had to lean against the cob wall. It wasn't merely that we had now raised a major structural element that would support our whole case; I was overwhelmed by the fact that the former wolf of Scotland Yard had trusted me with such information.

"So you're saying that everything that has happened revolves around Cole, not Florence?"

"That's just it, Christopher. I've held onto the idea for most of the day, and this only strengthens my belief."

Another thought occurred to me. "Might it not also suggest that we can now rule out the Wyndhams as killers?" He didn't need to respond; he looked a touch puzzled, and so I explained myself. "They would have no need to break in here. As they own the building, they must have a spare key."

He nodded but gave nothing else away. "Fine thinking, my boy, but if one of the Wyndhams had been here, they might have considered that very fact and broken into the house to throw us off their trail. Don't worry. If we're lucky, there will be something in this house that leads us to the killer."

Perhaps it was the weight of this statement that meant we both need required a little courage to step over the threshold. My grandfather looked at me, then placed one hand on the flat of my back, and we made the move together. It was lucky I'd left our purchases behind, or we wouldn't have fitted.

He was right about one thing – well, he was normally right about everything actually, but one fact in particular stood out in my mind. The cottage really was in a fine state and was furnished in a style that was far beyond the means of a village drunk.

Nobody had told us how Cole's parents had died. Perhaps it was another freak threshing accident. Either way, their presence was felt in the house. There was a small portrait of the Watkins family in the narrow entrance hall which showed baby Cole with his deathly serious father and pretty young mother. The only photograph on display was a cutting from the local newspaper when Cole was an adolescent. He was holding a large marrow with his still glum father and the caption said, 'Watkins win Produce Competition for Third Year Running.' I still thought we should interview Reverend Clarke in case vegetables were the motivating factor in the case.

Grandfather moved on, and I spotted his reaction as he paused in the first room off the passageway. He'd caught a glimpse of something that I, for one, had been waiting to see.

"The library," I said with some excitement.

We had come to a living room with a dining table on one side and two sofas positioned around a fire on the other. In comparison to this humble arrangement, the four walls of the room displayed a quite majestic assortment of old books. I had the feeling that the oaken shelves must have been designed for the room after the rest of the house was decorated. Not only did they have a different style from the other furnishings, they looked a great deal newer.

We didn't stand there gawping for long but dashed forward to inspect the substantial collection. The first shelf I looked at held books that were far older than the castle, but mainly seemed to contain endless accounts of the various tithes that were paid to the Wyndham family at their estate in Wales. The next shelf was more interesting. There were a number of handwritten journals from Algar's ancestors dating back to the sixteenth century. It must have been a family tradition, in fact, and I suddenly understood why Cole would have taken such interest in these dusty, and oddly powdery, old tomes.

That's right, powdery! I noticed marks time and time again on the spines of the books and along the edges of the shelves. I rubbed my fingers against one of them and discovered it to be a white powder. I noticed that Grandfather had spotted the very same thing and was already helping himself to a sample.

"There are no fingerprints in the powder," he reflected, peering into the envelope which he kept in an inside pocket of his coat for such moments. "How interesting."

"Yes, fascinating," I replied, though I would have struggled to say why.

I picked up one of the journals and found myself rather distracted by an account of a young chap by the name of Kit Wyndham who had come of age in the 1680s. Though separated by over two hundred years, it was incredible how much we had in common. He suffered all the same doubts about his life as I did, though in one respect, he had it easy. His parents had organised a marriage for him to the daughter of a wealthy family. It might not sound like the most romantic match but, had my parents hatched such a plan for me, it would have taken away my fears that no woman could ever love me and that I would die alone – possibly surrounded by the stuffed remains of my dear departed pets.

I would have enjoyed reading that pleasantly antiquated text for hours if my grandfather hadn't reminded me that there were more pressing matters for my consideration. He had sized up the collection before us and come away with a clear understanding.

"The shelves have been arranged chronologically. We're looking for the early eighteenth century, which would be approximately … here." He stopped a few shelves along from me and began to remove books, flick through a few pages and then return each one to the shelf. I suppose I should have helped him, but he seemed to know what he was doing without any assistance.

"It seems that Mrs Fox, the baker, may have been correct." He spoke in a way that was surely designed to prompt a question.

"Are you saying that the document Cole found really did relate to Lady Morgana?"

He paused with his finger to his cheek for three whole seconds before delivering me from the pain of anticipation. "Let us not get ahead of ourselves. That could well be the case, but it is clear that many members of the Wyndham family, going back centuries, have contributed accounts of their lives to the family library, and yet, if these are as well organised as they appear to be, there is nothing here

146

from the hand of Thomas Wyndham."

I considered his approach to our search once more and realised he had been assessing the dates to determine where the volume in which we were most interested would be found.

"And, of course," I began, while attempting to sound as though I knew what I wanted to say, "had his own journal been preserved, the mystery of Lady Morgana would have been solved years ago. It makes sense that he, or someone else in the family, hid the pages in another book."

"*Does* that make sense?" Trust the old genius to find a fault in the piffle and poppycock I was so confidently spouting. "Surely if he didn't want anyone to discover what had happened, he would have destroyed his memoir altogether?"

"Perhaps," I conceded. "But then... Well, it must be a difficult thing to do – destroying one's very memories, even in written form. It's almost like erasing yourself from existence. Don't forget that Thomas Wyndham would have lived the rest of his life with the knowledge of what happened to Lady Morgana. He would have been blamed for decades for her death. Perhaps he couldn't bear for the truth to be destroyed entirely, so he removed the key passage and hid it away in the dullest-looking book in the Clearwell collection. A text on average sheep weight in the Wyndham flock, or maybe the impact of inflationary rises on seed pricing." I sounded really rather clever summoning such hypothetical volumes from the ether, though, in truth, I'd spotted several such titles during my search.

"Christopher, I stand corrected."

I couldn't believe what he was saying. I stood waiting for a *however*... or some nasty quip at my expense, but it never came.

"That is sympathetic and well-formulated thinking. You have proven your point."

"Oh, gosh," I would like to have said more, but I couldn't think of anything, and so I repeated the sentiment. "Golly gosh!"

"Gosh, indeed. Now, we mustn't waste time looking for something that clearly isn't here. We can always ask the police to do that. I can only assume that there's an inspector bumbling about by now, though he hasn't exactly made his presence felt."

"So, what do we do next?"

His eyebrows rippled. A wicked smile erupted on his face, and he darted across to the fireplace on the far side of the room. Grandfather inhaled the air above the ashes in the grate. "It's less than a month old. This fire was lit after Cole died."

I had to take a deep breath before saying anything; he'd knocked the wind out of me. "You can tell that just by smelling it?"

He granted me a truly despairing look. "No, Christopher. I cannot smell the age of a fire. There's a singed ball of newspaper on the tiles with an article on this year's Epsom Derby on the second of June. The Derby was won by Joe Childs riding Coronach. He beat the field by five lengths and the horse was bred by Baron Woolavington."

I was about to ask him whether he had remembered all that, when I realised he must have read it on the paper.

"Which once again fits with what Florence Keyse told us." He seemed to say this as much for his own benefit as mine. "She saw smoke coming from the chimney some weeks after Cole died."

"It begs the question of why anyone would light a fire in June," I said, to brush over my previous imbecilic thoughts.

I'd clearly made up for my stupidity as he granted me a silent clap of his gloved hands. "An excellent point, indeed, Christopher. Although we've had plenty of rain since then, the weather has been mild and, in such a small dwelling as this one, a fire would be excessive."

He paused to smile at me expectantly. He was apparently hoping for an excellent answer to my excellent question. Sadly, all I could summon was, "Perhaps whoever came in here decided to cook some sausages. I adore a good sausage." It made me hungry just to think of such treats, and so I extracted a currant bun from my paper parcel. I offered Grandfather a bite, but he resisted.

"Hardly, boy. For one thing, there's a perfectly good kitchen here, but I also very much doubt that our killer broke into Cole's house in order to–"

"Or he burnt the document!" I interrupted before he could say anything more disparaging.

"An excellent alternative." My flights of genius and idiocy had just about balanced out one another, and he picked up an iron poker to see what the ashes might reveal. "Assuming I am not about to find a tiny fragment of paper with the words 'I killed Lady Morgana' on them, what do you imagine Wyndham's account would have revealed?"

It was an interesting point to consider. I must admit that I'd rather accepted Dante's idea that Thomas Wyndham was to blame for his fiancée's death, and yet, there was a significant issue with this.

"If Wyndham was a killer, that would suggest some loyal maniac here in Clearwell murdered Cole to keep the secret, then strangled Florence to hide the crime." I thought Grandfather might contribute something to the mental exertions I was undertaking. He remained silent and so I continued. "But if the contrary were true, that would point to the Mordaunts."

"And which do you think is more likely?" He fixed me with his unparalleled stare, and I suddenly felt rather hot.

"I... Well, it's hard to say. On the one hand, Sam Mordaunt had infiltrated the town and may well have been in the pub on the night Cole was killed. He was certainly present when Florence told us of the smoke she'd seen coming from this very chimney weeks after Cole's murder. So there is a strong possibility that the Mordaunts are responsible for the killings."

"And yet?" He could read me like a book – and not an old musty one, either, but a cleanly printed, modern one with well-defined margins and no ink smudges.

"And yet, it would have been a real risk for the Mordaunts to stalk about the town at night. Anyone could have seen them."

"That's possible." He had not been looking at me until this moment, but now peered back from his inspection of the ashes. To my surprise, he had extracted the tiniest scrap of paper that must have fallen from the fire to the dirty tiles beneath. He held it up between two gloved fingers and, in a curling, italic script on thick parchment, I could just make out the words 'my treasured innocent'.

CHAPTER TWENTY-TWO

There tended to be one key moment in each of our investigations at which we could finally see through the fog we'd entered. A turning point at which it was clear that our hard work had paid off and we were on the right path.

This wasn't that moment.

A disconnected phrase on a piece of burnt paper did not prove who was eliminating the inhabitants of a small Gloucestershire village, but it did provide us with a burst of excitement. Although we couldn't say what had caused Lady Morgana's death, or ascertain the part her intended had played in the mystery, it seemed likely that Cole and Florence had been killed to hide these ancient secrets. All we needed to discover now was why and by whom.

Simple.

We returned to the front garden to see that Delilah had finished her snack and was nosing around the bags I had left on the bench.

"You cheeky little mongrel," Grandfather threw his voice like a ventriloquist and scared the guilty creature. "Is your hunger never satiated?"

I must admit that, as I'd just bitten into a second bun, I took pause to reassure myself that this remark was not addressed to me. It goes without saying that, though the fruity, bready, sticky cake was a little past its best, it was still absolutely blooming delicious. I sometimes wished I had a voice in my head to tell me to stop thinking about cakes and concentrate on the life-and-death matter of our investigation. Regrettably, I did not.

A few things had changed since we'd entered Cole's cottage. For one, a storm had rolled over the village to lend an eerie light to the place. The clouds overhead contributed a crepuscular ambience, and such eerie atmospherics were only befitting of what was about to occur. The residents of Clearwell must have known the programme for that weekend's festivities and hidden away inside their homes. Even Jed Gibson had abandoned his chair near the petrol pumps, and a rather disturbing hush had fallen over Clearwell that was soon interrupted by the steady bang, bang, bang of a drum in the distance.

"Chrissy, do you know in what circumstances the compound *flux* is used?" Grandfather asked, as though unaware of the nightmare into which we were ambling as we left Rosebank Cottage behind and headed along the high street.

"I can't say that I do, Grandfather. Though I must declare it sounds quite otherworldly. Is it something from one of Todd's fantastical novels?" I sometimes wished I had a voice in my head to tell me to stop talking altogether.

"No, boy, it has nothing to do with fiction." He was past the point of shaking his head or rolling his eyes by now and proceeded with the explanation. "It is used by blacksmiths to stop metal from oxidising when it's heated. I believe that the white substance on the bookshelves in Cole's cottage could be flux – or rather a mixture of borax and ammonium chloride."

The incessant pulsation got louder the further we went. As the skies above us opened, and Delilah cowered behind my legs, I answered as though I was not the slightest bit intimidated by our predicament. "So the Mordaunts could be involved after all?"

"You tell me, Christopher."

The raindrops seemed to multiply in weight and size and, with my light summer outfit already soaking wet, we spotted the source of the drumbeat. I would much rather have sprinted back to the safety of the castle, but my superior came to a stop beside the Clearwell Cross to watch the human flood that was flowing towards us. At the front of the procession was one of the hooded demons who had greeted us on our arrival the previous day. He had a large Celtic drum in his hands and was providing the slow, steady encouragement for his kinsmen's vaguely bridal pace.

Just behind this monster were the Mordaunts themselves. Dressed in rather regal attire, Jimmy walked arm in arm with his wife. Their three children each held electric torches, as though they'd been told to illuminate their parents' path, while Uncle Cliff hung back from the others. It was clear that this was Jimmy's night.

I could see no sign of Sam, and I had to wonder what had happened to him after he'd been ejected from the pub. I doubt many people noticed he was missing, though. There must have been two hundred people from Scowles Folly there, all dressed in old-fashioned attire.

They were presumably harking back to the time of Lady Morgana, though they appeared to have mistaken the eighteenth century for the days of knights and dragons. I very much doubted the historical accuracy of the long gowns and tunics I saw on display.

"Guilty!" I heard a voice proclaim, though at least there was no fire or blood this time.

"Guilty," Jimmy echoed, before the devil continued with a list of accusations.

"Many are the crimes of Clearwell Castle. Many are the sins of Thomas Wyndham. Tragic is the tale of Lady Morgana, and perverse the betrayal of Scowles Folly."

They did not seem perturbed by the bad weather, and it almost looked as though they were bringing the clouds with them from the heart of the forest. What dark magic had they summoned to turn the sky black? Was this the curse of Lady Morgana made visible?

Grandfather simply smiled and raised his chin, as though he had gone to watch the Lord Mayor's Parade in London. I noticed that the mayor of Scowles Folly looked similarly jovial as he cheered on the caller, much to the delight of his people. His brother Cliff, like the good bodyguard that he clearly was, surveyed their surroundings but appeared to take no pleasure from the festivities.

We remained in that soggy spot for some time until the crowd turned right towards the castle and my grandfather sprang into life. My very own old devil could move quite swiftly when he wished and, with poor sodden Delilah at his heel, Grandfather managed to outmanoeuvre the invading army.

"That is far enough," he said, running into the middle of the road in front of St Peter's church and placing his cane down in front of him like a staff of old. I was worried they would march right over him, but the crowd stopped to hear what he had to say. "A tragedy has befallen this town this weekend, and your presence here will only make things worse."

Jimmy released his wife's arm and limped forward. "There is no tragedy so great as that which my people have lived through these last two centuries." We had heard this rhetoric before, and he evidently repeated it for the benefit of his followers rather than the impervious gentleman before him. "We have broken no laws. We are merely exercising our right to walk on public roads. If King George himself were here at this moment, he would confirm that there is nothing to stop any freeborn Englishman from going for a stroll."

"Freeborn Englishman" indeed! He sounded like he'd been born in the dark ages.

"That may be." Grandfather betrayed no fear as he stood before the throng. "But you should think of the people in this village whose wounds are still fresh. Many of the locals here have lost someone they love. Surely you can see that an innocent woman's death this very weekend holds more weight than whatever occurred all that time ago."

Jimmy had the bit between his teeth and would accept no counsel. "I concede nothing. This is our tradition, our right. We are upholding what's left of our pride."

With the rain pouring off the brim of his top hat, much as though he were standing beneath a waterfall, Grandfather breathed in slowly. "Do you want a war? Is that why you're here?" His voice was coated with not just anger, but disillusionment that anyone could be so pig headed. "Have you come in search of violence?"

I thought that the brief blink Jimmy gave in response suggested he would relent, but it was not to be. The devil with the drum fell silent, and so the mayor beat his hands together and simply walked past the only man who had stood up to him that day.

My grandfather would not give up on his task and appealed to the second in command. "Cliff, you're a reasonable man. Talk some sense into your brother."

The werewolf we had met that morning looked more like a whimpering puppy just then. He glanced between Jimmy and my grandfather but could only muster a weak reply. "This isn't my doing, but there's no standing in his way when he gets a mind to do something."

Jimmy looked back at Cliff, and I thought he would bark out an order as the rest of their brethren swelled around us. Instead, he wore his usual vacant expression and shuffled onwards.

"Have you seen my boy?" Cliff continued, pulling away from the others. "Have you seen Sam? I thought I'd find him here, but there's no sign of him."

154

"Not for an hour," I shouted over the deafening rain. "Perhaps he went back to your village, and you missed him."

The man looked quite chilled by this news but, shrugging in apology to my grandfather, he was carried along by the crowd. It was hard to imagine what would happen next. I had never seen my distinguished mentor defeated by anyone but himself before. He had attempted to turn back a tide, only for it to crash right over him – and that will be the last water-based metaphor I use for a while. Though, can you really blame me? I was soaked to the skin.

Once a lorry at the back of the procession had rolled slowly past us, a resolution formed in Grandfather's mind. "Quickly, Christopher. We must get to the gatehouse and make sure it is closed before they can penetrate the castle."

Delilah immediately shot ahead of us, presumably hoping to warn our compatriots herself.

"What do you think they'll do if they get inside the castle?" I asked, as I hurried to keep up with him.

"I'd rather not find out."

It must have been three hundred yards to the gatehouse, and I doubted that the old chap would have the puff, but I shouldn't have worried. He overtook the marauders at a canter, and I was the one who was soon out of breath – which is hardly surprising as I was still carrying all our purchases, and they were even heavier now that they were wet.

"Dorie, Todd, unnamed footman!" he shouted as we grew close.

Jimmy hadn't reacted when we'd first passed him, but as he saw what we planned to do, he urged his people to move faster.

"We're coming through now," I shouted. "Lower the drawbridge. Man the portcullis. Release the hounds." Though I had, admittedly, not noticed any of these things since my arrival in Clearwell, I lived in hope that they existed.

"Or more simply," Grandfather yelled, as we ran under the arch to safety, "close the gate once we're through!"

Dorie was still in position and, with perhaps the tiniest bit of help from the men alongside her, she pushed the heavy wooden gate into place and secured it with an enormous metal bar that slotted into the stone wall.

"Quick, Todd." Grandfather kept his head about him and issued more orders. "Run to the castle and get some guns in case things get out of hand."

"Quick, Dorie," I too knew how to bark at people. "Take this shopping; my arms are killing me."

I was quite exhausted but, as the enemy hammered on the door against which I had collapsed, I had rarely felt so safe. Well, until they started throwing projectiles over the walls, at least.

CHAPTER TWENTY-THREE

"What's happening?" Algar bellowed as he ran down the steps at the front of the castle.

We waited for the stones that were raining down around us to subside before darting across the garden to safety. The gate would hold without anyone standing there, and we were putting ourselves in unnecessary danger.

"What do you *think* is happening?" Grandfather could not hide his agitation as we ran for cover. "Morgana died two hundred years ago tonight, and the Mordaunts will not let you forget it."

I noticed Gertrude hanging a little way behind her father, looking quite racked with fear. She lingered at the entrance to the castle, apparently unsure whether to join us or retreat. Her mother was watching from the window of the dining room with her usual critical visage. She showed no sign of concern for us as a waxed-paper bomb filled with blood sailed over the wall and nearly splashed my trousers. Did those savages not realise they were linen? It was bad enough they'd been in the rain. If I'd stained them too, it would have been a disaster.

"This is terrible," the lord of the manor exclaimed, and he raised his coat high over his head to offer his friend some shelter. "Come inside, quickly."

"We're no closer to finding the killer," Grandfather explained in the entrance hall, as he brushed the excess water from his hat.

Delilah was watching him and must have concluded that this was her cue to do the same. She shook violently so that all her fur stood on end. She was standing just next to me at the time, and I was now even wetter than before. A footman came to rub her down and, had one appeared with a towel for me, I would almost certainly have allowed him to complete the task.

"There's something you're not telling me, Algar." Apparently unconcerned by the cold or damp, Lord Edgington fixed his eyes on our host and would not let him go until we had the answers we needed. "Something you know about this case that you should have already disclosed."

I had to stop him then as I realised that Gertrude had turned into a statue in the corner by the door. It was hardly out of character for her, but I didn't want her to be traumatised any further. I tapped my grandfather's shoulder, and I think he must have got the message as his voice fell quieter.

"The longer you resist, the harder it will be for you to confess your part in all this." He spoke through gritted teeth. "I've tried discretion, and I've tried asking nicely, but I'm running out of patience."

Algar said nothing. He was peering beyond his inquisitor at his frozen daughter. The poor girl looked half drowned by the rain, though she'd only been outside for a few seconds. Had I known something that could make her feel better, I would have said it but... well, I didn't.

"Come with me," Algar finally sputtered, and we followed him into a long, rectangular salon which we hadn't entered before.

There were Flemish tapestries on each wall depicting various biblical scenes, from Jesus healing the blind to Saul escaping from Damascus in a basket. The room was far gloomier than the others we had visited. This was not only because the night was falling outside; every last piece of furniture was dark and old fashioned. Dead-eyed hunting trophies lent an ominous feel to the place, and the portraits above each door seemed to have been created using nothing but shades of black paint.

"Is it because of Florence?" Grandfather asked when he was tired of waiting for Algar to serve up his confession. "You were having an affair with her, I assume?"

Algar looked quite aghast that the words had been spoken out loud. "How could you know?"

I would have required a good hour or so to piece together all the clues that had led Grandfather to this revelation. It was lucky, therefore, that he did it for me.

"It really wasn't so difficult. If your attentions to her in the pub last night weren't transparent enough, we spoke to her friends in the village today. She rejected the proposals of several suitors, which wouldn't mean anything in itself, if we hadn't learnt that she regularly took a bus eight miles to meet her fancy man.

"She clearly didn't want anyone in Clearwell to know who he was, and this led me to believe that it must be someone in a position of power. Though I suspected the Lieutenant-Colonel, we discovered his advances to Florence had already been rebuffed. Considering your comportment ever since we learnt of her death, you, my dear friend, were the obvious pick."

Algar crashed down in an armchair facing the window, just as a bolt of lightning split the sky. "There's no sense denying it now; it's true. I've been a fool. I never meant to fall in love with her. I've no idea what I was thinking, but you can't imagine what my life has been like these last years. You really can't."

"Is Cressida aware of the relationship?" Grandfather's tone had not lightened. He stood over the wretched man, and his eyes were just as troubled as the sky above the castle.

For a moment, Algar couldn't produce a sound but finally managed to shrug his shoulders despondently. "I suspect that she may be. She won't say it outright, but she talks more often than ever of my wicked nature. You see, my wife has a very simplistic view of human morality. There are only two types of people in this world: saints and sinners. And she's known for a very long time to which of those camps I belong."

For once, I knew what my grandfather was thinking; he had evidently hoped that Algar's affair with Florence could explain all the queer behaviour in the Wyndham family, but it was not to be. The rift between the earl and his wife had formed years before Florence Keyse had moved to Clearwell.

"Cressida's disdain for me goes back decades, almost to the time we were first married."

Oh, hurray for Christopher, I thought to myself, a touch vainly. *I was right on the bull's eye!*

Grandfather had another question that I could not have predicted. "Algar, can you promise that you remained here last night after we returned home?" He kept his steel-grey eyes locked on his prey. "Can I trust you?"

Our host for the weekend had fallen silent again. He evaded his old friend's gaze and peered down at the thick carpet beneath his feet. "Of course you can. You've known me since I was a boy." Any energy he once possessed had drained from him, and he delivered this response in a murmur.

"You didn't answer the first question," I pointed out, but my grandfather had already noticed.

"Tell me what happened."

My grandmother's cousin threw his arms in the air like a small child and responded in a shout. "Fine. I went back to the village to see her. She told me to come after the pub had closed but, by the time I got there, the place was dark. I assumed I'd misunderstood her and didn't think anything of it. I assumed that…"

Grandfather turned to me as though to ask, *Do we believe him, Christopher? Does that sound like the story of an innocent man?* He took a step backwards to remove himself from the conversation, and I understood what he wanted from me.

"Did you kill her, Algar?" I don't know if my voice had the same gravitas as my mentor's, but I did what I could. "Did you decide that the affair you were having had become too dangerous, and that it was time to bring things to a conclusion?"

He gripped the arms of his chair and pulled himself back against it as though trying to escape. "No, of course I didn't. I could never do such a thing." His eyes were like balloons then, but I was uncertain whether it was his fear of discovery or my accusation itself that scared him. "I left the village and came straight home. I didn't see anyone or anything."

"So you never hurt her?" Grandfather sought to confirm, his voice softer than normal.

Algar's head snapped in his old friend's direction. "I told you; I loved her. I loved Florence, and I never laid a finger upon her."

As his words echoed about the room, I heard a noise coming from the immense fireplace. It was little more than a gentle scuff and then a creak of metal, but it was enough to tell me there was someone hiding behind it. I didn't stay to hear the end of Algar's wailing denial but rushed across the room and launched myself against what I hoped would be the trick wall. Sadly for the right-hand side of my body, I'd picked the wrong one.

Once I'd recovered my senses, I tried the other wall and gained access to the tunnel to search for the eavesdropper.

"Dante!" I called after him. "I know it's you."

CHAPTER TWENTY-FOUR

There was just enough light to see him stop in his tracks. Rubbing my sore arm, I wandered along the tunnel to him. The swivelling wall closed behind me, and it was blacker than night in there. In fact, I would have been quite terrified if I'd been alone, but I knew my friend wasn't far away.

"It's not a crime." His voice travelled down to me, echoing off the four walls several times over so that it sounded like a choir was singing. "This is my house, and nobody's ever told me I can't explore it."

He sounded nervous, but I hadn't gone there to frighten him.

"I wasn't accusing you of anything." I drew level with where I assumed he was still standing. "But I'm as yellow as a canary, and the dark gives me the willies. So could we please go somewhere a little brighter?"

I thought I heard him smile then. Presumably it was just my imagination, as smiles don't generally make a lot of noise.

"Come along then," Dante agreed. "I'd know my way around these tunnels with my eyes closed. Though this certainly helps…" There was a rustle and a scratch that were significantly louder than the crack of a smile. A match flared into life, and my friend lit a candle on a looped ceramic holder. "You can get anywhere in the house if you know the layout of the place."

I could see his pale face in the glow of the flame as he turned to go. We followed the tunnel until we reached another false wall. Stepping aside, he let me go ahead of him, up a dusty staircase with a low ceiling, upon which I kept bumping my head.

"It's not funny," I insisted, but it did nothing to quell his laughter and, after the tenth or so bash, I barely felt it anymore.

I wondered how this hidden system of walkways fitted into the wider house. It was hard to imagine the original owners feeling the need for any such feature, but I suppose that, from everything we'd heard, Thomas Wyndham was a secretive chap. Before I could think too deeply about it, we emerged in Dante's bedroom on the first floor of the western tower.

"Welcome to my own private sanctuary," he said, as he went to sit on a padded bench in front of the window.

It certainly wasn't a bad place to hide away from the world. It was the same size as my grandfather's room on the other side of the castle, but instead of looking like the quarters of a medieval knight, it was chock full of all the objects a young man could desire. There were model planes flying around a solar system, which was suspended from the ceiling on cords. An illuminated globe with every country upon it lit up one corner of the room and, normally the first thing I attempted to locate wherever we went, a high bookcase behind the door held every fantastical title from the last fifty years of literature. It is possible that I spent too long gawping at all these marvels, as Dante looked a touch bored by the time I'd finished.

"There are some detective stories there if you fancy reading one," he said, so that we didn't have to talk of more serious matters. "Have you read any Christie? I've read all six of her books. Even the new one that was just released."

"You lucky thing. I've heard it's her best yet. I've become quite a fan of such literature since I've been working with my grandfather." I was smiling, until I realised just how easily he'd distracted me. "But I didn't come here to talk about books."

"Oh, very well. You caught me," he said with a guilty smile. "What of it?"

I'd already devised a curious theory when I found him in the tunnel, but the expression on his face served to prove it. "You already knew, didn't you?" He turned away from me, but I kept talking. "You knew about your father and Florence. You tried to tell me about them before the snake bit me in the forest."

He scoffed a little but would not reply. There was a loud crash from beyond the gatehouse, and I wondered whether the Mordaunts had taken up a battering ram to overcome the castle's defences.

"I'm right. I know I am. That's why you've been so skittish this weekend. Every time we're with your family, you become a different person. You're nervous and eager to please them. It's because you're worried, isn't it?"

I sat down beside him with my back to the window and he hugged his knees to his chest a little tighter. I considered laying out the evidence that proved my claim but had the feeling that I'd already said enough.

"Can you blame me for worrying? My father may well have destroyed our family." He exhaled loudly and shook his head, as though attempting to make sense of the whole sorry history. "I'm not saying we were ever perfect, and mother certainly doesn't make our lives easy at the best of times, but at least we're still together. I couldn't bear to think–"

His voice broke then, and he would not finish his sentence. I saw a lot of his father in the desperate glance he gave me. The pair of them couldn't have been more different in breadth and height, but the searching look that shaped his features was pure Algar.

"It can't be nice," I said in a softer voice. I wasn't trying to win him over in the hope he might know something useful. I really wanted to make him feel better. "I hardly see my father these days, but I know he's not far away, should I need him. And I do love him, even if he spends all of his time in the city. In fact, I'm sorry for even comparing the situation. It was really very self-centred of me."

He had to strangle a laugh then, as I was evidently being wet. "I'll let you off this once." Despite his jollier tone, it was clear that his fear had not abated.

"The thing is…" I didn't want to sound callous and was uncertain I should raise another awkward topic. "You see, I understand now why you and your father have been behaving so erratically, but I still can't grasp what's wrong with Cressida and Gertrude. They both seem so… miserable."

He snorted again, but in disbelief this time. "I wish I knew. Mother has always had a fiery temper, but she used to be tender sometimes too. Over the last year, she's acted as though she couldn't stand any one of us. As for Gertrude, well… we used to be friends and now she can be just as bad as Mummy. I feel sometimes that I'm the only one trying to keep our family together."

"Do you really not know what's got into them?"

He had seemed so debonair when we'd first met, but now looked just as scared as my chums had on the last day of school. We both faced an uncertain future, and though I might not have known where mine was heading, I wouldn't have swapped places with my friend.

Instead of answering my question, he wore a hangdog look and spoke in a low, sorrowful voice. "I just hope that things will go back to normal once your grandfather solves the case. He will work his magic, don't you think?"

"Of course he will." I could definitely have sounded more confident. It was not that I doubted my superlative companion's skills of deduction. It was more that I'd always assumed we would one day encounter a case that Lord Edgington simply couldn't crack. With all the twists, turns and complications we'd already encountered, I had to wonder whether we had finally found it.

"Do you have any sense of who might be to blame for Florence's death?" Dante's question was more than just a request for information; it was a plea for help.

I felt privileged to be in the know on such an important matter. "Grandfather thinks that her murder must be connected to Cole's."

"Young Cole Watkins?" I could see that this revelation had shocked him. I nodded, and he rocked gently backwards and forwards, as though trying to make sense of the news. "But what can any of it mean? Why would some monster want to murder the villagers?"

I struggled to remember all the things he'd asked me, let alone summon the answers. "Well, we've definitely formulated some theories. In fact, I'm of the opinion that the deaths could have something to do with Lady Morgana."

"So it's all because of the curse?" He managed to look even more frightened than before. "Could it have something to do with my sister's birthday? She's twenty-one in two days, you know."

I must confess that I had considered the curse of Lady Morgana in largely academic terms until now. I was aware of the fact that, were such a hex to exist, Gertrude could keel over dead at any moment, and yet I hadn't considered the impact this knowledge might have on her family. On hearing her brother's question, I realised what the presence of the enemy at the gatehouse must have done to the poor girl who had stood trembling in the rain as we arrived.

"The Mordaunts!" I was anxious myself by now. "You're right; they're here for Gertrude. Everything else is just a diversion. All these ridiculous festivities and even the murders could be a way to distract Grandfather from finding the real killer. Perhaps those barbarians are parading around outside so that they can deny responsibility when their assassin strikes from within."

"The tunnels!" we both said at the same moment and, with our moods, instincts and – no doubt – appetites in perfect synchronism, we flew from the room to save the castle, our families and, let's be honest, society as we knew it.

CHAPTER TWENTY-FIVE

In terms of my fledgling career as a detective, I'd had my good days and bad, my ups and my downs, my peaks and... well, I'm sure you get the idea. I was not a born investigator, and yet, for perhaps the first time, I was certain that I had uncovered a thread to our case that the former superintendent had overlooked.

And, yes, I'm aware I'd had this very same thought after every murder we'd discovered, but this time it simply had to be true. The venerated old chap had stated quite clearly that he had no idea why Gertrude was as nervous or temperamental as she'd appeared that weekend, but the truth had been staring us in the face all along; she was scared for her life, and rightly so.

Imagine that every young woman in your family going back two centuries had died in unusual circumstances before her twenty-first birthday. How do you think you'd feel about that rapidly approaching date? Especially in the presence of a pack of insurrectionists and with a murderer on the loose.

The poor creature must have been in a parlous state, but she needn't have feared. Her brother and I would do whatever it took to protect her. Our first task was to take up our candles and descend once more through the bowels of the house to the tunnel which led to the forest.

Perhaps inevitably, when we reached the concealed exit, I realised that we hadn't planned our valiant endeavour particularly well.

"What will we do if someone comes?" I asked, as we crouched down in the darkness to commence our watch.

"We'll clobber the blackguard!" Dante was more confident on the matter than I was, but at least his bravado was contagious.

"Perfect." I rubbed my hands together with great relish until another thought occurred to me. "Ummm... with what, exactly, will we clobber him?"

There was a faint light that penetrated the ivy to the spot where he was sitting, and I could just make out his change of expression. "Ah, you may have a point."

So we trudged back along the tunnel to look for weapons. Such quests are rarely a challenge in big houses. I could name fifty rooms in Cranley Hall where you could find a handy sword or axe, without even venturing into the armoury. On our way through the house, I spotted Delilah, who had been allowed to sleep inside for the night and lay at the bottom of the stairs, like a lion-skin rug. I had to assume that the others were tucked up in bed by now. There was no sign of anyone, not even a footman.

"Here we are," Dante declared, once we'd taken the stairs up to the most medieval-looking wing of the house.

I warily prised a spear from the clutches of a suit of armour. I'd had a run-in with just such a chap the previous Christmas, and I didn't want to take any risks. Dante found a broadsword that he claimed had once belonged to our great-great (etc. etc.) grandfather, who had led a battalion of Scottish Highlanders into battle against the Dutch marauders. I had a sneaking suspicion that he'd got his facts muddled, but then who was I to make such an accusation? It was really quite disturbing how little I knew about my grandmother's side of the family, let alone the wider history of the British Isles.

By the time we were both sufficiently armed, I couldn't help but imagine the sense of exhilaration our ancestor had experienced as he rushed into the fray with his kilt-clad comrades to put their clog-wearing enemies to the broadsword. Sufficiently motivated, Dante and I returned to our fox-hole. A mixture of nervousness and anticipation ran through my veins, and we chattered away together.

Sadly, the excitement did not last long. It turned out that sitting in a cold, damp pit on the off-chance that our enemies knew of the secret passageway into the castle wasn't as much fun as we'd imagined.

"Well, we've certainly done our bit, don't you think?" Dante asked after half an hour had passed, and our knees were aching from crouching in the shadows for so long.

"I'll say," I said. "If anyone was planning to invade the castle tonight, you can be sure they would have done it by now. They must have got scared that someone was on to them and scarpered."

"Oh, absolutely. Though no one will ever know it except for us, we almost certainly saved my sister tonight." There was a laugh in his voice, which confirmed that, like me, he didn't actually believe we'd achieved anything. Still, we'd made a good show of it, and our beds were calling.

I found myself wondering what my grandfather would have made of these theatrics. On the one hand, he would have criticised my haphazard approach to the investigation. We hadn't laid out any evidence in the scientific fashion he favoured and had rushed into danger with little hope of reward. But, then again, I was only going to be seventeen for a month or so longer. I hoped he would approve of my enjoying one last youthful escapade before the responsibilities of real life came to bear. He often spoke in fond terms of his own youth, spent running wild on our family estate with his older brother at his side. It only seemed fair that I should get the chance to do the same.

When we got back to the castle, Dante and I shook hands on the landing and went off to our separate towers. There was less noise from outside by this point, and I could only assume that the siege of Clearwell Castle had faded out with a whimper. It made me wonder how many siege armies – back in the days of yore – had set out to sack a rival fort, only to discover that the walls were too thick and so wandered back home with their swords between their legs.

As I curled up in bed and closed my eyes, I could sympathise somewhat with those unfortunate soldiers. It did not last long, though, as I soon fell fast asleep.

"Ahhhhhhhhh!" went the voice of my deceased headmaster in my dream as I imagined myself back at school on the last day of my exams. It was a terrifying moment as, not only was I without the pencil I would need to complete my final geography paper, I wasn't wearing any clothes.

"Ahhhhhhhhh!" Mr Hardcastle wailed once more, which made no good sense to me as he should have been saying something more relevant, such as, "Boy! Why are you naked?" or "Stop fussing, Prentiss. You can borrow a pencil from Master Adelaide."

I would stay asleep for a moment longer, with the old academic's ears puffing out smoke and the other boys in the exam hall laughing at my very visible bottom, before I realised that the scream did not originate in my subconscious mind but was echoing to me through the halls of the castle.

Within seconds, I was wide awake. I tossed aside the bed clothes, jumped up to standing and ran to the window to see whether the folk from Scowles Folly had mounted a second wave of attack. To my

169

surprise, the courtyard in front of the castle, and the world beyond it, looked quite peaceful. The storm had cleared, and a brilliant full moon shone from on high.

I rather thought that, in my hypnopompic state, I must have been confused and imagined the terrible wails I'd heard. But then they started up once more, and the estate came to life around me. Servants ran from their quarters in the gatehouse and dashed across the lawn to the castle. I saw Todd, club in hand, flanked by two of the Clearwell footmen, before Dorie bounded out, carrying what I could only assume in the darkness to be a blunderbuss. Even our Cook, Henrietta, was there. Dressed in her night cap and gown, she brandished her lethal rolling pin.

This display of allegiance was enough to stir me, and I shot from my room to descend the stairs. Delilah's barking helped me navigate the corridors and drew me up the western tower, past Dante and Gertrude's bedrooms, all the way to the top floor where their parents slept.

"This is punishment for your sins!" Cressida was kneeling in the corner of the room, as though at prayer. She was pointing at the immense wooden bed between two mullioned windows. "What greater symbol could God send us?"

It took me a moment to spot him, but Algar was on the floor by the bed. He was clutching his wrist with one hand and seemed to be in a terrible state. I had no time to worry about him, though, as I had more pressing concerns.

"Be careful, Delilah," I managed to yell, though I could do little else but hold my breath as that dear creature launched herself towards the source of the chaos.

In the centre of the unmade bed, positioned like a sprung coil, was a hissing serpent. There was enough light in the room for me to see that this was not the tetchy beast that had given me a peck on the nose in the forest. It had a brown zig-zag pattern along the length of its back and contrasting green sides. As my grandfather's gentle companion grasped the viper in her jaws, the words of my biology teacher finally came back to me.

Delilah was clearly a dog of action and showed no fear as she clamped her teeth down on Britain's only venomous snake and jumped back off the bed. Grandfather and Dante had arrived after me and stood aside as our canine heroine thundered past with the wriggling adder unable to bite her. I wondered if it was the already stricken Algar or the resilient dog who most deserved my concern. But from the determined look in her beautiful brown eyes as she passed, I knew that my dear, fluffy friend would be fine.

Grandfather evidently agreed as he stepped into the room to look at the wounded man. "What happened? How could that snake have got up here?"

He seized his old friend's wrist in his two hands and held it up to the beam of moonlight, which cut through the room like a saw.

"I don't see how the damn thing could have navigated the castle halls on its own," Clearwell's king pronounced. "It would surely have found a preferable place to hide before climbing all those stairs. Someone must have brought it up here."

Grandfather cast a glance in my direction, which I suppose was an accusation of sorts, but his gaze soon returned to the wound. "I don't see any sign of venom."

"How could you possibly know?" Cressida's voice shook and, though the threat had been removed, she huddled against the wall, perhaps still afraid of that ancient symbol of temptation and sin.

"There are no puncture marks as far as I can see. Despite their ill fame, adders are not typically aggressive animals. They only attack when afraid for their lives or defending their young." He paused to consider the implications of this statement. "Supposing someone placed the poor creature in the bed, he may have been feeling his way around when you rolled over and squashed him. He certainly wasn't trying to kill you if he didn't use his venom."

I thought it spoke volumes about my grandfather's kind nature that he could find sympathy for such a maligned beast.

"Are you going to be all right, Father?" Dante spoke in a timid voice and grasped hold of my arm for support.

"I'll be fine." Algar pushed himself up to sitting so that his back was against the bed. "It was a shock, that's all. I can't say I expected to wake up to find a snake taking a bite out of me."

Dante seemed to relax and went to attend to his mother, who had taken to pacing the far side of the room like a madwoman locked in a tiny cell. I would have stayed to see what more my grandfather had to say on the matter, but I could hear the staff amassing outside and a doleful bark from Delilah, so I descended to the ground floor of the castle once more. I must have been distracted, as it barely occurred to me how much I hate running up and down stairs!

"Great minds, Christopher," Grandfather appeared at the top of the stairwell to shout down to me. "The European adder is not a natural climber. I genuinely believe that someone was trying to kill our hosts. Find the culprit in my stead."

I can't say this was exactly what I'd been thinking when I left the bedroom, but it was not the moment to contradict him, and I rushed to find the search party.

"Someone was in here," I heard one of the footmen shout from the dining room. "The place has been ransacked."

"And in the east salon," a distant voice confirmed. "Tables overturned. Chairs smashed. Though they don't appear to have taken much time over it. I can see no sign of anything missing."

"Morning, Master Christopher." Todd passed me his club as I arrived in the entrance hall. "What's going on up there?"

"It's the Earl of Dunraven. It looks as though someone put a snake in his bed. It was an adder and things could have turned out rather nastily, but Grandfather says all's well."

"I wondered what Delilah had in her mouth as she ran past." Todd attempted a smile, though there was no joy in it. I doubted that he'd slept a wink; his eyes were quite wild and kept shifting around the room as though he expected some dark figure to emerge from the shadows.

"You don't think the assailant is still here, do you?"

Before he could answer, Delilah appeared from outside, sans serpent. As though very little of interest had occurred – and she in no way deserved a medal for her bravery – she returned to her spot at the bottom of the stairs and went back to sleep. She did not have a bloodhound's nose to aid us in our search, and I believed she had earned her rest.

Todd didn't answer the question directly but replied with another doubt. "Where could he be hiding if he's still in the building?"

The local staff were clearly busy searching the state rooms, and Dorie was patrolling the garden like an ogre, but there was one place which I deemed worthy of inspection.

"Come with me."

I entered the dining room and made my way through the previously described maze of broken furniture to the fireplace. Todd emitted a silent "wow" as I pushed open the hinged wall. I had no doubt he had read of such secret passageways in many of the adventure novels he so enjoyed, and his face spoke an equal number of volumes as I plunged into the darkness. I really should have known to bring a candle by now, but my capable companion could always be relied upon to think of such practicalities and nipped back into the room to illuminate matters.

"Incredible," he said as he held up the flame to look along the tunnel.

Despite his presence at my side, this was quite the most nervous I'd felt all weekend. The hour of night and the humidity in that cramped space combined to strike fear within me, so that every step I took felt like the ticking of some ominous clock. I think it's fair to say that, as these thoughts fogged my mind, I rather wished I'd taken big Dorie with me instead of the slim chap with the candle. At the very least, I could have hidden behind her if the snake-despatching killer jumped out on us.

We got to the first turn in the labyrinth without incident and pushed on, passing through the hollow spaces between the ballroom and kitchen, before descending the tunnel beneath the garden. Good old Todd showed no fear, which was a relief as I would probably have ended up in tears if he hadn't been steadfast for the both of us.

"Perhaps the blighter's already scarpered," he said, but even before the words were out of his mouth, the light that strafed ahead of us revealed a huddled shape on the floor near the end of the dank space.

For my safety, Todd put his hand out to hold me back, and, for his safety, I offered him the heavy wooden club which he'd previously given me for… for my… for protection.

And yet, I did not stay behind like a coward as the real hero put himself in danger. Even as the bundle on the floor appeared to shudder, I matched my companion step for step. A few feet from our target, I could make out a hood attached to a black cape, but no features of its owner were visible, and it was impossible to say whether the curled-up figure was there to attack us, or he had merely sought shelter from the rain.

We came to a halt out of arm's reach, but if the fellow had been sprightly, he might still have got the better of us. Any movement I had previously seen had now stopped, and it fell to me to seize the hood. As I peeled it back, it felt heavier than it should have, and some sticky substance seeped through it onto my hands.

The unconscious man was barely recognisable with the thick red liquid that had coloured his face. At first, I assumed it was one of the devilish upstarts from Scowles Folly, but I was only half right.

"That's the young chap from the pub last night," Todd said before I could.

"Yes." I held my fingers to the wound on the supine man's head and felt rather silly not to have identified the blood until now. "That's right, it's Sam Mordaunt."

CHAPTER TWENTY-SIX

As I attempted to solve the mystery of who would have murdered three largely unrelated people from the Forest of Dean, a million possibilities went spinning about my head like snowflakes in a blizzard. I wondered if Sam was the cloaked figure we had spotted leaving the castle on the night Florence Keyse was killed, and again in the forest when I was bitten by the snake. At first, I had to assume that someone from the household had delivered the blows that had felled him, but his assailant might just as well have been some double-crossing conspirator from his own village.

In fact, there was really only one thing that didn't occur to me. From the pallor of his skin and the sheer quantity of blood he'd lost, I didn't imagine for a second that Sam Mordaunt might still be alive.

"He's got a pulse," Todd declared, then craned his neck to listen. "Faint breath, too, but he's still with us."

He rose with unexpected alacrity and a strange noise carried down the corridor to us from some yards back. It was certainly the closest sound to a banshee's screech I will hear in this life. Though short and sharp it was amplified by the acoustics of that cavernous space to become a gasp of horror that seemed to last for days.

And in that time, Todd and I were able to peer back over our shoulders to catch a glimpse of the supernatural force that had discharged the uncanny emission. It was less than a moment, but I was certain of what I saw. For there, in the space where the sloping tunnel from the castle reached its lowest point, was Lady Morgana herself. Her pale face and almond eyes were unmistakable; it was the very woman I had seen in the portrait in the pub that afternoon.

But what convinced me that this was no human being we had encountered was the inexplicable flare of sulphurous fire that flashed before her. It seemed to consume her entirely from the bottom up and, in a moment, we were alone.

"Please tell me there's an entirely rational explanation for what we just saw," I begged of Todd, but he had extended one finger down the now empty tunnel and could not reply. "Please tell me that my imagination was playing a trick on me, and I didn't see a…" The word seemed too silly to even utter. But then I'm not one to shy away from silliness and gave it my all. "…a ghost!"

That gallant chap was still trembling as his eyes fixed on mine and he found his tongue. "There's a perfectly simple explanation, Master Christopher." He seized the lapels of my pyjamas at this moment, presumably for his own stability rather than mine. "The ghost of Lady Morgana Mordaunt is roaming the halls of the castle; the dead can walk the earth!" I was afraid he might melt in fear at this moment but, instead, a smile crossed his lips, and he began to laugh. "It's bally brilliant!"

I didn't like to curb the joy he was experiencing, but we did still have the matter of the wounded man to address and so I hurried him along. "Should I perhaps take his legs while you support his arms?"

Todd was looking into the darkness yet again, the disbelief still apparent on his face. "Pardon? Sorry?" His gaze widened, as he searched for understanding, but then my words must have reached him, and we got down to work. "That sounds like a plan."

Unable to comprehend how this sighting could fit into the wider case we'd been investigating, I focused on Sam Mordaunt. "If this is the snake-botherer we're carrying, how do you think he came by the gash on his head?"

"I'm afraid I haven't a clue." He adopted a less formal tone than the one he normally used. "To tell you the truth, Chrissy, I don't know how you and Lord Edgington do what you do. I'm sure I wouldn't be able to figure out half the cases that you can."

I considered the fact that, as I was yet to solve a case myself, and he had the capacity to solve half as many as my grandfather, that still put him some distance ahead of me on the scoresheet. I decided not to mention this but repeated something significant I had once heard.

"Now that I think of it, I don't believe you should move people when they have suffered an injury to the head." I was briefly worried about this before a consoling factor presented itself. "I'm sure it's fine just this once. But if he survives and makes a recovery, we'll have to tell him to steer clear of any such thing in the future."

"Very good, Master Christopher." He used his professional voice once more but offered a wink to show his amusement.

I backed down the corridor with Sam Mordaunt's ankles in my hands. He was much heavier than he looked, and I had to conclude that all the muscles he had were weighing him down. Does muscle weigh more than general corpulence? If so, I'll be sure to avoid gaining any. I am reliably informed that being over a certain weight is not conducive to one's health.

It was frankly rather tiring, and I was terribly relieved when I heard a grunt behind me, followed by a rush of pounding footsteps. Dorie must have been sent to check the tunnels as she popped up in the darkness.

"Hello, miniature Lord Edgington, sir," she called in a tone that always reminded me of a slightly terrifying child. "Would you like me to carry that dead man for you?"

"Thank you, Dorie," I consented. "He is a little heavy, though not quite dead, so you'll have to be careful how you hold him."

In the end, we decided that all three of us should help to transport the wounded fellow. Todd continued supporting Sam's upper body, Dorie dealt with the feet and such like, and I offered general encouragement. You know the sort of thing…

"That's right. Jolly good. Keep him coming. This way."

We soon had him back through the tunnels and laid out on a long wooden bench in the entrance hall. My grandfather looked perplexed by the events of that strange night, and Algar soon arrived, though there was no sign of the rest of his family.

"It's a nasty wound," the ex-policeman said as he examined the still unconscious interloper. Grandfather had no formal medical training, but he always spoke with authority on such matters and, in my mind at least, was as good as most of the quacks who had prodded and poked me over the years. At least he didn't suggest that his patient give up sticky buns or take up exercise!

I told him the circumstances in which we'd found Sam Mordaunt, and Algar seemed most offended by the presence of the enemy within the walls. "He must have been the one who put the snake in my bed. In fact, isn't that the same reprobate who's been sniffing about The Wyndham Arms for months?" He didn't wait for an answer but drew his own conclusions. "There's our killer, Edgington. The man can be linked to each crime."

Grandfather had certain mannerisms which I'd come to understand over the last year. For example, when he was tired, he would yawn –

like most of us, I suppose. When he was angry, his forehead would crease so that the deeply etched lines formed a V. And when he was incredulous on a particular subject, like now, he would often hide his emotions entirely, but pull at the right-hand cuff of his long, grey coat.

As he clearly wasn't going to deny Algar's accusation, it fell to me to do so. "Then how did he come to be wounded? It looks to me as though someone boshed him on the noggin!" I had spent too much time with Dante, and my speech was thick with argot.

"He could have banged his head in the tunnel," the earl growled. "There's nothing so strange about that."

I was not in an accepting mood and continued my argument. "Impossible. He was clearly attacked."

Perhaps to prevent our exchange of words from becoming more heated, Grandfather raised his hand to silence me. "We should take him somewhere comfortable and call for a doctor. In fact…" He looked towards the door at that moment, and I hadn't a clue what he was thinking. "Yes, I have an idea. Move him into the nearest bedroom. I have to fetch someone from outside. Christopher, with me."

There was no sense in arguing with him when he issued such orders, so I turned about and followed him. I couldn't have predicted what he had in mind but then seeing the future has never been my strong suit. He marched along the path beside the lawn, around to the gatehouse and straight up to the gate. The biggest surprise came when he unlocked the metal bolt and walked outside.

"We need a doctor," he exclaimed to the few remaining marauders.

The siege of Clearwell Castle had turned into a party. Several bearded men with their fingers looped through cider jugs were sitting around a bonfire that they'd built in the middle of the road. Someone had even thought to bring a fiddle and two unruly gents were having a bit of a dance.

There was little reaction to grandfather's statement and so he spoke again. "A man has been injured, and he's one of yours."

This at least caused a stir of activity as a few figures stood up from the fire. "What do ya mean, 'one of ours'?" a bare-chested chap who was wider than he was tall demanded, but his contribution was soon forgotten as Sam's own father stepped clear of his people.

Cliff Mordaunt was as fearsome as ever. "I was a stretcher bearer in the war. I had to patch up a fair few lads before we carted them back to safety. Will that do?"

Grandfather looked the man up and down, as though examining his credentials before admitting him to an important institution. I noticed his snake tattoo once more and could now see that the devious beast was spiralling around, not just his arm, but the outline of a metal pole. We turned back to the castle and Cliff followed, but it would be a moment longer before Lord Edgington revealed the name of the invalid.

"Cliff, I have to tell you that it is your son who's been injured. Christopher here found him in a tunnel on the grounds of the estate. I don't suppose you know how he got there?"

The man showed little emotion. He seized the loose tunic that had previously hung about his shoulders and pulled it over his head to hide his well-defined chest. "Take me to my boy."

I felt that he could have provided an answer to my grandfather's question but chose otherwise. I again had a sense of Cliff's quick wits, which matched well with his reticence to disclose any secrets to two practical strangers. It made me wonder once more how his idiot brother had become the mayor of Scowles Folly and not him.

He would say nothing else until we reached a spare bedroom in the eastern tower where his son had been placed. It was tucked away at the end of a corridor and had a slightly utilitarian feel to it. There was little to speak of in the way of decoration and the grey stonework was visible through patches of crumbling plaster.

Cressida and one of the footmen were already inside, tending to our patient (or perhaps our prisoner). They had tied a bandage around him and there were towels on hand should they be needed. Sam Mordaunt showed little sign of life, but I could make out the laboured rise and fall of his chest.

I expected his father to ask what had happened, but he simply sat down and set to work. "I'll need something to sterilise the wound. Has he gained consciousness since he was attacked?"

I was surprised to see the care with which Cressida attended to this envoy from the rival family. She rose from the bed to make room for Cliff and calmly answered his question. "He hasn't responded to our voices, but his breathing is steady, and he seems like a strong young man."

Her son and daughter were in the corridor peeking inside, and I noticed quite how nervous Gertrude still was. She looked at the unconscious blacksmith as though he was a dark spirit. She was so agitated that I was surprised she found the courage to stand there for as long as she did.

"Come along," Cliff barked when no one had reacted to his demand. "We need hot water, something for his fever and plenty of clean cloths. If his wound doesn't stop bleeding soon, I'll have to stitch it, but I won't allow infection to take hold. So move!"

With these last two shouted words, the staff scattered from the room like rabbits from a hound. The great hulking man tended to his son and the other souls who remained stood in silent reverence. I looked at my grandfather again to see what he thought of the mess in which we found ourselves, but he was typically inscrutable. All I could say for certain was that there was a reason he had brought Cliff Mordaunt into the house instead of immediately calling for a doctor. A reason that I couldn't fathom for one moment.

CHAPTER TWENTY-SEVEN

Once the requested supplies had been delivered, the panic subsided. It appeared that there was not a great deal that the lupine father could do for his son. Sam slept quite peacefully, but occasionally moved one arm or clutched his fingers more tightly. I had to hope that this was a positive sign and, when a doctor finally arrived with his Gladstone bag and stethoscope, the initial prognosis was good.

"I've no reason to think he's in any danger. The bleeding has been stemmed and his heart rate is normal," the tubby, bespectacled sort informed us, before leaving rather hastily.

We all breathed a sigh of relief, and Cressida took this as her cue to gather her children and leave. It was four in the morning by this point, and I rather wished I could do the same. I sat in an armchair in the corner, knowing full well that my grandfather would tut at me should my head start to nod and my eyes close. For some unknowable reason, I was more afraid of that soft utterance than any shouted rhetoric from my teachers at Oakton Academy. If tuts could kill...

"I can look after him myself," Cliff eventually informed us after I had long since begun to wonder what good we were doing there. Moral support is far more useful when the person one is supporting is conscious.

Grandfather would not take the hint and launched into the question he had been most eager to ask. "Do you know what your son was doing here in the castle?"

"I don't know what any of you are doing here. It's a cursed place and should have been knocked down decades ago."

Grandfather tilted his head from a forty-five-degree angle to its mirror image. "And yet, unlike your brother, you don't appear to hate the Wyndhams. How can that be?"

He huffed through his nostrils and glanced down at his boy. "I suppose I've learnt to look beyond the past better than some folk from my village."

Lord Edgington was perched on a stony windowsill, his profile visible against the bright moonlit sky. With his interrogation in full swing, he took a step forward, and I could see his face more clearly in the flickering light cast by the great brass candle ring overhead

"Not one to hold a grudge, then?" He nodded his approval. "The world would be a better place if more people were like you."

"I'm no angel." The blacksmith seemed to favour such short sentences and paused before continuing. "But I saw enough unnecessary pain during the war to know what pride and anger can reap."

"Ah, yes. You said you were a stretcher bearer." I think that the absence of any question in Grandfather's comment was intentional, and it drew the required response.

"I was in the Royal Army Medical Corps. Taught me a lot about the world… and myself. I don't think I would have survived a battle regiment. But instead of getting shot in no man's land, I helped save the lives of plenty who were."

"Did Jimmy serve with you?"

Cliff's eyes swung back to Sam then. "No, he stayed here, what with his limp. He hurt his leg just before the war. Never walked right after."

Despite the gruffness of his manner, the attention he paid his son was remarkably tender. And yet, he had shown no particular shock or sadness at Sam's condition when we broke the news. He was as hard a man to read as any I'd encountered.

"I'm sure your army training helped you turn off your emotion when necessary." Clever old Grandfather. Why hadn't I thought of that?

"No one can turn off what we feel. Not for long, at least. But we can bury it down when the moment calls for it." He sniffed then, and his eyes finally communicated a little of the love he had for his son. It was just a moment before he turned away to soak a fresh cloth in water and check that the bandage was correctly fixed, but I was confident of what I'd seen.

I could see the hesitation on my grandfather's face as he attempted to shift the conversation to the topic we most needed to address. "I'm sorry to press you, but I must ask what happened tonight. Did you see Sam again after we left?"

Cliff stared at the cloth that he held to his boy's head. "He turned up outside the castle once the gates were already closed. He was furious and said we were starting a war for no sensible reason." He shook his head a little, perhaps regretting his own role in the demented pageantry. "He wanted no part of it and walked off into the forest before I could ask where he was going."

"So who do you think is responsible for his condition?" I couldn't hold the question in any longer. It launched from my mouth like a cannon ball.

In a moment, the muscles in Cliff's neck seemed to double in size. It was almost as though he'd grown an extra pair of shoulders. "You think that someone did this to him?"

I was too nervous to respond to the formidable character, so my grandfather answered for me. "Surely you noticed the three distinct cuts? He didn't simply bang his head on a low ceiling. It looks to me as though he was struck several times with a blunt object."

In way of a response, Cliff glared out of the window. I wondered whether what he'd said about not bearing grudges would hold true if he discovered that someone had tried to murder his son.

Grandfather was tired of waiting and raised his voice. "Who do you think did it?"

"I don't know!" the giant snapped. "I don't understand anything that's happened here this weekend. First Florence, now Sam."

"Well, Cole Watkins was first, actually. And if—" I began, but he spoke over me.

"There you go then. I don't see why anyone would have attacked my boy, let alone killed those good people."

"You knew Cole Watkins as well as Florence Keyse?" Grandfather was quick to conclude.

It was curious just how willing Cliff was to discuss incriminating points such as this one. "Everyone in Scowles Folly knew Cole. He used to sell whatever he could get his hands on from the back of his cart. In fact, he was there the day he died. He couldn't get away with that sort of thing around here, mind. Not with the Wyndhams and that old soldier always on patrol. Cole was a chancer – there's no doubt about that. But I can't imagine anyone murdering him."

"We've heard the same thing all over the village," I revealed, while Grandfather was busy weighing up each word the man had spoken. "The victims have no great connection, and they were terribly nice people. But what if that's the point?" The two older, wiser and, let's be honest, better-dressed men looked at me with something approaching respect. "What if every last detail we've discovered – from old Thomas Wyndham's possible diary entry to Sam getting his head bashed in this evening – what if it's all just a ruse to stop us from focusing on the right crime. Perhaps someone was in love with Florence but she rejected him. Perhaps everything else we've witnessed was staged to hide the real motive."

"What an interesting idea, Christopher." Grandfather looked really quite serene at this moment. "Somewhat unlikely, but interesting nonetheless."

He fell to silent thought and, apparently sensing that it was time for us to leave the sickroom, Cliff mumbled a few last words for the night. "If you've nothing more to ask, I think the lad should get some rest. I'll let you know if anything changes."

Grandfather bowed his head a fraction to acknowledge this kindness, whereas I sped from the room hoping I might yet manage a few hours' sleep. I noticed two armed footmen stationed outside the bedroom door. The Wyndhams were clearly wary of a Trojan invasion.

I was more surprised, however, to see Gertrude still hovering about in the corridor. She was sitting in front of a window at the end of the hall, her eyes fixed on the gatehouse. I could only imagine the pain she was suffering. She must have wondered whether every moment she lived could be her last. In her place, I'd have spent that time with a nice slice of cake and a good book, but she was content – well, perhaps that's not the word for it – to sigh and look forlorn.

"Not so fast, Christopher," Grandfather's booming voice prevented me from running off to bed. "We have much work to do."

I was a little peeved by this. "And I have many sleepless hours to recover."

"You can sleep when you're old, boy. Young people are well known for staying up all night and seeking out adventures." He had caught up with me by now and wiggled his moustache defiantly, perhaps anticipating my next combative response.

"You're old. Why don't you sleep more?"

He clearly didn't enjoy the retort. "How can you say such a thing? I am not old. I have merely accumulated more time, experience and wisdom on this planet than you." He looked put out for a moment,

184

but then shook his head forcefully and recovered his train of thought. "Now, can we please address the matter at hand?"

"Which would be?"

"Our investigation, Christopher." Even in the dimly lit corridor, I could see him rolling his eyes ever so slowly, from one side to the other. "I imagine that you realised why I left the grounds in search of Cliff instead of calling a doctor."

I might have scoffed then to cover the fact that I really wasn't sure of the answer. "Of course I did. He was the closest person with medical training and would have been used to dressing nasty wounds on the battlefield." As true as this was, I failed to understand how Grandfather had known that the blacksmith had any medical experience.

He hummed appreciatively. "Good. And did anything surprise you about Cliff's manner in our interview?"

Feeling that my own grilling would probably take some time, I sat down on an intricately carved wooden chest. Grandfather frowned, as though to say, *really boy, that's a fine antique upon which you're lounging,* and so I stood back up again.

"He's certainly an interesting character." I had learnt to keep my answers suitably vague.

"That he is. And what of his attitude towards The Wyndhams? Did it not surprise you that he could be so forgiving when his brother Jimmy has spent his life strengthening the rivalry between the two towns?"

"Well, now that you mention it, yes, it did!"

"Excellent. And what do you make of your discovery of Sam Mordaunt in the tunnel beneath the forest?"

"I think it very strange." I hoped this would be a smart enough sort of response, but he clearly wanted more from me. "And I think that... Well, it doesn't make a lot of sense, does it?"

"What doesn't make a lot of sense?"

I would normally have ummed and ahhed and found an excuse as to why I had failed to summon a theory of my own but, rather unexpectedly, that would not be necessary. "The fact Sam Mordaunt was knocked out. If the assailant was from Clearwell, we would already know about it – if anything, it would be a point of pride for someone here to catch a Mordaunt red-handed. So who does that leave?"

It was time for my grandfather to look uncertain. How the tables had turned, how the mighty had fallen, how the– it didn't last long. "You mean to say you believe that Sam was attacked by his own people? But why on Earth would they have done such a thing? And how would someone from Scowles Folly have known about the supposedly secret tunnels in the first place?"

"That's obvious, isn't it? You see…" I started brightly enough, but soon ran out of steam. "No, sorry, I haven't a clue. Which is why I said from the beginning that it really doesn't make a lot of sense."

He had a good think on the matter before finding another way to contradict me. "In which case, I'm afraid I'll have to disagree with your previous observation, Christopher. There is nothing to say that one of the footmen here didn't knock out 'The Infiltrator' and feel guilt for what he'd done. Nor any evidence to point us in the direction of their rival village. Remember, Sam is the nephew of Scowles Folly's beloved mayor. Can you name with any certainty someone who wanted to harm him?" He glanced at the wall behind me and then straightened his posture, as though not wishing to be outdone by an inanimate object. "Perhaps the biggest question is what any of this has to do with the murders of Cole Watkins and Florence Keyse."

"That, I think I can answer." I was feeling rather confident again. "It's all down to the curse of Lady Morgana. When Todd and I found Sam's body, we saw her ghost wandering through the tunnel. She disappeared in a fiery flash, and I can only think that was how she died. Not pushed from a tower, or murdered in her bed, but put to the torch! I believe she wishes us to uncover her secret. Everything that has happened must be connected to her fate."

He breathed in slowly and carefully. "So your solution to the death of two real living humans is that a woman who died two centuries ago has come back to life to exact her revenge?"

I pulled at the collar of my pyjama top. It was really very loose but still felt as though it were strangling me. "When you put it like that, it sounds rather unlikely but…"

"Come along, Chrissy. We have a tunnel to inspect." He might have emitted a brief laugh as he marched away.

To be perfectly honest, I'd spent all the time I wanted underground that day and would have preferred to go for a walk on the ramparts to

186

admire the starry night or taken a turn around the garden to get some fresh air. On second thoughts, I'd rather have gone to bed – not that such considerations would have entered the old slaver's mind.

"Coming, Grandfather," I whispered, and ran after him.

"What is the foremost tool in a detective's arsenal, my boy?" he asked when we arrived at the spot at which I had seen the pretty apparition.

It was a difficult question to answer. He was forever stating such facts, and the precise details often changed from one case to the next. "The foremost tool in a detective's arsenal is… forethought?" I was fairly sure this was one of his golden rules, though, inevitably, not at that moment.

"No, Christopher. The foremost tool in a detective's arsenal is observation. Without our eyes, we are blind." I felt that he had simplified a more complex metaphor to make sure that I could grasp it.

Either way, he passed me his electric torch and bent down to grab a small stick from the floor. He held it up to the light, and I tried ever so hard to comprehend the significance of it. I was about to suggest that this twig was in fact the murder weapon, when he looped it through the handle of a candle holder that had been abandoned nearby.

"There is wax all over the floor." He used his free hand to draw my attention to the abundance of evidence. "The hellfire you saw was merely a fallen candle."

"In my defence, I was carrying our injured (and ever-so-heavy) suspect when I last passed through here." I sounded a touch sorry for myself. "You can't possibly claim it's my fault that I didn't spot it."

He shrugged before responding. "Perhaps not, but you might have wondered whence the light source to illuminate the supposed phantom had come and why it had extinguished itself so rapidly."

"So it wasn't Lady Morgana?" I asked, and he shook his head. "It was a real person who dropped a candle and ran away from us in the dark?"

"Quite. And as this was the only open point of access to the castle this evening, we can assume that your unsupernatural apparition is a member of the Wyndham household."

"There aren't many women here," I thought out loud. "I've spotted one young maid, and several old women. Except for Gertrude and

Cressida, of course."

"Of course." He smiled rather enigmatically, and I got the sense he was pleased with me. Sadly, I couldn't be sure why, and I really didn't see who could have dropped the candle, unless...

"So it was Gertrude!" I failed to hide my amazement. The figure had looked the very image of Lady Morgana. I didn't understand how my eyes had played such a trick on me. I should have worked it out before, as who else wore such old-fashioned clothes?

"That's right. And I can only assume that the ghostly sightings that the family had observed were her creeping about after dark as well. If she hasn't already gone to bed, we must find out what she knows."

I cleared my throat. "Ummm... and you're certain you wouldn't prefer to leave such an interview until the morning, when our brains are a little fresher?"

Instead of replying verbally, he whistled a merry tune as he walked back up the tunnel.

CHAPTER TWENTY-EIGHT

We found Gertrude in the exact same spot where we'd left her. She appeared to be one of those young people that my grandfather had described who enjoyed staying up late to seek out adventures. Based upon her melancholy expression, I couldn't say that it looked a great deal of fun. Give me a nice warm bed over such hijinks seven nights a week!

"I'm sorry to intrude," my learned companion intruded, and she jerked forward with a start. "We were hoping to speak to you, if you're not too tired, of course."

Her face was blank for a moment, and I once more noticed the familiar features I had seen in the tunnel when I'd thought her a spirit. "I'm sorry, Lord Edgington. I didn't hear you approach. Of course I'll talk to you. If there's anything I can do, just ask." There was a surprising amount of passion in her voice, and she swivelled her body away from the window to face us.

Not so subtly – so I can only assume it was for her benefit – Grandfather peered back at the two guards on duty outside Sam Mordaunt's infirmary. "Perhaps we could go somewhere more private?"

Still with that same intensity, she nodded and rose from her post. I was curious as to where she might lead us and rather hoped there would be some secret space in the castle reserved for such clandestine discussions. A hidden priest hole, maybe, or an oubliette. Wait a moment, what is an oubliette? I've clean forgotten.

In the end, she took us to the lounge where we had spoken to her father the previous evening. The upturned furniture had been righted, but the only light inside was from the embers of a half-lit fire. I thought she might switch on a lamp, or at least fetch an extra log, but she was evidently predisposed to such moody darkness and sat down in the flickering glow.

Grandfather took the armchair opposite, and I adopted my usual tactic of hanging about in the background somewhere, hoping that no one would pay me too much attention.

"My dear Gertrude," Grandfather began in a voice that was really very priestly – even if we hadn't found a hole for him. "My poor child, you must have suffered terribly these past days."

Instead of soothing the young woman's nerves, he seemed to have agitated her even more. She twisted her fingers together like a braid of hair. "What do you… I'm sorry, I don't understand what you mean."

The doleful expression on his face at that moment rather mirrored hers. "The curse, Gertrude. The curse of Lady Morgana must have upset you with your twenty-first birthday now imminent."

I believe that the old genius was just as surprised as I was by the girl's reaction. Instead of breaking into tears or wailing in agony, she released a fragile laugh. "Oh, the curse. Yes, that quite terrified me when I was a child. My mother seemed to thrill in telling me of it. She was certain that it was a punishment sent from God for each and every last one of our family's many sins."

She shook her head as though she still couldn't believe her unusual tale. "To tell the truth, I think it's all stuff and nonsense. There is no such thing as ghosts or hexes. I'm sure that the only curses that come true are self-fulfilling prophecies. If you tell yourself that you're unlucky, you're almost guaranteed to fail in your goals."

"So it wasn't the curse that upset you?" I had to ask, not because I didn't know the answer, but because I was struggling to believe it was true.

Her eyes flicked over to me, and she looked amused once more. "No, of course it wasn't. There are plenty of real things to be upset about in this world without superstitions. And besides, I've been so assured of my ill fate my whole life that I'm generally pleasantly surprised when things turn out well. It really doesn't seem much of a curse when we get to live in this beautiful castle and have such fine possessions."

She spoke in a tender voice, and I understood exactly what she meant. It seemed that everyone around her had worried about the family's history on her behalf, which had given her the freedom to focus on their otherwise good fortune.

"This does beg the question of what it is that has made you so withdrawn in your parents' presence, child." Grandfather allowed his words to mature a little before continuing. "I'm aware that I haven't spent a great deal of time with you this weekend, but it appears to me that there are two Gertrudes in the family. One is a relaxed, cheerful creature and the other a pale copy." His words chimed with my own thoughts on the matter.

I was less than amazed that our suspect should glance away at this moment. In fact, she was her fragile self once more, and the previously confident girl had disappeared. "I don't know what you mean."

Her shyness returned, and I knew it would take something special for Grandfather to get anything more from her. "I can see that you are afraid, my child. If it isn't the curse, my first thought would be that the murders have unnerved you. And yet, you were just as reticent when we arrived here. If you are willing to share your story with me, I can promise that whatever you have to tell me will go no further."

Her eyes scanned back to us, but her expression remained, for want of a better word, haunted. "I think you know what's wrong with me. You were there at lunch, after all."

I tried ever so hard to solve this equation – the ticking even started up in my head again – but it would do no good. All I could remember about our awkward repast in the lean-to conservatory was that she'd revealed more details about the curse and her forthcoming birthday. We'd already ruled out that reason, so what had upset her so?

"You're referring to your mother's behaviour," the far-cleverer-than-me lord deduced.

Gertrude stretched out her delicate fingers on her lap and responded in a broken voice. "I saw your face when she was talking about Cole Watkins. I could tell that you caught her in a lie. I thought for a moment that you would refute it, but you held your peace."

Grandfather nodded. "I did notice something unusual about Cressida's story. She seemed anxious to conceal Cole's connection to the family when, as far as I can tell, his claim of being descended from the Wyndhams is largely disbelieved in the village."

"That's what she does these days." Gertrude's deep well of sorrow had finally been tapped. "She rewrites the world around her to suit her own views. She changes history to agree with her skewed perspective. Growing up, I was told that Cole was a distant relation – if the truth be told, he even looked a little like Dante. My father once explained to me that this was the reason we housed his family in Rosebank Cottage. But as soon as he was dead, she claimed that he had nothing to do with us."

"Did you confront her on the matter?"

She breathed in softly and allowed the air back out again before delivering her answer. "Yes, of course I did. For the last year, I've found the courage to stand up to her, and she doesn't like it. But this time was worse. After the four of you went into the forest, I asked her why she had lied, and she became quite furious. She said that I had no right to accuse her of any such thing. She called me selfish and ungrateful and, when I wouldn't take back the question, she lost her mind entirely. She smashed her plate and threw a glass right past me. I have never seen her turn quite so demonic before. She was a woman possessed."

"But why do you think she changed the facts?" I asked. "Why would she want to hide Cole's connection to your family?"

The two of them turned to look at me. I felt that my grandfather might be better placed to answer the question than the woman's own daughter, yet it was Gertrude who responded.

"I think she absorbs guilt from any source she can find. She's addicted to the stuff. My mother has taken to shame and self-righteousness the way some people take to drink. She's like a medieval sin-eater, only instead of cleansing the world of wickedness, she stores up our indiscretions and grows more bitter."

"Has she ever struck you?" I couldn't ignore Cressida's viciousness. It was despicable to treat such a person as Gertrude so cruelly, let alone one's own daughter.

"She never did when I was her good, quiet girl. But she discovered that I'd left the house without her permission one night, and I genuinely believed that she would raise her hand to me. She lost all control of herself and said that I had the devil in my soul. If my father hadn't interrupted, I don't know what would have happened."

Though her words were full of anguish, she allowed another brief laugh to escape her throat. Her emotions came in rapid, distinct phases, and the laughter made way for tears. "If I'm telling the absolute truth, that is why I have appeared so nervous. I've been anticipating my birthday, not because I'm afraid of the non-existent curse, but because I will finally be of age and beyond my mother's control."

Leaning forward in his seat, Grandfather reached his hand out in front of the fire and gently patted the poor girl's arm. "Your mother has changed, and not only in the last year. When I first knew her,

192

she was quite different. But I believe that there is still good in her. Whatever she has said and however poorly she treated you, she has her own demons to fight. Perhaps, in time, you will understand her plight." I thought this a really very Christian position to take, and one which Cressida herself should have adopted.

Perhaps it was the careful attention he had shown her, or the shift in the conversation, but Gertrude suddenly became apologetic and shook her head from side to side as though to say, *aren't I silly?*

"I really don't know why I'm crying. I may not agree with my mother's behaviour, but there are far worse people in the world. The truth is that I do understand her. I understand that she feels she is a mere human and can never live up to holier examples. She is so consumed by what it means to be a good person that she's forgotten how to be one. And yet she was once a very loving mother." She reached into her long sleeve to extract a neatly folded handkerchief.

"But that's not the whole story, is it?" Grandfather's gaze was fixed on her. "There's something else that's been tormenting you."

Gertrude looked at me at this moment, as though I'd be able to save her from his questioning. She clearly didn't know me well enough!

"That's not true. I have nothing to hide."

"I didn't say that you were concealing something. In fact, I can see it quite plainly in every movement you make and every note in your voice."

She attempted to smile but was fooling no one. "This is ridiculous. What could you possibly mean?"

"As my grandson recently reminded me, I am an old man, but I still have eyes, my dear."

Becoming more agitated, she shifted in her chair. "I really don't know what you're implying."

Lord Edgington smiled a little patronisingly and patted her arm one last time before drawing back. "Then I am mistaken, and I must apologise." He adjusted his cravat and plucked a thread of cotton from his lapel before continuing. "Though I would still like to know what you were doing in the tunnel to the forest in the middle of the night."

CHAPTER TWENTY-NINE

Despite his best attempts to get to the truth, Gertrude would not be coerced into explaining herself. She insisted that her only dilemma was her mother's harsh temper and her father's appeasing nature. I saw nothing to suggest that she knew about Algar's infidelity, and yet she was clearly keeping something from us.

When our efforts came to naught, Grandfather accepted defeat. We left her staring into the fire, looking just as miserable as when we'd first encountered her upstairs.

There were a number of questions that I wished to put to the old policeman, but he spoke before I had the chance. "I simply wish I could say for certain what had brought about the change in Cressida. Until we can speak to her in person, I won't know how she fits into the wider picture we have been studying." He seemed quite perplexed by the situation, whereas I thought it really rather simple.

"It's obvious, isn't it? She suffers from the same disease as our school chaplain. My friend Marmaduke calls it Bible-itis; she's taken too big a dose of religion and is full to the gills with all that brimstone." I thought this rather witty, but Grandfather apparently disagreed.

"Really, Christopher, must you be so flippant? It's not her religion that makes her cruel. Faith can be a beautiful thing when coupled with a gentle soul. No, there is something terrible buried in Cressida which was not there when I first knew her. She is like the cursed figures in Hans Christian Andersen's 'Snow Queen'; she has a splinter of glass in her heart and eye and can find no goodness in the world."

"Oh, yes. I'm sure that's true. I just meant…" Seeing his stern expression, I decided to change the subject. "It's surely more important to discover what Gertrude was doing in the tunnel when I saw her."

He was at my side, walking back through the castle halls. "I think that's perfectly obvious. And if you don't understand why she was there, then remember what you told me you saw."

"The ghost that wasn't a ghost?"

"Correct. A ghost who has apparently been haunting this house for some time."

I did as he instructed and replayed the scene in my mind. That didn't work, so I tried it out loud. "Todd and I found Sam's body. He'd been covered over with his cloak and so I pulled it away to inspect his wounds. We heard a sort of gasp from along the tunnel and, when we looked back, she was standing there, her face illuminated by the candle which she instantly dropped."

"And?"

"And so… we… must… have…"

"It's terribly late, Christopher. Will this sentence be coming to a conclusion before daybreak?"

His cantankerous response must have sparked my brain into action. I fired off an answer as if it was the easiest thing in the world. "We must have scared her!"

He sighed and shook his head. "In a way, I suppose you're correct. But what does that suggest?"

I could no longer feel guilty for not being as smart as him, and so I told him just that. "You're the expert. You tell me."

"It suggests that Gertrude was shocked by what she saw there. Which means…" He stopped walking and wrinkled his nose. "Actually, no. I'm not going to give the game away. I think it would be better if you went to sleep to see what that brain of yours can summon in way of an answer."

This cheered me up, if only for the fact I would be allowed to get some more sleep. "Topper!" It seemed that, the longer I stayed in Clearwell, the more I sounded like Dante. "I'll have eighty winks or so, wake up with the answer we need, and see you for breakfast. How does that sound?"

"It sounds… optimistic."

I beat him about the back with a jovial palm and hurried off to bed before he could change his mind. I hadn't realised that there was actually very little of the night left. By the time I got into bed, there were birds singing outside and, approximately six seconds after I'd closed my eyes, I had to open them again as bright beams of daylight were streaming into the room. I did not feel strong enough to crawl out into the world, but there was a knock on the door and a footman entered to drag me down to breakfast.

The Wyndhams were all there except for Cressida. It being Sunday, I thought I might know where she'd gone. What confused me was the

196

fact that the rest of her family still looked so glum in her absence. Algar was staring at an egg in its cup, perhaps hoping it would offer the solution to all the world's problems if he could only work out how to crack it open. Dante wasn't much chirpier and made no attempt to animate his family for once, whereas Gertrude looked just as nervous as she had when we'd left her the previous night.

"Morning everyone," I tried to sound sunny for their sake, but was in a bad mood of my own. I'm like a grumpy mole when I haven't had enough sleep.

Grandfather, at least, had some urgency about him. He marched in as I arrived, dressed in his usual brand of detective's attire. "Christopher, have you only just risen? I've already been to see the inspector who's in charge of the case. Not the brightest chap I've come across, though he has at least confirmed Lieutenant-Colonel Stroud's whereabouts at the time Florence Keyse was murdered. It seems that he really was at his brother's house in The Pludds. A local bobby saw his car there, and his most belligerent brother confirms that he stayed all night."

It was too early in the day to make much sense of what he'd said, and I had other concerns on my mind. "Is there any news on the patient?"

The four of them stared at me as though I'd said something terribly cruel.

Even Grandfather looked melancholy. "I called to see his father. Sam's not out of the woods yet, but he's on the mend. His bleeding has stopped, and he regained consciousness on several occasions during the night. Time will tell what damage has been done."

His cautious response drew more frowns and sighs, not least from me. Tiredness is surely the opposite of a detective's foremost tool in his arsenal; it's more like the backmost stick of celery in his garden shed. I had no motivation to eat breakfast, let alone carry out a (practically) triple murder investigation. I was frankly exhausted and couldn't imagine finding the energy I needed to proceed. Instead, I hoped to linger in the castle all morning, being waited on hand and foot by the well-trained staff.

Sadly, Grandfather had other ideas. "There's no time to chat, I'm afraid. We have one last detail of the case to resolve and will be out for most of the morning." His announcement did not provoke much of a reaction from our hosts, but I was spurred into action. Having learnt from previous such disappointments, I shot to the breakfast table and took as much food as I could carry. Pastries, muffins, a crumpet or two and a glass of orange juice, which I drank immediately, rather than stuffing it into my pocket and having to bear a wet coat all morning.

"Did you really mean what you said about this being the final piece of the puzzle?" I asked the old fellow once we were out in the garden, with Delilah bounding along at my side.

"Did you really mean it when you said you would have worked out Gertrude's secret by now?"

"Of course I did." There was a channel of hurt audible in my voice. "I absolutely meant what I said, and the fact that I failed in my challenge doesn't take anything away from my strong commitment to the task."

"Very good, Christopher. In which case, your effort is commendable." He smiled at me, and we returned to more relevant discussion. "To answer your question, yes, I believe I know the identity of the killer and that we have almost every piece of evidence we require in order to tie up this twisting case. In fact, I feel I have been quite slow in my work. Perhaps it is due to the unreasonably hot weather, but I am rather disappointed in myself for taking so long."

I don't mind telling you that I was stunned by this announcement. "But… just last night you seemed so far from a solution. What has changed since then?"

"Everything, boy. Everything!" I thought he would be as opaque as ever, but he at least pointed me in the right direction. "In reverse chronological order, consider what Sam Mordaunt might have been doing in Clearwell – not just yesterday but the night before when we saw him on two different occasions. Consider the snake in Algar's bed and the attack on the castle, the burnt document of the late Thomas Wyndham and our trip to Scowles Folly. And, with all of this in mind, to arrive at the answer you must return to the original question of why Cole and Florence were murdered."

I tried to keep track of this long list of events and find a pattern through the evidence, but… well, it was rather difficult. Instead of coming across a solution, I thought of a new question to put to him.

"Wait just one moment. If you already know who the killer is, where are we going now?"

We'd passed through the gatehouse and left the grounds of the estate. The road outside had been scorched by the bonfire and there were piles of unburnt wood littering the ditches. There was even a drunken chap asleep in a bush. I wondered whether we should check that he was still alive, but Grandfather evidently had enough dead bodies with which to concern himself.

"We are going to plug the one gap in the story that I haven't yet filled." He wagged his finger like a belligerent judge. "We're going to see Cressida."

Some part of my brain must have already known this as, without thinking, I'd turned off the road into the churchyard.

"Oh, yes. Of course we are." I fell silent then as I wondered whether my grandfather was telling the truth. If he already knew the name of the culprit, it seemed foolhardy at best not to arrest the blighter forthwith. What difference did it make that we hadn't uncovered the reason for Cressida's bad temper? I could only conclude that there was more left to uncover than Lord Edgington would admit.

St Peter's looked as though it had been modelled on a toy church that someone found lying around in a nursery. Small and neat, with brightly coloured brickwork, it had an incredibly tall spire with stencilling to the roof in a vaguely gothic style. It was the kind of place in which I saw myself one day getting married to some kind-hearted, humble young lady who would love me (tummy and all). A distant cousin of my father's got married in Westminster Abbey, but this village chapel was much more to my taste.

"Really, Christopher?" Grandfather asked as I opened the door for him. "You wouldn't prefer somewhere a trifle grander?"

"No, I wouldn't. And stop reading my thoughts." I must have sounded defensive as he had a good laugh at this. "Besides, you've got nothing to worry about for the moment. First, I must find a trade, second, a woman silly enough to marry me and, third, I'll have to convince my mother that my fiancée is worthy of her beloved baby boy. Those are three things I don't see happening this century."

He paused beneath the pointed arch of the entrance. "Don't say that, Chrissy. I'd rather like to be alive when you walk down the aisle."

For a moment, I had to wonder whether Grandfather would make it to the twenty-first century. It might sound far-fetched, but I couldn't put it past him.

The interior of the church was perhaps even prettier than what we'd seen outside. A long aisle directed us towards an arched window that matched the portal we'd just come through and the front of the apse above the altar. I'd say the light that poured into the building passed through a rather nice example of curvilinear tracery, but my mother is the real expert on all things architectural, so please don't quote me on that.

Twelve elegantly carved wooden pews sat on either side of the aisle and, just beyond them, more arches were supported by barley stripe columns. I had not in any way changed my opinion that it would be a very nice place to get married. But we weren't there to plan a wedding or admire mid-nineteenth century architecture. We had a suspect to interrogate, and she was performing the most obvious ruse imaginable to appear innocent; she was organising the hymn books.

"May we talk to you, Cressida?" Grandfather's voice not only reached across to the countess, it filled the hallowed space around us and travelled up to the roof and back.

She stopped what she was doing to see which stray sheep had entered that lovely sanctuary. At first, she looked pleased to see us, but then her face fell, and I wondered whether she had some inkling of why we were there. Instead of replying, she placed the final book on the small wooden shelf and bustled over to us. She looked around the church as she went, as though afraid what the absent congregation might think of her. I have no doubt that tongues wag in small villages like Clearwell, and I didn't blame her for being wary.

With his usual quiet warmth, Grandfather allowed her to lead us back outside – much as a gentle wave will carry shipwrecked sailors to safety. We circumnavigated the building and found a quiet spot in which to talk. As far as I could see, St Peter's had no graveyard, but there was a long rectangular garden with fruit trees and bushes that surrounded the church. It was a peaceful morning, and I settled down on a bench just as a roar of anger rent the very air.

"What on Earth do you mean by coming here?"

CHAPTER THIRTY

Cressida's furious words remained there with us, like the headline on a newspaper masthead. Rather than react in kind, my grandfather simply smiled.

"There's really no need to worry yourself," he began with an uncharacteristic – and dare I say foppish – flick of the wrist. "We have good news. I believe I have identified the killer."

This seemed to soothe the nervous woman somewhat, but she still fidgeted with her fingers in the pocket of her woollen cardigan. "I'm sorry if I sounded curt. I appreciate everything you've done for us, but I'm sure you can imagine why I've been on edge."

While Grandfather interrogated our suspect, I decided to catch up on breakfast. I must say though, I found it odd that she didn't ask who the killer was and had to wonder whether she already knew.

"It's interesting you should say that." He gripped the smooth amethyst ball at the top of his cane as Delilah ran between the rows of neatly trimmed privet bushes. "It's the one thing I have been unable to determine."

She brought her hand to the buttons at her neck. "I beg your pardon?"

"Since we arrived at Clearwell, you have been nervous, aggressive and endlessly critical of your family. I cannot fathom what could make you act in such a fashion, especially in the presence of guests."

I was even more surprised by his bluntness than our suspect. I nearly choked on my croissant.

She bit her lip but would not respond, and so Grandfather continued. "In light of this conduct, I have a question for you. I'd like to know what happened to the real Cressida Wyndham. The young woman who welcomed my family here all those years ago."

I gasped then, before realising that he was not suggesting that Cressida had been replaced by an impostor; he was speaking metaphorically.

She fell back in shock and landed beside me on the slatted bench. "Why are you tormenting me? I've received you with the generosity I would extend to any visitor, yet you stand there insulting me."

As unrelenting as ever, Grandfather took a step closer and raised his voice. "It is not your generosity to guests that concerns me. It's your cruelty to your family. You call yourself a God-fearing woman and yet, the Bible that I know speaks of familial loyalty and love to all mankind. You show more kindness to the books in your church than your own son and daughter. So tell me why."

I can't say it was particularly comfortable to sit next to that slightly dazed woman as she endured Lord Edgington's barracking. He was a storm wind, blowing iron nails in place of hailstone.

Cressida could no longer look at him, and her gaze fell to the floor. I'd rarely seen my grandfather take such a confrontational approach with a suspect. If anything, I often found him to be more tender with the women he interrogated. He had never been the typical growling policeman type, and it was hard to know what had come over him.

"If you won't explain, perhaps I should present my own theory." It was a question in the form of a statement and, as the countess didn't answer, he persevered. "I remember what Algar was like before you married him. I remember his father telling me – with some pride, I might add – about his son's reputation in the village. Your husband-to-be was an idle lothario. But after the two of you met, he seemed to change. When I last came to Clearwell, you appeared most contented together. I can only imagine that this was a façade, and Algar's romantic dalliances never truly stopped."

She glanced over her shoulder. It was no longer the fear of being overheard by her neighbours that worried her, but that such words could be uttered before the house of God. Perhaps reassured that the old stones were not eavesdropping, she finally produced a response.

"No, it was…" Well, it actually took her one more go to get started, but after that, she was away. "Algar really had changed. To give him the credit he deserves, he was a true and gentle husband for many years when we were first married. I was only twenty-one at the time, but I loved him. I felt quite giddy every time we were together and, after our children were born and we inherited the castle, I thought that my every dream had been fulfilled."

Her eyes took a brief stroll about the garden and came to settle on our lovely dog, who was rolling about in the shade of an apple tree.

I had assumed that Grandfather would soften his approach now that she had begun to explain herself, but his ferocity only increased. "I see. Then it did not start immediately, but he eventually strayed." It was not just that the old fellow was angry, he sounded quite arrogant. For all his bravado and determination, I had always found him to be a polite sort of bulldog. "That's surely why you took so strongly against your own husband."

"No, you're wrong." Cressida's words launched through space to knock her inquisitor back a step. "You can jump to conclusions if you like, but it won't tell you what really happened to my family."

Grandfather observed her for a few moments, perhaps aware that she had already made a salient point and would not be moved by his usual stratagems. We'd dealt with some despicable characters in our investigations. Some had been wise, others quite foolish, but few had been strong enough to hold their nerve before the force of former Superintendent Edgington's immense brain.

Her initial hesitance had subsided, and she seemed to enjoy the confrontation. "If you have nothing more to say, I'll be leaving." Despite this statement, she stayed right where she was and waited to see what her opponent would try next.

"In which case, I must apologise." Grandfather's face turned a little paler as the confidence drained from him. It really was a sight to behold, but I didn't trust him for one second. "I've made a fool of myself this weekend. I'm a shadow of the man I once was." The words were nothing more than a hesitant scratch that crept from the base of his throat.

I could see what he was doing, of course. It was the tactic of an infant; when shouting doesn't work, try a plea for sympathy. That isn't to suggest it was a poor plan. I merely doubted that Cressida would be swayed by such an obvious manoeuvre. But then, what do I know?

"I'm not saying you've failed in your task." Her expression became unexpectedly earnest. "I just wanted you to see that you can't predict human behaviour. Life doesn't always play out to the rhythm we would like; there is no drumbeat to guide our footsteps."

Lord Edgington (or the version of himself he was inhabiting at that moment) would not be comforted by her words. "I discovered that Algar had been untrue to you, and I thought that would be the key to the whole case. I thought I could finally make sense of this chain of uncanny events. Florence Keyse's death, the storming of the castle last night, even the poisonous snake in your bed."

I was curious that he had not laid out any evidence against her. It was as though he was keeping the most pertinent details close to his chest. His usual system of methodically constructed facts had been discarded, and he was happy to confront her with vague suspicions.

I was not a total idiot – or perhaps that should be, *I was only a partial idiot*. I could tell that he was trying to evade her defences. I watched in silence as he continued his act as a defeated old man in need of reassurance. He was quite the thespian, but he couldn't fool me. Whenever Cressida looked away, I saw his expression change and a hungry look in his eyes. He was prodding and probing, and I thought I knew why.

He'd led me to believe that he had identified our culprit, but what if she was already there in front of us? What if Cressida was the killer? It made sense that she would want to dispose of Florence Keyse, her husband's lover. And as for Cole... Well, Cole had been the great unknown from the beginning. He was surely the hole in the case which Grandfather had gone to the church to plug.

But then... perhaps Cole knew something about Algar and had to be silenced. If this hypothesis were true, the murders had nothing to do with Lady Morgana or Scowles Folly. Everything that had occurred had been spurred by the pride of the Wyndhams. Dante had thought that his mother's bizarre behaviour would tear the family apart, and his fear had only deepened when he'd learnt of his father's affair. But what if she'd been doing what she deemed necessary to keep them together?

In a sudden rush, everything made sense. Cressida was our culprit! She'd killed out of love for her family. I still couldn't fathom where Sam Mordaunt fitted into the plot, but I was sure that Grandfather would tie up the loose ends. All in all, it was a successful investigation, and the case was closed. Well, not really of course, but you can't blame me for trying.

"There was one thing that never sat right with my theory," Grandfather said when several seconds of silence had passed. "Sometimes, a police officer can overlook minor details and focus on the main facts of the case in order to arrive at the correct conclusion. But I can't simply ignore one of the murders. You see, Cole doesn't appear to have any connection to the other crimes. It was wishful thinking to imagine that I could ignore his part in everything."

Cressida sneered at this. I couldn't understand what so unnerved her, but Grandfather's eyes flared again, and I realised that this was the reaction he required.

"I'm sorry. Did I say something funny?" His eyebrows travelled further up his forehead in an approximation of an innocent look.

"No, no." Her voice was faint, and it was hard to believe even this simple denial.

"Oh, how silly of me." He smiled just a fraction and tapped his head to suggest the fallibility of his memory. "Cole was related to the Wyndhams, of course. That's why you paid for his cottage, wasn't it?"

She made no answer this time but shifted her weight on the bench.

"A distant cousin of Algar's great-grandmother. Something along those lines, wasn't it?"

She looked away again, and it was clear that she was trapped. If she denied the connection between Cole and her family, she would only show how deeply it had affected her. And yet, if she confirmed the story, that would prove she had lied to us, at lunch the previous day, when she had poured scorn on Cole's connection.

The great Lord Edgington's gaze was glued to our suspect. "It struck me as strange that your family would be so supportive of a distant relative, a bastard, no less. By the sound of things, Cole could not prove his relationship to the long-dead earl from whom he claimed to have descended."

"*Bastard* is just the word for him," she said in a low growl.

"It wasn't until Cole was born that he and his family were given their cottage in the village. Isn't that correct?"

She would not answer but looked straight through him.

I saw what he was trying to prove at last and blurted out the facts that they both already knew. "If Cole was descended from the Wyndhams, one of his parents would be too. So why was it only after he was born that you did anything for them?"

Grandfather's smile bloomed on his face like a happy sunflower in an otherwise barren field. "That is my question precisely." He crossed his arms and waited for a retort that would never arrive. "When did the piece of glass pierce your heart, Cressida? When was it exactly that you decided the only way to save your family from sin was to spend the rest of your life condemning them?"

"He duped me!" Her response was so loud I was surprised it didn't shake the apples from the tree. "Algar knew full well what he'd done, yet he married me all the same."

I finally understood what my grandfather had been doing since the interview had begun; he was jiggling a key in a tricky lock. He'd tried turning it in one direction, then another, before shaking it about any which way until the door burst open.

"Cole was Algar's son." Still standing in front of her, he placed his palms together. "You've made your children live through misery because your husband had a baby before you were married, and you couldn't forgive him."

"It is not for me to forgive." She had returned to her usual strained tone of voice. The veins in her forehead were pulsing with each word she spoke. "Only God forgives, but it's too late for any of us." Her nerves snapped and her whole body began to shake as though some spirit had possessed her. "Algar cast sin upon our family. He defied the will of God."

I thought she might combust, or perhaps just explode, but, to my wonderment, my grandfather darted forward to support her. "You poor soul. I am sorry for all you have suffered. But you said it yourself; it is not for us mortals to judge. Your husband was a foolish boy, but when he met you, he grew up and changed for the better. I could see back then just how much he loved you, and I believe that he still does."

"I wish he'd never told me," she said between sobs. "I wish I had lived my life in joyous oblivion."

Grandfather pulled her closer, and her words died away. With the three of us squashed together on that small wooden bench, he peered across at me keenly. He was no doubt attempting to communicate something hugely significant, but I couldn't fathom for a moment what it might be. I was too busy wondering how any of this was related to the murders we'd been investigating.

CHAPTER THIRTY-ONE

It was quite the equation; I can tell you that!

Two dead bodies and an unconscious blacksmith. A family consumed by past sins, not to mention a two-hundred-year-old rivalry, a ghost who wasn't a ghost and all that business with the snake. Which, now that I thought of it, still didn't make any sense. Did the fact we discovered Sam Mordaunt in the castle mean that he was to blame for the hissing reptile's presence there?

That was one mystery I couldn't solve, but I realised that, if you were looking for a veil for your murderous intentions, you could do a lot worse than using the complex history of a town. However, if Cressida was not to blame for the killings, who did that leave?

This was the question that most taxed me as my grandfather and I escorted the countess back to Clearwell Castle. Such chaos had whirled around us for the last two days that I'd hardly had time to make a list of suspects. This seemed like as good a time as any and so I began to tot them up in my head.

Jimmy Mordaunt – mayor of the rival village. A rather dim-witted fish if ever there was one and, in some ways, the obvious suspect. If he discovered Cole's secret, he might have taken the necessary steps to conceal it. Few people hated the Wyndhams and the village of Clearwell as much as Jimmy, but why would he have attacked his own nephew?

His brother Cliff – a loyal, smart fellow. I couldn't see him being the killer, so it was probably him. He might have gone along with his brother's plans to mark the anniversary of Lady Morgana's death, but he surely wouldn't have hurt his son, would he?

Lieutenant-Colonel Stroud – the retired soldier was certainly a cantankerous sort, but he was out of town at the time that Florence was killed. Though Cole had died in front of his house, we had amassed very little evidence of his guilt and his alibi suggested I should cross him off the list.

Jed Gibson – we'd found no sign that the musical garage owner was involved in any of the crimes, and I thought this highly suspicious. What's more, he'd taken advantage of my kindly grandfather to sell him all sorts of expensive things from his shop. The man was evidently a scoundrel – but probably not our culprit.

Algar Wyndham – we now knew that Cole was his son. Perhaps the young wastrel had intended to blackmail his good old dad with the information he'd discovered in the family library. Algar was at the pub on the night his lover was killed and went back alone to see her, but… it was hard to say exactly, but… well, I just didn't think he was the one. Perhaps it was his warm personality or the love he showed for his family, but I couldn't see him killing his secret son or his secret paramour. And why would he have put a snake in his own bed?

Gertrude Wyndham – no, impossible! Who would even suggest such a thing? She was barely allowed out of the castle by her mother and would have found it difficult to enact such elaborate plans. And besides, though I was aware of the odd exception or two, I still found it difficult to believe that pretty young ladies could be killers!

Cressida Wyndham – I believe we'd recently ruled out her involvement, hadn't we?

Dante Wyndham…

I stopped myself then as I couldn't bear to think of my new friend being responsible for such barbaric crimes. He was too good a chap. He'd welcomed me into his home and treated me like a brother and yet…

Dante Wyndham – all of the evidence I'd collected to explain why his mother would be the killer applied to him, too. He had been terribly nervous around his family the whole time we'd been in Clearwell. I'd taken this as a sign of his fears for his parents' marriage, but what if it was something more? What if he'd been cleaning up after his father's indiscretions and feared discovery?

Perhaps he'd realised what shame that his father's bastard son could have brought upon the Wyndhams and dealt with the problem. He'd definitely knew about Algar's affair with Florence. Maybe he'd seen their flirtation at the pub that night and gone back to murder her. If even I had noticed how affectionate his father had been, you can be sure that Dante had.

A searing pain tore through my stomach as the case built against him. This was the very worst outcome I could imagine. I didn't want my cousin to be responsible, and yet the longer I thought about it, the more likely it became. Grandfather had his arm around our teary companion as we walked through the gatehouse, but I could only think of this new possibility.

If Dante had already committed the two murders, confessing to the attack on Sam Mordaunt might have incriminated him in the other crimes. He knew those tunnels better than anyone. So let's say Sam planted the adder in the castle and was trying to escape when Dante clobbered him. The reason Gertrude dropped her candle when she'd seen his body was the simple fact that she suspected her brother's involvement. Perhaps she knew what a perverse mind the boy had and was horrified to see another victim fall by his hand.

This was the closest I'd come to a coherent theory for the complex case, and it made me feel quite awful. Why couldn't the killer have been someone nasty? I didn't particularly like that grumpy old Lieutenant-Colonel. And the policeman we'd met was rather a pain. Why couldn't it have been one of them instead of my jolly new friend?

There was no time to curse my luck, as we were soon back in the castle. Grandfather took Cressida to see Algar in the lounge, and I would have gone in with them, but I felt that it was not my place. I had to wonder if my esteemed mentor would sit them both down and tell them to stop behaving so irrationally. They had both done wrong – both acted like fools – but if they loved one another and cared for the family they had formed together, it surely wasn't too late to put things right.

Of course, if it turned out that their son had been sauntering about the town, strangling young women and pushing drunken peasants down wells, that would be the straw that broke the dromedary's back.

I tried to be positive. As I sat outside the door, making out very little of their muffled conversation, my stomach felt as though a family of bluetits had recently built a nest inside me, but I tried to think of an alternative to Dante being the killer. I still didn't see how we could rule out the staff at Clearwell, or even one of the old men in the pub whose names we hadn't learnt and who had barely featured in the case.

Just imagine! Imagine that, despite all the history and anger, shame and recrimination, the killer was one mad old chap from the pub who was angry about the best cake award at the Clearwell fete, or a disagreement over an overgrown rhododendron! I'm not sure it would be a satisfying conclusion to the case, but at least my grandfather would have to admit that his method wasn't foolproof.

The only thing loud enough to penetrate the thick oaken door was a shouted phrase from Algar that left nothing but silence in its wake. "I wanted to love you…" he cried with all the passion of a young Don Juan. "I do love you."

In time, the mumbling resumed, and my grandfather opened the door for Algar and Cressida to leave the room. Their faces were stony, and they could barely meet my gaze, but their fingers were entwined, and there was a nervous energy to them that was visible in the earl's great swaying form and his wife's shifting gaze. I don't know what my mercurial forebear had said to our hosts, but it appeared to have done the trick.

He kept his counsel then but bowed low, – an odd concession considering their relative titles – and we waited for husband and wife to stroll out of sight. I rather hoped that they were off for a cheek-to-cheek dance in the ballroom or a reaffirmation of their love for one another in the forest. Of course, I'm something of a romantic, and they had probably just gone for a cup of tea.

"Christopher," my companion began once we were alone. "Our investigation is concluded. I have filled in every hole in our knowledge, identified our culprit and solved various mysteries along the way." He did not inject his voice with a great deal of emotion and might well have been informing me of a list of train times or the results of a tennis match. "All in all, I would say it has been a successful weekend and, as ever, you have helped me immeasurably."

I shuddered a little as I worried what this news spelt for Dante.

"Without one particular observation you made last night, I might never have come to the right conclusion." He brushed an invisible speck of dust from his lapel and turned to leave.

I was rather distracted and pushed on with what I wished to say. "Wait, just a moment, Grandfather. I have a question for you." I took a deep breath before broaching the painful subject. "I must ask whether Dante is the killer."

His pupils shrunk a little as he turned to face the bright window at the end of the hall. "I'm interested to know why you would posit such a suggestion."

210

Though I examined his face for some evidence that my suspicion was correct, he gave nothing away.

"I've been considering the possibility since we left the church." I glanced down self-consciously at my fingers. They were not quite as sausagey as they had once been. Perhaps, as I grew, they would become fine and graceful like a piano player's. I wouldn't hold my breath. "It seems to me that Dante had both the opportunity to carry out the three attacks and the knowledge of various secrets that might have forced him to commit them for the sake of his family."

I hadn't stood up from the slung leather chair and so he knelt down in front of me. I was surprised his knees could manage it at his age – not that my knees were any better.

"Will you do something for me, Christopher?" he asked, and so I nodded. It was an understatement, of course; I would have done *anything* for him. "Will you explain the thinking that led you to your culprit?"

I looked into his eyes to see a galaxy of thoughts and complex emotions. It felt as though I was peering at the workings of his brain for a moment. I was quite hypnotised, but I did as he requested.

"I suppose that my suspicions were first aroused when I caught him listening to our conversation last night. I immediately realised that, of everyone in the family, he would know most about the different threads we have been weaving together." A tiny nugget of wisdom came to the forefront of my mind. "I doubt there is any such thing as a secret in a house with hidden passageways. And yet it was more than that. You see, when he took me up to this room, although I was the one asking the questions, it felt at one moment as though our roles had reversed. He claimed to be concerned that you would never find the killer, but I wonder now whether he was fishing to discover what I knew."

When a short period of contemplation had concluded, he asked another question. "But what of concrete evidence? Surely you have something that could support this assertion?"

I tried to get my own thoughts in order before I answered. "If we consider the fact that there are two dead bodies and one injured man, opportunity is surely a major factor in choosing our culprit." I was terribly proud of how this sentence fell from my lips. I almost sounded like a real detective. "How many people can we honestly say would have had the chance to murder Cole and Florence and the knowledge to locate the tunnel and knock out Sam Mordaunt?"

He straightened up then, so that his eyes were almost level with mine. "That is an interesting point, but I'm afraid the answer is *"more than one"*. You'll need to do better than that to convince a jury of a man's guilt."

"But Dante was in the pub before Florence died, and I remember Jed Gibson telling us that there were Wyndhams about on the night Cole was murdered too."

"The same could be said for Algar, though. You must explain what it is about Dante that led you to believe he could be responsible for the crimes."

I genuinely tried, but as soon as I had to explain my ideas in front of my teacher, they seemed too small and unlikely. "Well... he's desperate to keep his family together, so what if we were wrong and the document that Cole discovered implicated the modern-day Wyndhams? Perhaps-"

"Rest your mind, boy." Grandfather placed his hand ever so purposefully on my sleeve. I was gripping my seat so hard that my nails were digging into the leather. "Dante is not the killer."

I didn't know whether to feel disappointed that I'd failed to solve the case, or relieved that my friend was innocent. I managed to experience both emotions at the same time, which was... shall we say... unusual?

"Opportunity and motive must never outweigh the evidence before us. We mustn't bend the facts to fit a hypothesis, and yet you have sewn together an interesting analysis of the case. You should be proud of your work." He let out a heavy breath and picked over his own words. "*I* am proud of what you have achieved this weekend – with the possible exception of that business with the grass snake. In fact, that was really rather-"

Noticing my vexed expression, he decided not to finish that sentence. "You have done extremely well, and it is almost time." I didn't follow his meaning, but he rose and helped me up to standing before brushing off a speck of cobweb from the breast of my white cotton shirt. "We have a killer to unmask."

That ever so rare and ever so encouraging smile broke out on his face. "But first, I have a few small matters to which to attend. Meet me in the garden in five minutes. Tell Todd to get the car ready and Dorie that her services may be needed. If Henrietta has her rolling pin at hand, she's welcome to join us, too."

I was carried along by this burst of positivity and barely squeaked a note in reply. He understood my meaning, though, and winked at me as he disappeared into the lounge where the telephone was located. I walked through the castle, aware that we would not stay in Clearwell much longer now that Grandfather's task was complete, and my job standing alongside him had been carried out to perfection.

It made me feel rather homesick. I don't know if that's quite the word for it, but generations of my ancestors had lived in that strange abode, and I had only enjoyed two days there. I very much wondered if I should ever go back again, and a pang of sadness briefly passed through me as I broke free from the castle into the clean, fresh air of that warm summer's day.

CHAPTER THIRTY-TWO

I was not the only one issued with instructions. Algar and Cressida had clearly been told to gather their offspring and prepare to depart the grounds. I hadn't a clue what Lord Edgington had in mind, but I knew I wouldn't have to wait long to discover his plan.

My family of cousins wore grim expressions. They reminded me of the time I'd got into trouble at school and been sent to the head of the sixth form for my punishment. I waited in that corridor for an hour in a state of intense fear before realising that Mr Munroe wasn't at school that day. I got off scot-free, but certainly learnt my lesson; it was the last time I ever whistled 'Land of Hope and Glory' in the middle of a maths class!

Algar and Cressida's hands were still connected, though I was sure they had much to discuss before they could return to something resembling the happy life they had once enjoyed. When I saw my friend Dante again, I felt a little guilty for suspecting him. He greeted me with a shy smile and a punch on the arm, and I decided that he was a forgiving sort and wouldn't have objected to the thorough job I had done.

Our loyal assistants from Cranley Hall were already waiting on the drive. Grandfather soon appeared, and I think that every last one of us gasped when we saw that he was not alone. He was supporting a rather lethargic Sam Mordaunt, with the man's father taking the other arm. The invalid looked exhausted but very much alive and unleashed a winning smile in our direction which soon spread around the group. His father couldn't resist the temptation, and even the Wyndhams were happy that he had come through the worst of his ordeal.

Grandfather waved his free hand rather regally and deposited Sam into the Rolls for Todd to drive him into town. With this done, he marched straight past us to leave the Clearwell estate, and we all trailed after him. With our car at the rear, it was very much like a funeral procession. Happily though, the body we were escorting was still alive.

Grandfather's normally speedy gait had slowed to a steady stroll. He even swung his cane through the air like the leader of a marching band. Behind him, the Wyndhams walked shoulder to shoulder in a line of four, and then the misfits (Dorie, Delilah and I) kept pace in front of the Rolls. It was lucky that they lived so close to the village, as our progress was far from swift.

"Does anyone know where we're going?" Dorie loudly whispered, and Todd leaned out of the car window to reply.

"It's the last day of the Lady Morgana memorial. One of the footmen told me that the folk from Scowles Folly stage a wedding banquet in the town each year to commemorate the nuptials that never took place." We could always rely upon our chauffeur to be well informed.

"Oh, that's nice." Dorie scratched her nose and eventually offered an explanation. "I hope there'll be grub."

We paraded all the way to the high street where, sure enough, those loveable scamps from the neighbouring village had once again painted the streets with blood. There was a large table laid out for the banquet and a bride sitting at one end in a tattered and torn wedding dress.

For all these macabre touches, I must admit that they'd put on a good spread. There were sandwiches cut into little triangles, (fantastic!) sausages on sticks, (delicious!) dates wrapped in bacon, (yum yum!) and even a freshly roast chicken that one of the Scowles Folly lot was busy carving. The thirty or so members of the party were arranged around the table, and I was interested to spot a look of apprehension on Cliff Mordaunt's face in the back of the Rolls as we came to a stop. I wondered if his fellow villagers would consider him a turncoat to be arriving in such company.

It was not just the town's invaders who were present. Many figures we had come to know in Clearwell were there as spectators. Jed Gibson from the garage had a bottle of cider which he passed about among his friends from the pub. I noticed the butcher, the baker and Lieutenant-Colonel Stroud with sour faces and balled up fists as they endured the sordid spectacle. In fact, almost everyone we'd met that weekend was on hand, and I could only imagine that Grandfather had rung ahead to invite them.

In a moment, all attention was turned to the huddled figure in white at the end of the table. The bride was about to make a speech.

"For two hundred years, my wedding has gone uncelebrated."

Though I could not see the face behind the shabby veil, the voice floated over as a ghoulish moan. "For two hundred years, I have suffered the indignity of my rejection, betrayal and brutal murder. But my time has finally arrived. I am here to claim my rightful dominion, to ascend to the ranks of–"

"Oh, do be quiet, you fool." Grandfather slammed down his amethyst-topped cane on the table with a most impressive *thwack!* that caused the wine glasses to sing and the plate of jelly to wobble. "We haven't come here today to listen to you peddling your ridiculous stories. It's time I told everyone the truth about the crimes of Clearwell Castle."

Whoever was in the wedding dress cackled and hunched a little lower. This was as much as my grandfather could bear before he walked the length of the table to grasp hold of the bride.

Jimmy Mordaunt did not look happy to have his veil pulled back. What was more surprising, however, were the lengths he had gone to in order to embrace his role. I'm fairly certain that he was wearing makeup.

CHAPTER THIRTY-THREE

There was not the gasp I might have expected. Perhaps everyone else there had realised that the strange chap was otherwise missing and solved this simple conundrum. I, on the other hand, had not.

"It's lucky you're such a complete buffoon, or I might have considered the possibility that you killed Cole and Florence." Grandfather's insult drew some laughter from a surprisingly large swathe of the audience. Even Jimmy's nephew, who was being helped from the car into a seat at the table, looked cheered by the words.

"Who are you calling a buffoon?" The mayor of Scowles Folly… scowled.

"I would have thought that was obvious." Grandfather was simply a genius at rolling his eyes, and he now indulged in one of his greatest performances. "I used the second-person pronoun and looked at you as I spoke. Now, if you'll stop your inane chattering, I will explain exactly what has happened in Clearwell this weekend."

With his rich tone and lively delivery, he'd managed to silence the street. The locals from the village stood before The Butcher's Arms, apparently anxious to discover Lord Edgington's findings. Perhaps more surprisingly, their rivals looked just as curious and, except for the odd sound of drinks being refilled or someone munching a stick of carrot (very well, that was me) the masses would remain quiet for some time.

"Crimes have been committed here in Clearwell. Wrongs have been perpetrated, but not against Lady Morgana Mordaunt." Standing ramrod straight, Grandfather delivered this opening salvo from behind the grim bride. The sun shone down to turn his silver hair gold, and he surveyed the stone-faced onlookers for a moment before continuing. "Two residents of this village have been murdered and a third man almost died. But these were no ordinary killings, and I was forced to call upon my years of experience as a police officer in order to solve them."

There was a brief murmur of appreciation, and a new reality settled in the minds of his audience; yes, he really did know the name of the killer, and we would soon be privy to the knowledge.

"We all know of the bitterness that has passed between your two villages, but what if a document existed in Thomas Wyndham's own hand that could lay to rest the rumours and hearsay once and for all? What if we could read about the events of the fateful night Lady Morgana died?"

Grandfather looked from one party to the other, and the Lieutenant-Colonel seemed to shudder in apoplectic rage. It was a fairly mild reaction by his standards.

"It is my belief that the discovery of such a document brought about the death of Cole Watkins. Due to his connection to the Wyndhams..." Lord Edgington chose these words carefully, clearly unwilling to expose Algar's dirty secret to the world. "...Cole was in charge of the family's collection of books and documents dating back over three hundred years. On the day he died, he told many of you that he planned to reveal a particular discovery at the village fete, and that what he had to share would change Clearwell for ever."

It was at this moment that my esteemed forebear decided to take a stroll. He pottered along past the seated revellers all the way to the crowd of locals. "The question I couldn't answer until last night was who would have wanted to keep Lady Morgana's secret so desperately as to resort to murder? It seemed to me that there were two possible solutions. Either someone from Clearwell believed that the document would prove that Thomas Wyndham really had murdered his wife-to-be, or someone from Scowles Folly believed that it wouldn't. But, whatever the reason, Cole had to die, so down the Lieutenant-Colonel's well he went."

He stopped at this moment to look Stroud in the eye. "Of course, Cole was a drunkard and, by all accounts, he had been imbibing heavily that night. No one believed that there was anything suspicious in the poor chap's death. Well, no one except the landlady of The Wyndham Arms, at least.

"Florence Keyse saw smoke coming from the chimney of Rosebank Cottage weeks after Cole died, and she shared the information with the drinkers at her pub on Saturday night. A few hours later, she met a similar fate. She was strangled with a length of cord behind the bar where she worked. At the scene of the crime, we found a military button with the crest of the Royal Army Medical Corps and the loaded gun which she had attempted to reach in order to defend herself – a gun which, as my grandson correctly deduced, had no bearing on the case whatsoever."

This seemed a rather unnecessary detail to include, but it did comfort me that I'd got at least one thing right. He winked across the table, and I gave dear Delilah's floppy ears a stroke as I listened to his tale.

"The two victims were beloved local characters, and we struggled to find anyone who thought badly of them. Cole was a figure of fun, known for his singing, drinking and storytelling. Florence was the woman who kept him in his cups, though the two had little to do with one another outside of the pub. I found almost nothing else to connect them, but then I'm certain the killer knew that would be the case."

He started his walk back up the other side of the table, taking in each face that he passed. Jimmy Mordaunt's whole family was there. One of his daughters kept looking at me as though she wanted to pop me into her mouth and chew me up. It was most disconcerting, and I wasn't sure I liked it.

"As landlady of the jolliest pub in the village, Florence was a popular presence here, and her beauty and charm had not gone unnoticed. Her refusal to accept marriage proposals from suitors young and old may have turned some people against her. But I could find no evidence of a particular vendetta, and so I returned to my original hypothesis.

"There was no shortage of people in Clearwell who wished to tell me of the wickedness of Scowles Folly nor a lack of evidence of that village's hatred towards the Wyndham family. The mummery and theatrics that Jimmy Mordaunt has directed this weekend – the devilish parades, attacks on the rival castle and this very wedding feast – all showed me just how important the grudge between you had become. And if that wasn't enough, our trip through the forest to Scowles Folly proved it."

He stopped beside a small group of Clearwell's farmers and turned his back to them so that, for a moment, it looked as though they were a mob, and he was their leader. "Everything in that town is held together by the bitter regrets that have accumulated over two hundred years. From The Lady Morgana public house to the crumbling folly which gave the place its name, it does not feel so much a village as a living museum.

"The only thing stopping me from rounding up the grandees of Scowles Folly and charging them with murder was that, as the obvious culprits, they would have had to be fools to murder their enemies in such a fashion." He stopped to examine Jimmy Mordaunt's vacant smirk. "No, I was certain that a far cleverer stratagem was at play and turned my attention to town in which I stand.

"Clearwell, just like so many villages across Great Britain, is filled with honest, hardworking people, who enjoy nothing more than a little gossip and backstabbing. A quick trip around the shops provided us with a report of the final hours of Cole Watkins' life, knowledge of Florence Keyse's mystery man and the key to Rosebank Cottage. The house had been generously lent to Cole's parents when he was a baby and housed the Wyndham Family's personal library."

It seemed that, with each element of the story he recounted, a different member of the audience became more nervous, and my suspicions changed. At that moment, Gertrude looked quite as terrified as I'd seen her all weekend and I was a little concerned that I'd judged her too kindly.

"My grandson and I inspected the cottage and discovered traces of a burnt document in the fireplace grate. The only words we could decipher, in an ancient, scrawling hand, were 'my treasured innocent' the meaning of which I could not initially ascertain. More interesting, however, were the traces of white powder on the bookshelves and certain spines. I cannot be certain until I get a sample of the substance analysed in the police laboratory in Scotland Yard, but I'm fairly sure that it was blacksmiths' flux."

In a moment, he crossed from one side of the table to the other and peered down wolfishly at Cliff Mordaunt. "Cliff, can you tell me for what purpose borax is commonly used in a forge?"

The beast-man showed no fear and, if anything, grew in confidence as he replied. "We use it for welding. It creates a barrier to reduce the amount of oxygen present."

This was all a bit too scientific for my liking, and I didn't actually know what any of it meant – although it was the second time I'd heard such an explanation. What I did understand was that the presence of the powder surely linked the Mordaunts to Cole's cottage. It seemed as though we'd found the culprit, but I'd come to such conclusions before (that very day) and waited for Grandfather to continue before leaping forward to pick the wrong killer.

"Yes, borax is often used by blacksmiths, but it has countless other uses in everything from cooking to gardening and such evidence would not send a man to the gallows. What struck me in this find was that there were no fingerprints in the powder, and so I could only conclude that it had been intentionally planted to incriminate the only family of blacksmiths in the area."

I had already observed the high regard in which Grandfather held Cliff Mordaunt, and the two men now nodded to one another in solidarity. I was terribly glad he was not the killer, as he was the sort of capable, masculine man that I longed to become, but presumably never would.

"However, like many of you here, Cliff Mordaunt served in the war. Anyone who has seen the tattoo on his left arm will be able to tell you that he was a soldier in the Royal Army Medical Corps. And it just so happened that the snake curling around a metal rod was the same insignia as the button we found in the pub when Florence Keyse was killed." Evidently, I had not drawn this conclusion at all, and I felt dreadful until, glancing across at me, Grandfather put me out of my misery once more. "Which served as yet more evidence that the real killer was trying to throw me off his path."

"Oh, thank goodness…" I believe I said this out loud as I was reassured for the second time that Cliff was not the killer. No, honestly. He wasn't!

CHAPTER THIRTY-FOUR

Lord Edgington had fallen silent and appeared to be debating with himself how best to continue his analysis. I was confident that he was about to reveal the murderer, and yet I felt no closer to knowing who it would be. Was he being a clever old soul and ruling out each of our suspects only to present a new piece of information that would turn the case on its head? Or was there some fresh name yet to emerge that I had failed to consider?

"My thoughts have rarely strayed far from another Scowles Folly resident," Grandfather began once more and, by this stage, my insides were in such agony that it felt as though I'd eaten a spoonful of red ants. "Cliff's son, Sam, has earned a nickname in Clearwell. The locals call him The Infiltrator, as he has been coming here to drink for months. As far as I have heard, he has caused no trouble, but there must have been something that drew him to the village. Something which took him to the castle last night, and the night before, in fact, when we spotted him lurking nearby."

I remembered the cloaked figure we'd seen when we'd returned from the pub on our first night in Clearwell. I could only assume that Sam was the distant shape that Dante had spotted in the woods, too.

Grandfather paused again and watched the slightly nervous faces of the seated banqueters. I really couldn't say what he was about to disclose and so I took a handful of sandwiches from the table and continued in the essential role of *peckish spectator*.

"My grandson and our chauffeur discovered Sam unconscious in the tunnels beneath the castle shortly after a poisonous snake had been placed in the Earl and Countess of Dunraven's bed. The Wyndhams took the injured man into the house and made sure that he was given the attention he required, despite the fact that his presence on their property made him the likely culprit for the poorly planned assault. Sam had been struck about the skull with a heavy object; the barrel of an electric torch, for example, could cause such damage.

"And yet, as his wounds were not life-threatening, I initially wondered whether his attack had been staged in order to infiltrate the castle. But I should not have been so cynical. Sam Mordaunt has been coming to Clearwell for a much higher calling than hatred or revenge."

The young chap smiled at this and sat up in his chair, though it was clear that such effort caused him pain. It was not my grandfather he sought. He turned to look at Gertrude, who was standing perfectly still beside her family, apparently more nervous than anyone else there.

"I cannot tell you when it happened, and I'm sure no one but the greatest poets could put their finger on why such romantic reactions occur, but Sam Mordaunt fell in love with Gertrude Wyndham."

There was a communal gasp from every last person. I would have done the same, but I had a mouth full of ham and bread. It was interesting to watch the revelation wash over the crowd. At first, there were noises of amazement and even anger that these two rival houses should have crashed up against one another in anything other than fury.

But then an unusual change occurred. Starting with Jed Gibson and the other shopkeepers, a cheer went up across the scene. Applause broke out and Cliff put his arm around his boy in celebration. There was still the odd grumpy face – Lieutenant-Colonel Stroud was presumably incapable of anything but a grimace – but the majority of those present could see the good in two young people falling in love.

"When I went to speak to the Mordaunts in their village yesterday, it was clear to me that, while most of you knew nothing, Sam's father understood where his son had been going in the evenings. He'd been using his visits to The Wyndham Arms to cover his real intentions, and I can only assume that, after his single pint in the pub, Sam would meet his beloved in the forest."

I fixed my eyes on the Wyndhams then. Gertrude was peering into her parents' faces, attempting to garner some inkling of their thoughts on the matter. I was worried that the centuries of division would be too painful to forget, but then Algar kissed his daughter gently on her forehead and urged her to go to the man she loved.

It took little persuasion to send her skipping off along the table to throw her arms around Sam, who had to grimace a little as she almost bashed his wounds in her excitement. Cliff seemed quite moved by the moment and, with the lovers decoupled once more, he held his hand out to meet… his future daughter-in-law? It was hard to say what would happen, but Grandfather had some thoughts on the matter.

He placed his hands on the couple's shoulders before speaking.

"If allowed to bloom, I am confident that your love will achieve great things. You must have already applied for the wedding licence you require. That is what has made you so nervous this weekend, is it not, Gertrude?"

The princess of Clearwell Castle did not respond. She was too amazed by the detective's intuition to do anything but stare back in wide-eyed wonder.

"Together," Grandfather continued, "you will lay the so-called curse of Lady Morgana to rest and unite two families and towns that have been separated on the basis of a falsehood." I would like to have asked what he was implying at this moment, but he steamrollered on. "As a testament to your love, the affection you hold for one another has already enabled me to solve two murders."

We had all fallen silent to hear the conclusion of his tale. Seeing him unravel a case was like having a private audience with one of the theatrical greats. He was the Henry Irving of the detective world.

"You see, I have been looking for a masterful solution to a terrible case. I've spent this weekend searching out the criminal who could construct such an intricate and complex plan filled with traps and double bluffs, when, in actuality, he never existed. I must admit that I have been outwitted by a witless man, but it was only when I discovered the love that Sam Mordaunt had for Gertrude Wyndham – only when I saw how she suffered when he was injured last night – that I realised my mistake."

He walked back to where he had started the presentation some minutes earlier. "I believed from the very beginning that the document Cole Watkins found would have cleared Thomas Wyndham's name and proven that Lady Morgana had not been murdered. And, if that were true, it would point to someone from Scowles Folly, not Clearwell, as the murderer."

"Where's your evidence?" Jimmy Mordaunt demanded in a cold voice as he tore his veil from his head entirely. "Morgana was slain in her home. How can you say what happened all that time ago?"

Grandfather rounded on the chap. "How can you? You've been whipping up your townsfolk for years to hate the Wyndhams, but why? You have no proof of what happened to the poor woman." He waited to ensure that the ignorant fellow would not interrupt again.

"If an inhabitant of Scowles Folly was to blame for Florence's death, he would have had to know what she said in the pub on Friday. She'd seen someone inside Cole's cottage weeks after he died, and the killer didn't want her telling anyone else about it.

"But Sam Mordaunt was the only Scowles Folly-er in The Wyndham Arms that night, and he wouldn't wish to create further discord between his own family and that of his secret fiancée. So who informed Cole's murderer that Florence would need to be killed in order to cover up the first crime?"

"I did," Sam interjected, his voice weak. "I would have said something, but I didn't realise what it meant until now. You see, I passed a message to my uncle."

CHAPTER THIRTY-FIVE

There was a brief burst of noise as the audience made sense of the young chap's statement. The gang of Clearwell farmers looked as though they wanted to take up arms – or pitchforks, at least – against the lad, but one rather astute spectator realised something significant.

"Sam left that night with the Lieutenant-Colonel," I said, recalling the scene quite clearly. "The old soldier sat writing something and, when Sam got up to leave, he darted outside." I looked across at the man, but he showed no emotion. "It was just before the road was set on fire and, with all the excitement that ensued, I clean forgot the whole thing."

There was a further point to extract from what Sam had said, but I wasn't fast enough to do so, and it fell to Dante to ask the key question. "So then who killed Cole and Florence and who bashed Sam on the noggin? Was it the Lieutenant-Colonel or Jimmy Mordaunt?"

Grandfather was in the spotlight once more and couldn't resist a triumphant smile. "I told you that I was looking for the mastermind who had perpetrated the murders, when in fact, I should have been looking for two complacent fools."

I'd always known Jed Gibson was a good chap! The Wyndham Arms' favoured accordionist seized hold of the blue-blazered soldier and held him in place until a few of the burly farmers could get a proper grip on him. I still wasn't sure what part Stroud had played in the proceedings, but his arrogant expression confirmed that he was a bad sort. Jimmy Mordaunt, meanwhile, displayed his usual oafish grin, as though unaware of the peril in which he now found himself.

Grandfather would soon set him straight on that score. "I knew from the first moment I met you, Jimmy, that you were no great thinker. You stirred up anger in your village in order to maintain your influence. While your ancestors may have been worthy nobles, you are no match for them. Like so many politicians, instead of finding solutions to your town's problems, you decided to blame someone else. So you resurrected the ancient hatred for your rivals here in Clearwell.

"But a house built on such unstable foundations needs an awful lot of care and, when Cole Watkins appeared in your village claiming to have discovered a document that could correct a great mistake in history, you realised what you needed to do."

The Lieutenant-Colonel had heard enough. "There you go, then. That nincompoop in a dress is to blame. It's got nothing to do with me."

I often admired the quiet patience my grandfather displayed at such moments. He wore a positively saintly smile as he replied to the odious character. "On the contrary. The well down which Cole was pushed was in front of your property. And, for events to have unfolded as they did, I believe you saw the act take place."

The soldier's rather weaselly face puffed up in indignation. "It's not a crime to witness someone else being murdered."

Grandfather was too quick for him and was ready with a response. "Oh, I don't know. The police might have something to say about withholding information, not to mention the lack of civic duty you showed when you failed to assist them with such a serious investigation. The real reason you didn't tell anyone what you'd seen, though, was that you simply couldn't stand Young Cole Watkins. You were no doubt only too happy for his late-night singing to be brought to a permanent conclusion."

The farmers pushed their duplicitous captive forward, and he sputtered out a response. "That's neither here nor there. I am as innocent as the day I was born." He evidently enjoyed the sound of his own voice and practically sang his defence.

"Perhaps… but then you got a taste for the savagery you'd witnessed and plotted a second murder. As her friends informed me, you were in love with Florence Keyse, but she did not return the sentiment. She could barely stand to serve you on Friday night in The Wyndham Arms, which is when you saw your opportunity to reap revenge without getting your hands dirty. You knew that Jimmy Mordaunt would kill to protect his petty empire, and so you sent him a note explaining that Florence had seen something incriminating. It was a neat piece of work to drive to your brother's house that night and provide yourself with an alibi, but the fact remains that you were complicit in Florence Keyse's death."

"Hang on… one of *them* and one of us worked together to murder them poor folk?" a woman at the table puzzled. "How did they ever trust each other?"

"They didn't," Grandfather explained. "Which is why Jimmy tried to implicate the Lieutenant-Colonel in Florence's murder by cutting off a button from his brother's military uniform to leave at the scene of the crime – foolishly overlooking the fact that each corps within the army has its own unique insignia. Stroud wasn't much wiser, of course. I can only assume he broke into Rosebank Cottage to incriminate Jimmy knowing that he would use the fool for his own ends."

"So why didn't he simply tell the police what he'd seen when Cole was murdered?" This was another of my fine questions.

There was so much I didn't know and so little time to explain, but Grandfather did his best. "If he'd done that, Jimmy would have been sent to gaol before Florence could be killed. The Lieutenant-Colonel bided his time and waited for the perfect moment."

Grandfather paused his performance for us to make sense of the strange case. There was no one standing near me, so I had a word with Delilah.

"Well, I never!" I exclaimed. "Did you ever hear such a tale?"

She responded by cocking her head at an angle, as though to say, *I suppose it was all right.*

Jimmy had been rather discreet this whole time, and I wondered whether he thought that, by remaining quiet, he might evade arrest. This hope was soon abandoned, and he stood up from the table in that mouldy old wedding dress. He was quite the least attractive bride I'd ever seen, and my father's cousin Rachel – who married a judge in Sussex last year – was certainly no Gainsborough.

"They're trying to hang me for something that I didn't do, lads. The Wyndhams are behind this; you can bet they are."

"Oh, please." Grandfather had rarely looked so unmoved by a suspect's pleas. "It's a little much for you to beg for loyalty from your people after you attempted to murder your own nephew to keep the feud alive."

Perhaps unsurprisingly, Jimmy could summon no response to this, and Lord Edgington continued to lay out the man's nefarious scheme. "You were suspicious when he appeared after the siege, and so you followed him to the passage that Gertrude had shown him. You knocked the poor boy out before he could return to his sweetheart, and then you attempted the most poorly conceived murder of the century.

Seeing your chance to access the castle undetected, you cast about for a weapon. You may have the ability to capture a wild snake without getting bitten, but you failed to realise that Adders are not the vicious killers that their reputation would suggest."

The dim-witted mayor had started to panic, and he pleaded with his compatriots. "I'm no killer. You've got to believe me."

He pushed his chair back, and I could tell that he would do something idiotic – it was simply his way. Spotting a gap through the crowd, he spun on the spot and bolted. I noticed that the limp with which he normally walked had mysteriously disappeared, and he sprinted towards freedom, only to trip over his long skirt and fall flat on his face. Even his own people laughed at that.

"It's not fair!" he complained from his new altitude. "The law's always been on the Wyndhams' side; they hushed up what happened to Lady Morgana. What hope have I got of a fair trial?"

Jimmy's hard-done-by act would come to nothing, and as some burly farmers pulled him up to standing, my grandfather delivered another unexpected revelation.

"I've already told you; Morgana wasn't murdered. She died in childbirth."

A wave of surprise passed across the assembly. My grandfather had clearly observed any number of things that I had failed to register. This was an accepted fact in all of our investigations, and yet we had learnt so little about Lady Morgana that I couldn't imagine how he had arrived at such a conclusion.

After all, I had been with him the whole way. I was there when we found the single fragment of Thomas Wyndham's document, but Grandfather had acknowledged that the three singed words we'd discovered could refer to almost anything. And that was as close as we had come to the fabled lady. I had briefly believed that I'd seen her ghost in the tunnels of the castle, but that had turned out to be–

"Gertrude is descended from Lady Morgana!" I declared, and a ripple of excitement travelled about like a stone dropped in a lake. "It's the only thing that makes sense. Lady Morgana died in childbirth, but the Wyndhams couldn't admit as much as Thomas was not due to marry his fiancée until she turned twenty-one. That was why there was so much secrecy over her death, and why he married so swiftly after his true love died. It was to hide the scandal because the baby lived, and Gertrude is his descendant."

"Excellent work, Christopher!" Gosh, it had been weeks since my grandfather had uttered these words. I was beginning to think I was no longer worthy of them. "That's exactly it. The words we found in Thomas Wyndham's hand never sounded to me as though they referred to his beloved. 'My treasured innocent' sounded more like something you would say to a child. When you told me of the supposed ghost you saw in the castle last night, it occurred to me just how great a similarity there was between the painting of Morgana we had seen in Scowles Folly and Gertrude herself." He paused before concluding this point. "It became clear to me then that Morgana and Thomas's child had survived and that the Wyndhams are descended from him."

I'm sure we all looked quite stunned as we made sense of this final part of the story. If Gertrude and Dante, and even Algar for that matter, were Lady Morgana's descendants, it meant that the Mordaunts had been fighting their own kin all this time. It was the definition of a fruitless endeavour, and Grandfather couldn't resist underlining the fact.

"Not all murderers are clever. Some attempt to kill by placing easily frightened animals in their enemy's beds. With Lieutenant-Colonel Stroud's assistance, Jimmy killed two innocent people and attacked his own nephew in order to preserve the rivalry between two families that are, in fact, one. Such was the idiocy of this plot it was almost beyond my comprehension, but I got there in the end." He took a moment to enjoy the two characters' pitiful expressions. "Officers, arrest these men."

He extended an arm to point at the culprits before realising that no one had actually called the police. "Oh, dear. I really should have thought ahead."

CHAPTER THIRTY-SIX

Jimmy's part in the case was evident, and Grandfather hoped that, when the local bobby we'd seen the day before finally appeared, Lieutenant-Colonel Stroud would be arrested for soliciting the murder of Florence Keyse.

I must say, I found the whole thing terribly sad. Good people had died because of two men's vanity. They were one as bad as the other, though I couldn't understand how Grandfather had been able to pick the culprits so effortlessly.

"I'm afraid you're missing the point, Christopher," he told me as we sat beside the fireplace in the castle. "I chose the right killers. What more do you want me to say?"

"I'm not trying to be obstinate, Grandfather. It just seems there were a great many variables that must still be explained. For example, how did you know that it wasn't Stroud himself who pushed Cole to his death?"

"Because he wouldn't have sent a message to Jimmy Mordaunt expecting him to murder Florence if he hadn't known that Jimmy was already a killer. In fact, it wouldn't surprise me if he'd used that information to blackmail him into committing the second crime. The Lieutenant-Colonel was certainly eager to link the two murders when we first spoke to him."

I think I might have scratched my head at this point, before realising it made me look a little ignorant and cutting the gesture short. "Very well then. How did you know the Wyndhams weren't to blame? Algar might have murdered Cole to maintain the secret of his parentage and then Florence in order to hide their affair. What did he do to convince you that he wasn't the killer?"

"Well…" The old chap was surprisingly reticent on the matter. "Can we just say that I carefully examined a good friend's character and came to the conclusion that he was not to blame?"

I had to swallow a gulp then. This was the last thing I'd expected him to say. "No, you cannot. Where's the logic in such a statement? You're forever telling me that I must support my theories with evidence. The fact that you've known Algar since he was a boy is hardly proof that he isn't a murderer."

He laughed at me then. He had a good old belly-shaking chortle and clutched his side in agony – which served him right for being so mischievous. "Oh, Christopher, I accept defeat. I admit that I couldn't rule out Algar's involvement entirely but, as I told you before, motive and opportunity do not make someone a killer." He shook his head fondly as he looked at me, and I felt rather capable for once. "The bigger issue you should be discussing is the fact that I wouldn't have done any of this without you."

"I'm sorry, but I don't see how I've helped you in the slightest."

"Don't you?" He waited a moment while I stared back agog. "So you don't remember suggesting that the curse and the rivalry could be a distraction from the real motive for the murders? You even said that one of Florence's suitors could be to blame. It didn't seem likely to me at first, but when I considered the possibility that there were two people behind the killings rather than one, the pieces fell into place."

"Well, I…" I allowed his words to slosh about my head in the hope I would eventually believe them. Before that could happen, Todd came in with a trolley of cocktails, and Algar and his wife were not far behind.

"I asked your man to prepare something a little unusual," the Earl of Dunraven explained, as Todd set about pouring the drink he had mixed in the kitchen.

Cressida had not lost her hesitant air. "We thought the children deserved something special, considering…" I didn't believe she would get the words out, but she took a deep breath and tried once more. "… considering that we are due to have a wedding."

Delilah was pretending to be a lion skin again but gave a woof of appreciation. She was very much a romantic at heart.

"We have been divided for too long." Algar spoke in a slow, heavy voice, as though he needed to consider the impact of each word. "My darling Cressida suggested that Sam and Gertrude should wed in St Peter's this evening. No banns have been read, but they have the marriage licence and, besides, the archbishop is a close friend of mine."

I must say, I was surprised by the rush to see the young lovers married, though I thought I knew the reason for it. Gertrude's twenty-first birthday was only a day away.

"We decided it will be safer if they are married today." A nervous smile momentarily reshaped Cressida's lips. "Under the circumstances."

It was rather wonderful that any reservations she might have had to the wedding were overruled by her superstitious nature. The curse of Lady Morgana had finally delivered a happy ending.   I sincerely hoped that Algar and Cressida could return to the happy life they had once led. I wondered if Sam and Gertrude's marriage could be the spark that the family needed to put things right.

The happy couple soon arrived, along with Sam's father, and Gertrude had a request of her own to make. "We were hoping you would be a witness, Lord Edgington." In her long white gown, she looked as though she'd dressed that morning on the off-chance she'd have to get married. "After all, without you and Chrissy, it's unlikely we would have got this far."

"I'd probably still be lying unconscious in the tunnel," Sam added, and this memory seemed to remind him of the pain he'd endured, as he touched the back of his head a little tenderly.

"Of course I will," Grandfather replied, as our flexible chauffeur handed him a sparkling flute. "What exactly are we drinking, Todd?" he asked after he'd consumed half the glass.

"It's my own invention, M'Lord." The smart chap bowed a fraction as he spoke. "It contains red grape juice, vodka, a dash of Angostura bitters and Veuve Clicquot champagne."

"Does it have a name?" I felt I should ask, and Todd smiled as he'd clearly been expecting this very question.

"Yes, Master Christopher. I've christened it the Lady Morgana."

To put our expert cocktail maker to the test, we all sampled his new creation. It managed to be simultaneously sweet and sharp, fizzy and fruity, and I found it quite delicious.

"The Lady Morgana?" Cliff said, regarding the glass in his large hands with some distrust. "Whatever you call it, that's a tasty concoction. I'll have another."

Dante popped out of the fireplace at this moment to give us all a fright, and I spent the next hour running about in the forest with him before Cressida forced us to get changed into more formal attire.

It was a different kind of parade that we enjoyed that afternoon.

Gone were the thoughts of funerals and demons, buckets of blood and ancient curses. We were a wedding party and everyone there looked thoroughly happy to be alive. Taking up the rear of the procession, I had another question for my grandfather.

"You know, old man," I began rather impertinently. "I can't say that I was sad not to spot the killer this time. I was so worried that Dante was to blame, and it gave me the most enormous sense of relief to discover otherwise."

His smile straightened out, and he looked a touch sterner for a moment. "You came very close, Christopher. You mustn't be so hard on yourself."

"Yes, that's all well and good, but I was still largely wrong. And what I need to know is... well, what I need to know is how I'm ever going to be *not wrong*. We've investigated any number of murders at this stage, and I still haven't picked the absolute, one hundred per cent correct culprit."

"That is true." He looked straight ahead as he walked and placed his cane down with a resounding tap every other step. "But I have a question for you, Christopher. Have you ever played chess?"

"Chess?" I thought I should make sure that I'd heard him correctly. "The game with the little horses and such?"

He managed to frown without actually moving his mouth. "That's right; chess."

"Yes, of course. In fact, Marmaduke says I'm quite the marvel at it. I'm the only boy he has repeatedly beaten in just five moves."

"Impressive." His frown became a little less... frownsome, if that's a word. "So, then I'm sure you'd concur that you can't play chess unless you know how each piece moves."

"Oh, quite." The truth was that I had once attempted to play without having the first idea of the rules. I was in no way tempted to explain this, however, and said no more.

"Very good. And the same holds true for detective work."

"I need to know how the pieces move?"

"Well, yes. Just as you can't sit down at a chessboard and expect to understand the game, you cannot turn up at a crime scene and hope to solve a murder. There's a lot you still have to learn, and I'm going to teach you."

"Isn't that what you've been doing for the last year?" I was really rather confused on the matter.

"Oh no, my boy. We've only scratched the surface. And yet you've already come on in leaps and bounds."

It was my turn to feel a little more cheerful. "Gosh. Just imagine how good I'll be once you've actually taught me something."

He did not respond to this but puzzled over a question of his own. "What I still haven't discovered is how the delightful lovers crossed paths in the first place. Did Gertrude pop out to the pub one night for a pint of Shires, or did the pair of them bump into one another in the forest?"

It took me a moment to realise that he expected me to answer. "Oh… ummm… perhaps they– Oh, look. Here's the church."

I was pleased to see the priest standing at the door to welcome us. Reverend Clarke was a jolly chap with a round belly and a rounder head, and I had to ponder where he'd been all weekend as chaos consumed his parish. It was too late to worry about such things now, though. He was probably just tending to his vegetable garden.

As Sam and Gertrude walked down the aisle to be united in eternal matrimony, Grandfather and I were at the front of the church to enjoy the blessed spectacle. I can't say with absolute surety, but I had the definite sensation that, if no one had been watching, the renowned Lord Edgington would have shed a tear. His eyes looked red. He covered his mouth with his hand, and he had to keep blinking as the couple read their vows to one another. I don't mind telling you that I was a touch emotional myself.

It was a wonderfully simple service with only a few guests in attendance and, when Grandfather stepped forward to be their witness, I felt rather good about the world. Yes, there were murderers lurking around every corner that we inspected, and, yes, I was coming to see just how selfish humans could be. But by visiting Clearwell to meet a group of relatives I hadn't previously known, it felt as though my family had grown by some measure. It was truly lovely.

"Do you think this means the curse is now forgotten?" Dante asked me as we stood outside the church where half the village had come to throw petals at the blushing groom and his beautiful bride. "A Wyndham has finally married a Mordaunt. Sam might not be Lady

Morgana, but I should think that he'll do the job."

I was about to tell him that I didn't believe there had ever been a curse, but he seemed quite excited by the idea.

"Yes, Dante. I'm sure that you'll have no more trouble from now on."

He smiled a truly gleeful smile, and we took a handful of petals from Jed Gibson's basket and tossed them into the air. Saying goodbye to my friend was no fun, but when Todd brought the Aston Martin around for Grandfather to pilot, I was quite happy to be setting off somewhere new.

"Next stop King Arthur's birthplace?" I asked, as Grandfather tossed me the keys and I immediately passed them back to him – I'd tried driving once and it hadn't gone well.

"You decide!" he responded, and it was almost as much pressure as if I'd been the one behind the wheel.

I opened the door for Delilah to hop into the sporty grey car before climbing aboard myself. Grandfather started the engine and our friends yelled and waved as we departed. Even the newlyweds took the time to see us off, and it was with some sadness that I called a final "Toodle-oo!" to my cousin Dante. I craned my neck to look back at him until the church, the gatehouse in the distance and everything behind us was a blurry dot.

"Come along, Chrissy." My grandfather took one hand off the wheel to ruffle my hair. "Don't be so blue. There are adventures to be had…"

I interrupted him before he could finish the sentence. "…and mistakes to be made."

"That is not what I was going to say." He looked glum for a moment, but his smile soon returned. "Oh, very well. Yes, it was. England is our large, flat oyster!"

The End (For Now…)

240

Get another

LORD EDGINGTON ADVENTURE

absolutely **free**…

Download your free novella at
www.benedictbrown.net

"LORD EDGINGTON INVESTIGATES..."

The eighth full-length mystery will be available in **November 2022** at amazon.

Sign up to the readers' club on my website to know when it goes on sale.

ABOUT THIS BOOK

These days, most of the ideas for my books start with the setting, and the setting is often inspired by the front cover. As we include a preview of the next book at the back of each release, I always have to be planning ahead, and so does my wife (who happens to also be my graphic designer.) Together, we scour stock photo sites looking for beautiful pictures of old buildings that I feel would suit the series. However, it's very difficult to find images that have the correct licence and so, a couple of months ago, I decided to e-mail the owners of some incredible buildings I came across. The first people to get back to me were the managers of Clearwell Castle, which is now a wedding venue.

Without their permission to use an image of the castle, and even the name of the building in the title, this book wouldn't exist. So much of this story was suggested by the myths and history related to the area around the real town of Clearwell. Even the characters and the gothic feel of the book are due to all the amazing things that I learnt about the Forest of Dean and that imposing building on the cover of the book.

Of course, Clearwell Castle is not an ancient medieval monument, it was only built a few hundred years ago (only!) and, as a result, there is a sense of medieval theatricality that runs throughout the book. I like to think of the inhabitants of the two villages as being more like historical reenactors than authentic representatives of, as Chrissy puts it, "the time of knights and dragons", and this idea certainly shaped a lot of the plot and the book's relationship to history and mythmaking.

The Forest of Dean, as well as being a truly beautiful setting, is another place of which I have fond memories from visiting with my family as a child. I was also happy to set a book there as it lies right on the border with Wales. I believe this is my sixteenth novel and it's quite amazing that I haven't written a book yet about my motherland. My mum was born in the Rhondda Valley, I went to university in Aberystwyth and moved to Swansea afterwards to look for work. I spent every summer of my childhood visiting my cousins there, and probably know the area better than anywhere else in Britain, and yet the closest I've got to writing a book about it is the Forest of Dean. At least Lord Edgington likes the idea of travelling to "the land of song" – if only to sample the cheese – so I'm sure it will happen before long.

There's a lot about my research in the next chapter, but, first, I really wanted to acknowledge the impact that the e-mail reply from the castle owners had on this book. This is probably the closest I will come to Influencer-style advertising, but I genuinely hope that someone will get married in that beautiful place because they've read my book or even just seen the cover. Thank you so much to the generous people at **countryhouseweddings.co.uk,** if you hadn't responded to my e-mail, I don't know what I would have written!

If you loved the story and have the time, please write a review on Amazon. Most books get one review per thousand readers so I would be infinitely appreciative if you could help me out.

THE MOST INTERESTING THINGS I DISCOVERED WHEN RESEARCHING THIS BOOK...

This book was quite different from its predecessors in that most of the research I had to do was centred around the real-life setting of Clearwell in Gloucestershire. I was lucky enough to have permission from the current owners of the castle – where you can and, let's be honest, probably should get married, as it is now a stunning wedding venue. They also allowed me to use the real name of the castle in the title, and this set me off on a brilliant tangent, as I dug deep into the local history. As the brief disclaimer at the front of the book suggests, I did not attempt to create a perfectly accurate recreation of the village and its surroundings, but I tried to imbue the story with as many local details as possible.

This meant that – despite the fact I built a sturdy wall all the way around the castle that doesn't actually exist, invented the neighbouring village of Scowles Folly, allowed the forest to reclaim some of its land and changed certain features of the village (I moved the well, for one thing!) – I tried to reflect something of the character of the area. The Wyndham family really were the owners of the previous manor house who knocked it down to build the current castle in the eighteenth century – though, as far as I know, they were not cursed by their rivals. The Countess of Dunraven really was the person who commissioned the current church and school of the village. It sounds as though she was a real character, and I even found a photo of her online from the mid-nineteenth century – No, she didn't have Facebook, someone must have scanned it! In it, she stands imperiously in front of the castle, looking a bit like a ghost and that's what gave me the idea for Lady Morgana and that whole plotline.

The castle itself, which looks so beautiful on my cover thanks to the generous photographer Dan Morris (he photographs weddings, just saying) is considered one of the very first examples of Gothic Revival architecture which became popular in England over a decade later. Its architect, Roger Morris, was registered as a mere bricklayer before the castle was completed but, within a few years would be officially listed as a gentleman. He had a lengthy career building spectacular examples of gothic and Palladian architecture for some of the wealthiest and most fashionable aristocrats of his day, not least The Column of Victory in the grounds of Blenheim Palace.

After the Wyndhams sold Clearwell, it passed through different owners and was badly damaged in a fire in 1930, before being restored and then falling into near total disrepair. This was handy for me plotting my book as it gave me free reign to lay the building out as I wished. I based my layout, partly on the modern interior of the wedding venue – did I mention you can get married there? – partly on photos from before the fire, but largely on my imagination – I don't think it was ever quite as medieval looking as I decided it should be for the sake of this extremely gothic book.

Perhaps the best part of Clearwell Castle's story, though, is the most recent chapter. Not only was the building saved from demolition when it was bought by the son of the former gardener, who was himself born on the grounds. In the seventies, it was used as a recording studio by bands like Queen, Black Sabbath and Led Zeppelin, while the new owners brought the building back to life.

All the shops mentioned, and even the names of many villagers in the book, are taken from the real people who lived there at the time – though that's where the similarity ends. I was lucky enough to find a list of the people who were living in the village shortly after the book is set, along with a description of their jobs and residences. I spent a lot of time wandering Clearwell village on Google maps, trying to work out where everything would have been, and it became the perfect canvas onto which to sketch my outlandish plot.

The story of the poor murdered bears is famous in the Forest of Dean. It actually took place in 1889, a little way away from Clearwell but... well, poetic licence! Four Frenchmen were travelling with their two dancing bears through Gloucestershire when a rumour started that the animals had attacked and killed a child. In the spirit of all good baying mobs, a group of workers killed the bears and beat the Frenchmen but were soon hauled up before a magistrate as, in fact, the bears were innocent. "Who killed the bears?" became an insult and, I thought, the perfect brush with which to tar the imaginary inhabitants of Scowles Folly.

The incredible forest hideaway where Chrissy gets bitten by a snake is a real place called Puzzlewood. The unique, moss-covered warren of paths, boulders and scowles (ancient natural pits and hollows that lent themselves to the extraction of iron ore from the Roman times onwards) was originally overlaid with paths by a rich family in the nineteenth century. It has doubled as a magical land in countless films, including Star Wars, Harry Potter and The Secret Garden. If you can't visit, I'd recommend searching for pictures online, as the mysterious place really has to be seen to be believed.

The town of Cheddar, by the beautiful gorge, really does lay claim to the oldest cheese shop in the world. William Small's Genuine Cheddar Cheese Depot, as it was known in the twenties, first opened in 1870 and has remained a family business ever since. I'd also like to point out to my international readers that good mature cheddar cheese is the most delicious substance known to man and, were I not able to buy it here in Spain, I really might have to move. British food gets a bad rep internationally, but I really do believe that we have fantastic ingredients and an amazing restaurant culture – and that's all I'm going to say on the matter.

Much like Chrissy and his grandfather, I do enjoy taking out my map of Britain from the 1920s and charting a path across the country to see what interesting stops there might be on the way. The journey in this book is as circuitous as ever, but I couldn't resist giving them the chance to call in on that most majestic city of Bath. It's a particularly interesting place as it is so associated with various historical periods from Roman times right through to the nineteenth century. All the facts I mention in the book are true, though the picture I paint of it is probably a little too old-fashioned for the twenties. I just felt that Lord Edgington would have fitted in beautifully in the Regency Era, and so I decked out the women there with cotton parasols and crinoline dresses. Perhaps one day I'll write a Jane Austen style romance with him as the hero. He's certainly proud enough.

In order to complete their journey, they must cross the Severn estuary and, luckily there was a tunnel for that very purpose. Completed in 1886, the Severn Tunnel took nearly fourteen years to build and is seven kilometres long, which made it the longest underwater tunnel in the world for the next hundred years. From 1910 to 1966 there was a train service which carried motorist's cars on wagons, though the cars had to be covered with tarpaulins as so much water gets into the tunnel from the river above.

We still have my father's Hornby toy trains from when he was a boy, and I've always loved steam trains, so it was a lot of fun going down this particular rabbit hole. I must admit that, when I jumped out of my seat with joy having found a 1920s timetable of the service from Pilning railway station, I knew that I'd gone too far.

The very first scene I wrote in this book was when Chrissy and his grandfather go to Cole's cottage to look for clues and find a newspaper which mentions the 1926 Epsom Derby. My secondary school was a couple of miles from the famous racecourse, and I was amazed to discover that a video newsreel still exists from the time. It's available on the British Pathé website, which is an incredible resource for researching the twenties. On derby day, there was torrential rain, but people still showed up by the busload to have a flutter on the horses and perhaps get a glimpse of King George.

In my first draft I'd, anachronistically, referred to Cliff Mordaunt as a medic, but the closest such role in the First World War was occupied by stretcher bearers. Groups of men, often with little medical training, would risk their lives, running into no man's land to look for still breathing bodies. They were required to bandage their fallen compatriots and carry them back to hospital tents, where doctors could care for the wounded, or they'd be taken away in ambulances.

I had to look into the age at which women could marry, both at the time of Lady Morgana and in the twenties. And, luckily for my plot, not that much had changed. In the eighteenth century, girls could marry from as young as twelve, though records suggest this was extremely uncommon, and despite what we may know assume, over 90% of women married in their twenties. More importantly for the plot, though, both in the seventeen hundreds and the nineteen twenties, women could not get married without their parents' permission until they turned twenty-one.

One of my early readers wanted me to remove the snakes, but I thought they were perfect considering the themes of the book. The Forest of Dean really does have Britain's largest population of adders, and grass snakes really can change the shape of their heads to look like the deadly species that share their territory. Adders have more triangular heads compared to non-venomous snakes and, in other countries, some grass snakes will even flatten the head and neck to imitate a cobra's hood. In fact I found out all sorts of interesting things about them. When faced with a foe, the barred grass snake may play dead and can even secrete blood from its mouth to sell the act. In reality, they rarely bite and are more likely to make a stinky garlic smell to scare off their enemies. Much like a boy I was at school with, in fact.

Another fun tangent I went off on was when I spent an hour reading about lightning. I don't know why I started, (it barely gets a mention in this book) but what I discovered was rather amazing. Depending on the country in which you live, you're around a hundred times more likely to die of a lightning strike if you are poor. The reason for this isn't as simple as you might think, though. At the end of the nineteenth century, most people in America who died from lightning strikes were at home in bed at the time. In the last twenty years, there are no reports of people in the US dying in such a manner. Why? Because modern plumbing and wiring tend to ground lightning strikes, and so people almost never die in their homes in Western countries. Poorer countries have fewer modern amenities (along with far more people working out of doors) so such tragedies still occur.

It's always nice to finish with a song, and there were two real beauties in this book. The first, which poor Cole Watkins sang in his final night on Earth, is possibly as old as Clearwell Castle and belongs to the British folk tradition of drinking songs – of which there are hundreds. I changed the verses around to fit the story, and tweaked a few lines, but the original song of "Come Landlord, Fill a Flowing Bowl" is at least two centuries old and – though I can find no record of its authorship – it appears to be English… or Scottish.

250

For anyone familiar with my Izzy Palmer stories, you'll know how much I enjoy making up my own songs to include in my books. I thought it was about time that Lord Edgington and Chrissy had one of their own. There is a poem in the local Forest of Dean vernacular called "Who Killed the Bears?" but, as I could only just about understand it, I decided to make up a similarly titled song for our heroes to entertain the people of Clearwell. I particularly like Chrissy's effort.

Music is an important part of my life. Singing along to a beloved song at a concert is one of my favourite things, and I sing all day at home with my daughter. I think that songs add a lot to animate each scene and help set the atmosphere. Before finishing this book, I gave a final listen to the audiobook of **"The Mystery of Mistletoe Hall"**, and I was amazed at the impact George Blagden's brilliant interpretation of the carols had on the mood of the story – moving us from the sombre tones of "The Coventry Carol" to the singalong fun of "Ding Dong Merrily on High". I have promised him that four songs per story is the absolute maximum, though, as I don't want my mystery novels to turn into hymn books.

ACKNOWLEDGEMENTS

This book was rather difficult to write as I was on holiday for the greater part of it. It was written in Spain, England, Italy and France and, when first completed, was the longest in the series so far – before I hacked away at a lot of unnecessary twaddle. That hacking would not have been possible without my incredibly generous first wave of readers who supported me massively this time around.

Thank you, too, to my crack team of experts – the Hoggs, the Martins, (**fiction**), Paul Bickley (**policing**), Karen Baugh Menuhin (**marketing**) and Mar Pérez (**forensic pathology**) for knowing lots of stuff when I don't. Thanks to my fellow writers who are always there for me, especially Pete, Catherine, Suzanne and Lucy.

Thank you, many times over, to all the readers in my ARC team who have combed the book for errors. I wouldn't be able to produce this series so quickly or successfully without you, so please stick with me, Izzy and Lord Edgington to see what happens next…

Rebecca Brooks, Ferne Miller, Melinda Kimlinger, Deborah McNeill, Emma James, Mindy Denkin, Namoi Lamont, Katharine Reibig, Sarah Dalziel, Linsey Neale, Karen Davis, Taylor Rain, Terri Roller, Margaret Liddle, Esther Lamin, Lori Willis, Anja Peerdeman, Kate Newnham, Marion Davis, Sarah Turner, Sandra Hoff, Karen M, Mary Nickell, Vanessa Rivington, Helena George, Anne Kavcic, Nancy Roberts, Pat Hathaway, Peggy Craddock, Cathleen Brickhouse, Susan Reddington, Sonya Elizabeth Richards, John Presler, Mary Harmon, Beth Weldon, John Presler, Karen Quinn, Karen Alexander, Mindy Wygonik, Jacquie Erwin, Janet Rutherford, Anny Pritchard, M.P. Smith, Robin Coots, Molly Bailey, and Keryn De Maria.

READ MORE LORD EDGINGTON MYSTERIES TODAY_

- **Murder at the Spring Ball**
- **Death From High Places** (free e-novella available exclusively at benedictbrown.net. Paperback and audiobook are available at Amazon)
- **A Body at a Boarding School**
- **Death on a Summer's Day**
- **The Mystery of Mistletoe Hall**
- **The Tangled Treasure Trail**
- **The Curious Case of the Templeton-Swifts**
- **The Crimes of Clearwell Castle**
- **A Novel Way to Kill** (Free ebook available from October 2022)
- **The Snows of Weston Moor** (Coming November 2022)

Check out the complete Lord Edgington Collection at Amazon.

The first three Lord Edgington audiobooks, narrated by the actor George Blagden, are available now. The next release, **"The Mystery of Mistletoe Hall"** will be out in October 2022.

"THE CRIMES OF CLEARWELL CASTLE" COCKTAIL

Our resident Lord Edgington cocktail expert, François Monti, was on holiday when I wrote this book and so I decided to do something different. By this point in his varied career, Todd would have had some good ideas on what makes a tasty cocktail. I, meanwhile, am a total ignoramus, but I did my best to create something which, as Chrissy says is "simultaneously sweet and sharp, fizzy and fruity".

The Lady Morgana cocktail originally started out with crème de cassis, but the blackcurrant liqueur dominated the flavour, and so I went back to the drawing board. François tells me that grape juice cocktails are rare. My daughter loves the stuff, so I gave it a shot. By the end of my experimentation, I'd gone through a bottle of champagne and finished off some left-over vodka from our last party, but I came up with something that I really enjoyed.

> **15ml / 0.5 fl oz vodka**
> **70ml / 3 fl oz red grape juice**
> **1 teaspoon (5ml/ o.2 fl oz) of Angostura Bitters**
> **90ml of champagne** (Veuve Clicquot if you'd like to be as fancy as Lord Edgington, supermarket's own brand if you don't want to waste your money, and Spanish Cava or Italian Prosecco if you're sensibly keeping the costs down.)

It's very easy to make. Simply mix the ingredients together in order, then fill the glass with champagne. There is no mixing or shaking required as the champagne being poured over the initial mixture should do the job for us. Serve chilled!

You can get François's brilliant book "101 Cocktails to Try Before you Die" at Amazon...

WORDS AND REFERENCES YOU MIGHT NOT KNOW

Rag (verb) – to tease or bully.

Fudge (verb) – to do something in a vague manner in order to conceal something.

Mrs Beeton – the first superstar cookery writer from the nineteenth century.

Navvies – British slang for a general labourer.

Cap-a-pie – Antiquated French loan expression to mean from head to toe.

Neoteric – something new or forward-looking.

"You know, I'd be off my bean if I couldn't keep my pecker up, but I suppose I'm just that sort of bird," – You know, I'd go crazy if I couldn't remain positive, but I'm just that sort of person.

Upkeep (verb) – well, this isn't actually a verb. I just thought that Jed Gibson might try to use it as one to impress Lord Edgington.

Tout de suite – French for *right now!*

Fuddle – it originally meant "to get drunk" then it came to mean "confused as though drunk" before finally meaning simply confused. The more common term "befuddle" is far newer and fuddle dates back to the sixteenth century.

Lycanthrope – a werewolf or someone who believes themselves to be one.

Jejune – a simple and unsophisticated person.

Pint of Shires – a fictional brand of ale in the rural British radio program, The Archers. I grew up having to listen to this near-daily show and hated it as a child, but now really love it, and my writing is more influenced by it than I've ever admitted. It's not only the longest-running drama in the world, it is also just about the cosiest show on radio and can be listened to all over the world via the BBC.

Rig-outs – an antiquated term for outfits.

Chin-wag – British slang for a chat.

Somnolence – sleepiness.

Herpetologist – an expert on snakes.

Cooper – a barrel maker.

Supernal – divine or celestial.

Miffed – British slang for being annoyed

Bullyrag (verb) – to bully or bother, though its etymological root is thought to be independent from the older word "bully".

Piffle and poppycock – nonsense and chatter

Hypnopompic – I knew the word hypnogogic, which refers to the state between waking and sleep, well this is the state between sleep and waking.

Argot – slang.

Oubliette – I've forgotten... No, hang on! It means a dungeon which is only accessible from above, in which people would be placed in order to be.... wait for it... forgotten! From the French word for forget (I hope I've underlined the joke enough times now).

Sin-eater – a person who would be paid to eat a meal beside a dying or dead person that would absolve the unlucky soul of their sins. What I didn't know was that such an occupation was largely confined to Wales and its neighbouring English counties, so this reference is quite fitting for a book set so close to the Welsh border.

Curvilinear tracery – tracery is the word for dividing up architectural features such as windows with stone bars or moulding. Curvilinear tracery is a later development of this technique, which is characterised, as its name suggests, by curved lines.

Henry Irving – one of the great actors of the Victorian era. He was well known for directing, designing, writing the theme tune and starring in major productions of Shakespearean and contemporary plays. Well, part of that might be an exaggeration. He was also notoriously manipulative and is considered the main influence for the character of Dracula as the writer, Bram Stoker, worked as Irving's business manager.

Frownsome – no, Chrissy, it's not a word. The commonly used adjective is frowny.

Surety – a nice, antiquated word meaning certainty. Today, it more commonly means a deposit paid on the promise of the fulfilment of a certain deed or action.

CHARACTER LIST

Clearwell Residents

Young Cole Watkins – a cheerful drunk who claims to be related to the Wyndham family. He's dead before the story begins!

Algar Wyndham – The Earl of Dunraven – the owner of Clearwell Castle and Chrissy's grandmother's cousin.

Cressida Wyndham – The Countess of Dunraven – Algar's Wife. A nervous, zealous woman who foresees damnation in everything.

Dante Wyndham – their blithe and adventurous teenage son.

Gertrude Wyndham – their mopy yet lovely daughter.

Lieutenant-Colonel Stroud – a grumpy former soldier who lives in village

Florence Keyse – lovely young landlady of The Wyndham Arms pub.

Shopkeepers – Mrs Fox, the baker. Mrs Yarworth, the butcher. Jed Gibson, grocer and garage owner.

Scowles Folly Residents

Jimmy Mordaunt – the rather clownish mayor who sustains the rivalry between the villages.

Cliff Mordaunt – his brother. A huge, hulking blacksmith.

Sam Mordaunt – Cliff's son.

CHARACTER LIST

Regular Characters

Lord Edgington – "The Most Honourable Marquess of Edgington, Lord of Cranley Hall" – The main detective of my series. Retired Metropolitan Police superintendent, owner of the grandest estate in Surrey, and Christopher's grandfather.

Christopher Aloysius Prentiss (Recently turned seventeen!) – Kind-hearted, well-meaning and somewhat sentimental, Christopher is Lord Edgington's loyal assistant.

Delilah, the golden retriever – she is also very loyal!

Albert Prentiss – Chrissy's soppy, heartbroken brother.

Marmaduke Adelaide – Chrissy's former bully, turned schoolfriend.

The Three Williams – Chrissy's best friends at Oakton academy.

Lord Edgington's Staff

Todd – chauffeur and Jack of all trades. Mixes a mean cocktail and is always on hand when action is needed.

Dorie – supposedly a maid but employed more often as Edgington's massive body guard.

Halfpenny – Cranley Hall's Footman.

"Cook" – Henrietta – Cranley Hall's somewhat experimental cook.

Alice – Cranley Hall's maid and Chrissy's (former) one true love.

Patrick Driscoll – Her husband, Cranley Hall's head gardener.

THE IZZY PALMER MYSTERIES

If you're looking for a modern murder mystery series with just as many off-the-wall characters, try **"The Izzy Palmer Mysteries"** for your next whodunit fix.

Check out the complete Izzy Palmer Collection in ebook, paperback and Kindle Unlimited at Amazon.

ABOUT ME

Writing has always been my passion. It was my favourite half-an-hour a week at primary school, and I started on my first, truly abysmal book as a teenager. So it wasn't a difficult decision to study literature at university which led to a masters in Creative Writing.

I'm a Welsh-Irish-Englishman originally from **South London** but now living with my French/Spanish wife and presumably quite confused infant daughter in **Burgos**, a beautiful mediaeval city in the north of Spain. I write overlooking the Castilian countryside, trying not to be distracted by the vultures, hawks and red kites that fly past my window each day.

When Covid 19 hit in 2020, the language school where I worked as an English teacher closed down and I became a full-time writer. I have two murder mystery series. There are already six books written in **"The Izzy Palmer Mysteries"** which is a more modern, zany take on the genre. I will continue to alternate releases between Izzy and Lord Edgington. I hope to release at least ten books in each series.

I previously spent years focussing on kids' books and wrote everything from fairy tales to environmental dystopian fantasies, right through to issue-based teen fiction. My book **"The Princess and The Peach"** was long-listed for the Chicken House prize in The Times and an American producer even talked about adapting it into a film. I'll be slowly publishing those books over the next year whenever we find the time.

"The Crimes of Clearwell Castle" is the seventh novel in the "Lord Edgington Investigates…" series. The next book will be out in November and there's a novella available free if you sign up to my readers' club. If you feel like telling me what you think about Chrissy and his grandfather, my writing or the world at large, I'd love to hear from you, so feel free to get in touch via…

www.benedictbrown.net

Made in the USA
Coppell, TX
10 June 2023

17926487R00152